HAUI

STORIES

KINGFISHER
An imprint of Kingfisher Publications Plc
New Penderel House, 283-288 High Holborn
London WC1V 7HZ
www.kingfisherpub.com

First published by Kingfisher 2002
This edition published by Kingfisher 2005
2 4 6 8 10 9 7 5 3 1

A CIP catalogue record for this book is available from the British Library

ISBN-13: 978 0 7534 1153 7
ISBN-10: 0 7534 1153 9
1TR/THOM/MAR/80NS/F

Printed in India

HAUNTED
STORIES

CHOSEN BY
AIDAN CHAMBERS

ILLUSTRATED BY
TIM STEVENS

KINGFISHER

CONTENTS

INTRODUCTION

G HOST STORIES come in two kinds.

There is the sensational kind. They tell about ghosts you can see and hear and touch and even smell. (I haven't read any that describe the taste of a ghost.) These spooks clank chains, appear in weird shapes, send shivers down your spine and make your hair stand on end. The other is the psychological kind. They tell of ghosts that never appear in the flesh, so to speak, but invisibly invade your mind and haunt your soul. Both kinds are included in this collection of some of my favourite spectres.

The Haunted and the Haunters by Edward Bulwer-Lytton is one of the best sensational ghost stories ever written. It was based on the true story of a house in London that was abandoned for forty years because of the terrifying experiences people endured while living there. It was also written during the period when the ghost story was at the peak of its success and popularity, the Victorian age of the nineteenth century. Candles and oil lamps throwing their wavering, spooky shadows were still the main means of lighting houses. Streets were dark and often dangerous at night. People were not as sceptical as we are these days and believed more than we do in the supernatural. So it was easy for them to imagine that houses were haunted and that ghosts stalked the unlit streets.

In *The Canterville Ghost*, written at that time, Oscar Wilde pokes fun at the sensational ghosts. It is a rare example not only of a humorous ghost story but also of one told from the ghost's point of view.

Both stories have been favourites of mine since I first came across them. As has one of the earliest of the psychological kind. In *The Tell-Tale Heart* by Edgar Allan Poe a murderer believes he is haunted by the sound of the beating heart of his dead victim, whereas of course we know that it is all in his mind. He is indeed being haunted, not by his victim's heart, but by his own guilt.

7

The ghost in August Derleth's *The Lonesome Place* is all in the minds of the children who imagine it. And yet is it? It just *might* be there! That's how the best psychological ghost stories work. And *The Lonesome Place* is a classic of the kind. Children's imaginations can be so powerful that what is fantastic becomes real to them, so real it can lead to death. Which is a thought as scary as any ghost can be.

I particularly enjoy stories that combine sensational and psychological hauntings, which is why I tried to write one of my own in *Room 18*. Like many such stories, it began with a real event. A friend went to stay in a Dublin hotel. He was given room 18 and had a dreadful, haunted night. On another visit he stayed at the same hotel and asked about the room, because he did not want to sleep in it again. But the receptionist said there was no room with that number. My friend went to look for it. And indeed, not only was there no room of that number, but there was no room where the one he had slept in had been.

Many of the stories in this collection were written especially for me by some of the best short story writers: John Gordon, Jan Mark, Lance Salway, Catherine Storr, William Trevor and Robert Westall.

There is something else I like about the stories I've chosen. They are well written. Even when they use elaborate language, as in *The Haunted and the Haunters*, they do not waste words, they keep moving along, produce surprises and are never boring.

Though they were meant mainly as entertainments, these stories all manage to explore, below the surface of the spooky fun, eternal truths about human nature. They remind us of the mystery of life and the strangeness of death, and help us to think about life and death in an enjoyable way. Perhaps that explains why ghost stories are so popular.

AIDAN CHAMBERS
April 2002

THE LONESOME PLACE

AUGUST DERLETH

YOU WHO SIT in your houses of nights, you who sit in the theatres, you who are gay at dances and parties – all you who are enclosed by four walls – you have no conception of what goes on outside in the dark. In the lonesome places. And there are so many of them, all over – in the country, in the small towns, in the cities. If you were out in the evenings, in the night, you would know about them, you would pass them and wonder, perhaps, and if you were a small boy you might be frightened. Frightened the way Johnny Newell and I were frightened, the way thousands of small boys from one end of the country to the other are being frightened when they have to go out alone at night, past lonesome places, dark and lightless, sombre and haunted . . .

I want you to understand that if it had not been for the lonesome place at the grain elevator, the place with the big old trees and the sheds up close to the pavement, and the piles of lumber – if it had not been for that place Johnny Newell and I would never have been guilty of murder. I say it even if there is nothing the law can do about it. They cannot touch us, but it is true, and I know, and Johnny knows, but we never talk about it, we never say anything. It is just something we keep here, behind our eyes, deep in our thoughts where it is a fact which is lost among thousands of others, but no less there, something we know beyond cavil.

It goes back a long way. But as time goes, perhaps it is not long. We were young, we were little boys in a small town. Johnny lived three houses away and across the street from me, and both of us lived in the block west of the grain elevator. We were never afraid to go past the lonesome place together. But we were not often together. Sometimes one of us had to go that way alone, sometimes the other. I went that way most of the time – there was no other, except to go far around, because that was the straight way down town, and I had to walk there, when my father was too tired to go.

In the evenings it would happen like this. My mother would discover that she had no sugar or salt or bologna, and she would say, "Steve, you go down town and get it. Your father's too tired."

I would say, "I don't wanna."

She would say, "You go."

I would say, "I can go in the morning before school."

She would say, "You go now. I don't want to hear another word out of you. Here's the money."

And I would have to go.

Going down was never quite so bad, because most of the time there was still some afterglow in the west, and a kind of pale light lay there, a luminousness, like part of the day lingering there, and all around town you could hear the kids hollering in the last hour they had to play, and you felt somehow not alone. You could go down into that dark place under the trees and you would never think of being lonesome. But when you came back – that was different. When you came back the afterglow was gone; if the stars were out, you could never see them for the trees, and though the street lights were on – the old-fashioned lights arched over the crossroads – not a ray of them penetrated the lonesome place near to the elevator. There it was, half a block long, black as black could be, dark as the deepest night, with the shadows of the trees making it a solid place of darkness, with the faint glow of light where a street light pooled at the end of the street. Far away it seemed, and that other glow behind, where the other corner light lay.

And when you came that way you walked slower and slower. Behind you lay the brightly lit stores; all along the way there had been houses, with lights in the windows and music playing and voices of people sitting to talk on their porches. But up there, ahead of you, there was the lonesome place, with no house nearby, and up beyond it the tall, dark grain elevator, gaunt and forbidding. The lonesome place of trees and sheds and lumber, in which anything might be lurking, anything at all. The lonesome place where you were sure that something haunted the darkness waiting for the moment and the hour and the night when you came through to burst forth from its secret place and leap upon you, tearing you and rending you and doing the unmentionable things before it had done for you.

That was the lonesome place. By day it was oak and maple trees over a hundred years old, low enough so that you could almost touch the big spreading limbs; it was sheds and lumber piles which were seldom disturbed; it was a pavement and long grass, never mowed or kept down until late autumn, when somebody burned it off; it was a shady place in the hot summer days where some cool air always lingered. You were never afraid of it by day, but by night it was a different place.

For, then, it was lonesome, away from sight or sound, a place of darkness and strangeness, a place of terror for little boys haunted by a thousand fears.

And every night, coming home from town, it happened like this. I would walk slower and slower, the closer I got to the lonesome place. I would think of every way around it. I would keep hoping somebody would come along, so that I could walk with him, Mr Newell, maybe, or old Mrs Potter, who lived farther up the street, or Reverend Bislor, who lived at the end of the block beyond the grain elevator. But nobody ever came. At this hour it was too soon after supper for them to go out, or, already out, too soon for them to return. So I

11

walked slower and slower, until I got to the edge of the lonesome place – and then I ran as fast as I could, sometimes with my eyes closed.

Oh, I knew what was there, all right. I knew there was something in that dark, lonesome place. Perhaps it was the bogey-man. Sometimes my grandmother spoke of him, of how he waited in dark places for bad boys and girls. Perhaps it was an ogre. I knew about ogres in the books of fairy tales. Perhaps it was something else, something worse. I ran. I ran hard. Every blade of grass, every leaf, every twig that touched me was *its* hand reaching for me. The sound of my footsteps slapping the pavement were *its* steps pursuing. The hard breathing which was my own became *its* breathing in its frantic struggle to reach me, to rend and tear me, to imbue my soul with terror.

I would burst out of that place like a flurry of wind, fly past the gaunt elevator, and not pause until I was safe in the yellow glow of the familiar street light. And then, in a few steps, I was home.

And mother would say, "For the Lord's sake, have you been running on a hot night like this?"

I would say, "I hurried."

"You didn't have to hurry that much. I don't need it till breakfast time."

And I would say, "I coulda got it in the morning. I coulda run down before breakfast. Next time, that's what I'm gonna do."

Nobody would pay any attention.

Some nights Johnny had to go down town, too. Things then weren't the way they are today, when every woman makes a ritual of afternoon shopping and seldom forgets anything.

In those days, they didn't go down town so often, and when they did, they had such lists they usually forgot something. And after Johnny and I had been through the lonesome place on the same night, we compared notes next day.

"Did you see anything?" he would ask.

"No, but I heard it," I would say.

"I felt it," he would whisper tensely. "It's got big, flat clawed feet. You know what has got the ugliest feet around?"

"Sure, one of those stinking yellow soft-shell turtles."

12

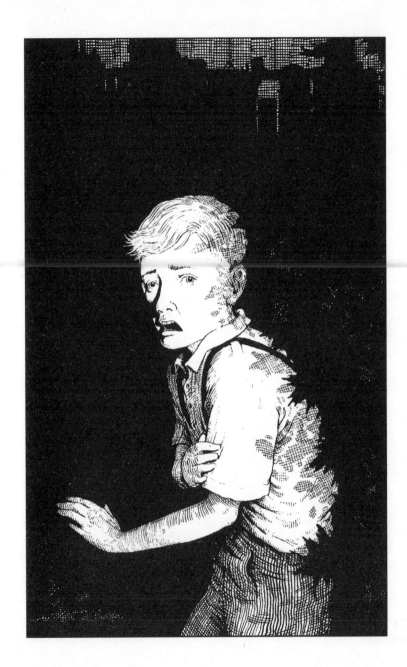

"It's got feet like that. Oh, ugly and soft, and sharp claws! I saw one out of the corner of my eye," he would say.

"Did you see its face?" I would ask.

"It ain't got no face. Cross my heart an' hope to die, there ain't no face. That's worse'n if there was one."

Oh, it was a horrible beast – not an animal, not a man – that lurked in the lonesome place and came forth predatorily at night, waiting there for us to pass. It grew like this, out of our mutual experiences. We discovered that it had scales, and a great long tail, like a dragon. It breathed from somewhere, hot as fire, but it had no face and no mouth in it, just a horrible opening in its throat. It was as big as an elephant, but it did not look like anything so friendly. It belonged there in the lonesome place; it would never go away; that was its home, and it had to wait for its food to come to it – the unwary boys and girls who had to pass through the lonesome place at night.

How I tried to keep from going near the lonesome place after dark!

"Why can't Mady go?" I would ask.

"Mady's too little," Mother would answer.

"I'm not so big."

"Oh, shush! You're a big boy now. Your Sears-Roebuck pants are long ones," she would say.

"I don't care about any old Sears-Roebuck pants. I don't wanna go."

"I want you to go. You never get up early enough in the morning."

"But I will. I promise I will. I promise, Ma!" I would cry out.

"Tomorrow morning it will be a different story. No, you go."

That was the way it went every time. I had to go. And Mady was the only one who guessed. "Fraidycat," she would whisper. Even she never really knew. She never had to go through the lonesome place after dark. They kept her at home. She never knew how something could lie up in those old trees, lie right along those old limbs across the pavement and drop down without a sound, clawing and tearing, something without a face, with ugly clawed feet like a soft-shell turtle's, with scales and a tail like a dragon, something as big as a horse, all black, like the darkness in that place.

But Johnny and I knew.

"It almost got me last night," he would say, his voice low, looking anxiously out of the woodshed where we sat, as if *it* might hear us.

"Gee, I'm glad it didn't," I would say. "What was it like?"

"Big and black. Awful black. I looked around when I was running, and all of a sudden there wasn't any light way back at the other end. Then I knew it was coming. I ran like everything to get out of there. It was almost on me when I got away. Look there!"

And he would show me a rip in his shirt where a claw had come down.

"And you?" he would ask excitedly, big-eyed. "What about you?"

"It was back behind the lumber piles when I came through," I said. "I could just feel it waiting. I was running, but it got right up – you look, there's a pile of lumber tipped over there."

And we would walk down into the lonesome place at midday and look. Sure enough, there would be a pile of lumber tipped over, and we would look to where something had been lying down, the grass all pressed down. Sometimes we would find a handkerchief and wonder whether *it* had caught somebody.

Then we would go home and wait to hear if anyone was missing, speculating apprehensively all the way home whether *it* had got Mady or Christine or Helen, or any one of the girls in our class or Sunday School. Or whether maybe *it* had got Miss Doyle, the young primary grade teacher who had to walk that way sometimes after supper. But no one was ever reported missing, and the mystery grew. Maybe *it* had got some stranger who happened to be passing by and didn't know about the Thing that lived there in the lonesome place. We were sure *it* had got somebody.

"Some night I won't come back, you'll see," I would say.

"Oh, don't be silly," my mother would say.

What do grown-up people know about the things boys are

15

afraid of? Oh, hickory switches and such like, they know that. But what about what goes on in their minds when they have to come home alone at night through the lonesome places? What do they know about lonesome places, where no light from the street corner ever comes? What do they know about a place and time when a boy is very small and very alone, and the night is as big as the town, and the darkness is the whole world? When grown-ups are big, old people who cannot understand anything, no matter how plain?

A boy looks up and out, but he can't look very far when the trees bend down over and press close, when the sheds rear up along one side and the trees on the other, when the darkness lies like a cloud along the pavement and the arc-lights are far, far away. No wonder, then, that Things grow in the darkness of lonesome places the way *it* grew in that dark place near the grain elevator. No wonder a boy runs like the wind until his heartbeats sound like a drum and push up to suffocate him.

"You're white as a sheet," Mother would say sometimes. "You've been running again."

"You don't have to run," my father would say. "Take it easy."

"I ran," I would say. I wanted the worst way to say I had to run and to tell them why I had to. But I knew they wouldn't believe me any more than Johnny's parents believed him when he told them, as he did once.

He got a licking with a strap and had to go to bed.

I never got licked. I never told them.

But now it must be told, now it must be set down.

For a long time we forgot about the lonesome place. We grew older and we grew bigger. We went on through school into high school, and somehow we forgot about the Thing in the lonesome place. That place never changed. The trees grew older. Sometimes the lumber piles were bigger or smaller. Once the sheds were painted – red, like blood. Seeing them that way the first time, I remembered. Then I forgot again. We took to playing baseball and basketball and football. We began to swim in the river and to date the girls. We never talked about the

Thing in the lonesome place any more, and when we went through there at night it was like something forgotten that lurked back in a corner of the mind. We thought of something we ought to remember, but never could quite remember; that was the way it seemed – like a memory locked away, far away in childhood. We never ran through that place, and sometimes it was even a good place to walk through with a girl, because she always snuggled up close and said how spooky it was there under the overhanging trees. But even then we never lingered there, not exactly lingered; we didn't run through there, but we walked without faltering or loitering, no matter how pretty a girl she was.

The years went past, and we never thought about the lonesome place again.

We never thought how there would be other little boys going through it at night, running with fast-beating hearts, breathless terror, anxious for the safety of the arc-light beyond the margin of the shadow which confined the dweller in that place; the light-fearing creature that haunted the dark, like so many terrors swelling in similar lonesome places in the cities and small towns and countrysides all over the world, waiting to frighten little boys and girls, waiting to invade them with horror and unshakable fear – waiting for something more . . .

Three nights ago little Bobby Jeffers was killed in the lonesome place. He was all mauled and torn and partly crushed, as if something big had fallen on him. Johnny, who was on the Village Board, went to look at the place, and after he had been there, he telephoned me to go, too, before other people walked there.

I went down and saw the marks, too. It was just as the coroner said, only not an "animal of some kind", as he put it. Something with a dragging tail, with scales, with great clawed feet – and I knew it had no face.

I knew, too, that Johnny and I were guilty. We had murdered Bobby Jeffers because the Thing that killed him was the Thing Johnny and I had created out of our childhood fears and left in that lonesome place to wait for some scared little boy at some minute in some hour during some dark night,

17

a little boy who, like fat Bobby Jeffers, couldn't run as fast as Johnny and I could run.

And the worst is not that there is nothing to do, but that the lonesome place is being changed. The village is cutting down some of the trees now, removing the sheds, and putting up a street light in the middle of that place; it will not be dark and lonesome any longer, and the Thing that lives there will have to go somewhere else, where people are unsuspecting, to some other lonesome place in some other small town or city or countryside, where it will wait as it did here, for some frightened little boy or girl to come along, waiting in the dark and the lonesomeness . . .

SUCH A SWEET LITTLE GIRL

LANCE SALWAY

I T WAS AT BREAKFAST on a bright Saturday morning that Julie first made her announcement. She put down her spoon, swallowed a last mouthful of cornflakes, and said, "There's a ghost in my bedroom."

No one took any notice. Her mother was writing a shopping list and her father was deep in his newspaper. Neither of them heard what she said. Her brother Edward heard but he ignored her, which is what he usually did. Edward liked to pretend that Julie didn't exist. It wasn't easy but he did his best.

Julie tried again. She raised her voice and said, "There's a ghost in my bedroom."

Mrs Bennett looked up from her list. "Is there, dear? Oh, good. Do you think we need more marmalade? And I suppose I'd better buy a cake or something if your friends are coming to tea."

Edward said sharply, "Friends? What friends?"

"Sally and Rachel are coming to tea with Julie this afternoon," his mother said.

Edward gave a loud theatrical groan. "Oh, no. Why does she have to fill the house with her rotten friends?"

"You could fill the house with *your* friends, too," Julie said sweetly. "If you had any."

Edward looked at her with loathing. "Oh, I've got friends all right," he said. "I just don't inflict them on other people."

"You haven't got any friends," Julie said quietly. "You haven't got any friends because no one likes you."

"That's enough," Mr Bennett said, looking up from his paper, and there was silence then, broken only by the great rumble-slush, rumble-slush of the washing machine in the corner.

Edward chewed a piece of toast and thought how much he hated Julie. He hated a lot of people. Most people, in fact. But there were some he hated more than others. Mr Jenkins, who taught maths. And that woman in the paper shop who'd accused him of stealing chewing gum, when everyone knew he never touched the stuff. And Julie. He hated Julie most of all. He hated her pretty pale face and her pretty fair curls and her pretty little lisping voice. He hated the grown-ups who constantly fluttered round her, saying how enchanting she was, and so clever for her age, and wasn't Mrs Bennett lucky to have such a sweet little girl. What they didn't say, but he knew they were thinking it behind their wide bright smiles, was poor Mrs Bennett, with that lumpy, sullen boy. So different from his sister. So different from lovely little Julie.

Lovely little Julie flung her spoon on the table. "I *said* there's a ghost in my bedroom."

Mrs Bennett put down her shopping list and ballpoint in order to give Julie her full attention. "Oh dear," she said. "I hope it didn't frighten you, darling."

Julie smiled and preened. "No," she said smugly. "*I* wasn't frightened."

Edward tried to shut his ears. He knew this dialogue by heart. The Bennett family spent a great deal of time adjusting their habits to suit Julie's fantasies. Once, for a whole month, they had all been forced to jump the bottom tread of the staircase because Julie insisted that two invisible rabbits were sleeping there. For a time she had been convinced, or so she said, that a pink dragon lived in the airing cupboard. And there had been a terrible few weeks the year before when all communication with her had to be conducted through an invisible fairy called Priscilla who lived on her left shoulder.

And now there was a ghost in her bedroom.

Try as he might, Edward couldn't shut out his sister's voice. On and on it whined: ". . . I was really very brave and didn't run away even though it was so frightening, and I said . . ."

Edward looked at his parents with contempt. His father had put down the newspaper and was gazing at Julie with a soppy smile on his face. His mother was wearing the mock-serious expression that adults often adopt in order to humour their young. Edward hated them for it. If he'd told them a story about a ghost when *he* was seven, they'd have told him to stop being so silly, there's no such things as ghosts, why don't you grow up, be a man.

"What sort of ghost is it?" he asked suddenly.

Julie looked at him in surprise. Then her eyes narrowed. "It's a frightening ghost," she said. "With great big eyes and teeth and horrible, nasty claws. Big claws. And it smells."

"Ghosts aren't like that," Edward said scornfully. "Ghosts have clanking chains and skeletons, and they carry their heads under their arms."

"This ghost doesn't," Julie snapped.

"Funny sort of ghost, then."

"You don't know anything about it."

Julie's voice was beginning to tremble. Edward sighed. There'd be tears soon and he'd get the blame. As usual.

"Come now, Edward," his father said heartily. "It's only pretend. Isn't it, lovey?"

Lovey shot him a vicious glance. "It's *not* pretend. It's a real ghost. And it's in my bedroom."

"Of course, darling." Mrs Bennett picked up her shopping list again. "How are we off for chutney, I wonder?"

But Edward wasn't going to let the matter drop. Not this time. "Anyway," he said, "ghosts don't have claws."

"This one does," Julie said.

"Then you're lying."

"I'm not. There *is* a ghost. I saw it."

"Liar."

"I'm not!" She was screaming now. "I'll show you I'm not. I'll tell it to *get* you. With its claws. It'll come and get you with its claws."

"Don't make me laugh."

"*Edward*! That's *enough*!" His mother stood up and started to clear the table. "Don't argue."

"But there isn't a ghost," Edward protested. "There can't be!"

Mrs Bennett glanced uneasily at Julie. "Of course there is," she said primly. "If Julie says so."

"She's a liar, a nasty little liar."

Julie kicked him hard, then, under the table. Edward yelped, and kicked back. Julie let out a screech, and then her face crumpled and she began to wail.

"*Now* look what you've done," Mrs Bennett snapped. "Oh *really*, Edward. You're twice her age. Why can't you leave her alone?"

"Because she's a liar, that's why." Edward stood up and pushed his chair aside. "Because there isn't a ghost in her bedroom. And even if there is, it won't have claws." And he turned, and stormed out of the kitchen.

He came to a stop in the sitting room, and crossed over to the window to see what sort of day it was going to be. Sunny, by the look of it. A small tightly-cropped lawn lay in front of the house, a lawn that was identical in size and appearance to those in front of the other identical square brick houses which lined the road. Edward laughed out loud. Any ghost worthy of the name would wither away from boredom in such surroundings. No, there weren't any ghosts in Briarfield Gardens. With or without heads under their arms. With or without claws.

He turned away from the window. The day had started badly, thanks to Julie. And it would continue badly, thanks to Julie and her rotten friends who were coming to tea. And there was nothing he could do about it. Or was there? On the coffee table by the television set there lay a half-finished jigsaw puzzle. Julie had been working on it for ages, her fair curls bent earnestly over the table day after day. According to the picture on the box,

the finished puzzle would reveal a thatched cottage surrounded by a flower-filled garden. When it was finished. If.

Edward walked across to the table and smashed the puzzle with one quick, practised movement of his hand. Pieces fell and flew and scattered on the carpet in a storm of coloured cardboard. And then he turned, and ran upstairs to his room.

He hadn't long to wait. After a few minutes he heard the sounds that he was expecting. The kitchen door opening. A pause. Then a shrill, furious shriek, followed by loud sobbing. Running footsteps. A quieter comforting voice. Angry footsteps on the stairs. The rattling of the handle on his locked bedroom door. And then Julie's voice, not like a seven-year-old voice at all any more but harsh and bitter with hate.

"The ghost'll get you, Edward. I'm going to tell it to get you. With its claws. With its sharp, horrible claws."

And then, quite suddenly, Edward felt afraid.

The fear didn't last long. It had certainly gone by lunchtime, when Edward was given a ticking-off by his father for upsetting dear little Julie. And by the time Julie's friends arrived at four, he was quite his old self again.

"The ugly sisters are here!" he announced loudly as he opened the front door, having beaten Julie to it by a short head.

She glared at him, and quickly hustled Sally and Rachel up the stairs to her room.

Edward felt a bit guilty. Sally and Rachel weren't at all ugly. In fact, he quite liked them both. He ambled into the kitchen, where his mother was busy preparing tea.

She looked up when he came in. "I do hope you're going to behave yourself this evening," she said. "We don't want a repetition of this morning's little episode, do we?"

"Well, she asked for it," Edward said sullenly, and sneaked a biscuit from a pile on a plate.

"Hands off!" his mother said automatically. "Julie did *not* ask for it. She was only pretending. You know what she's like. There was no need for you to be so nasty. And there was certainly no excuse for you to break up her jigsaw puzzle like that."

Edward shuffled uneasily and stared at the floor.

"She *is* only seven, after all," Mrs Bennett went on, slapping chocolate icing on a sponge cake as she did so. "You must make allowances. The rest of us do."

"She gets away with murder," Edward mumbled. "Just because she's such a sweet little girl."

"Nonsense!" his mother said firmly. "And keep your mucky paws off those ginger snaps. If anyone gets away with murder in this house, it's you."

"But she can't really expect us to believe there's a ghost in her bedroom," Edward said. Do *you* believe her? Come on, mum, do you?"

"I –" his mother began, and then she was interrupted by a familiar lisping voice.

"You *do* believe me, Mummy, don't you?"

Julie was standing at the kitchen door. Edward wondered how long she'd been there. And how much she'd heard.

"Of course I do, darling," Mrs Bennett said quickly. "Now run along, both of you. Or I'll never have tea ready in time."

Julie stared at Edward for a moment with her cold blue eyes, and then she went out of the kitchen as quietly as she'd entered it.

Tea passed off smoothly enough. Julie seemed to be on her best behaviour but that was probably because her friends were there and she wanted to create a good impression. Edward followed her example. Julie didn't look at him or speak to him but there was nothing unusual about that. She and the others chattered brightly about nothing in particular, and Edward said nothing at all.

It was dusk by the time they'd finished tea and it was then that Julie suggested that they all play ghosts. She looked straight at Edward when she said this, and the proposal seemed like a challenge.

"Can anyone play?" he asked. "Or is it just a game for horrible little girls?"

"Edward!" warned his mother.

"Of course you can play, Edward," said Julie. "You *must* play."

"But not in the kitchen or in the dining room," said Mrs Bennett. "And keep out of our bedroom. I'll go and draw all the curtains and make sure the lights are switched off."

"All right," said Julie, and the other little girls clapped their hands with excitement.

"How do we play this stupid game?" said Edward.

"Oh, it's easy," said Julie. "One of us is the ghost, and she has to frighten the others. If the ghost catches you and scares you, you have to scream and drop down on the floor. As if you were dead."

"Like 'Murder in the Dark'?" asked Sally.

"Yes," said Julie. "Only we don't have a detective or anything like that."

"It sounds a crummy game to me," said Edward. "I don't think I'll play."

"Oh, *do*!" chorused Sally and Rachel. "Please!"

And Julie came up to him and whispered, "You must play, Edward. And don't forget what I said this morning. About my ghost. And how it's going to get you with its claws."

"You must be joking!" Edward jeered. "And, anyway, I told you. Ghosts don't have claws." He looked her straight in the eyes. "Of course I'll play."

Julie smiled, and then turned to the others and said, "I'll be the ghost to start with. The rest of you run and hide. I'll count up to fifty and then I'll come and haunt you."

Sally and Rachel galloped upstairs, squealing with excitement. Edward wandered into the hall and stood for a moment, wondering where to hide. It wasn't going to be easy. Their small brick box of a house didn't offer many possibilities. After a while he decided on the sitting room. It was the most obvious place and Julie would never think of looking there. He opened the door quietly, ducked down behind an armchair, and waited.

Silence settled over the house. Apart from washing-up sounds from the kitchen, all was quiet. Edward made himself comfortable on the carpet and waited for the distant screams that would tell him that Sally had been discovered, or Rachel.

But no sounds came. As he waited, ears straining against the silence, the room grew darker. The day was fading and it would soon be night.

And then, suddenly, Edward heard a slight noise near the door. His heart leaped and, for some reason, his mouth went dry. And then the fear returned, the unaccountable fear he had felt that morning when Julie hissed her threat through his bedroom door.

The air seemed much colder now, but that could only be his imagination, surely. But he knew that he wasn't imagining the wild thumping of his heart or the sickening lurching of his stomach. He remembered Julie's words and swallowed hard.

"The ghost'll get you, Edward. With its claws. With its sharp, horrible claws."

He heard sounds again, closer this time. A scuffle. Whispering. Or was it whispering? Someone was there. Something. He tried to speak, but gave only a curious croak. And then, "Julie?" he said. "I know you're there. I know it's you."

Silence. A dark terrible silence. And then the light snapped on and the room was filled with laughter and shouts of "Got you! Caught you! The ghost has caught you!", and he saw Julie's face alive with triumph and delight, and, behind her, Sally and Rachel grinning, and the fear was replaced by an anger far darker and more intense than the terror he'd felt before.

"Edward's scared of the ghost!" Julie jeered. "Edward's a scaredycat! He's frightened! He's frightened of the ghost!"

And Rachel and Sally echoed her. "He's frightened! He's frightened of the gho-ost!"

"I'm not!" Edward shouted. "I'm not scared. There isn't a ghost!" And he pushed past Julie and ran out of the room and up the stairs. He'd show her. He'd prove she didn't have a ghost. There were no such things as ghosts. She didn't have a ghost in her room. She didn't.

Julie's bedroom was empty. Apart from the furniture and the pictures and the toys and dolls and knick-knacks. He opened the wardrobe and pulled shoes and games out on to the floor. He burrowed in drawers, scattering books and stuffed animals

27

and clothes around him. At last he stopped, gasping for breath. And turned.

His mother was standing in the doorway, staring at him in amazement. Clustered behind her were the puzzled, anxious faces of Sally and Rachel. And behind them, Julie. Looking at him with her ice-blue eyes.

"What on earth are you doing?" his mother asked.

"See?" he panted. "There isn't a ghost here. She hasn't got a ghost in her bedroom. There's nothing here. Nothing."

"Isn't there?" said Julie. "Are you sure you've looked properly?"

Sally – or was it Rachel? – gave a nervous giggle.

"That's enough," said Mrs Bennett. "Now I suggest you tidy up the mess you've made in here, Edward, and then go to your room. I don't know why you're behaving so strangely. But it's got to stop. It's got to."

She turned and went downstairs. Sally and Rachel followed her. Julie lingered by the door, and stared mockingly at Edward. He stared back.

"It's still here, you know," she said at last. "The ghost is still here. And it'll get you."

"You're a dirty little liar!" he shouted. "A nasty, filthy little liar!"

Julie gaped at him for a moment, taken aback by the force of his rage. Then, "It'll get you!" she screamed. "With its claws. Its horrible claws. It'll get you tonight. When you're asleep. Because I hate you. I hate you. Yes, it'll *really* get you. Tonight."

It was dark when Edward awoke. At first he didn't know where he was. And then he remembered. He was in bed. In his bedroom. It was the middle of the night. And he remembered, too, Julie's twisted face and the things she said. The face and the words had kept him awake, and had haunted his dreams when at last he slept.

It was ridiculous, really. All this fuss about an imaginary ghost. Why did he get in such a state over Julie? She was only a little kid, after all. His baby sister. You were supposed to love your sister, not – not fear her. But no, he wasn't *really* afraid of her. How could he be? Such a sweet little girl with blue eyes and fair bouncing curls who was half his age. A little girl who played games and imagined things. Who imagined ghosts. A ghost in her bedroom.

But he *was* frightened. He knew that now. And as his fear mounted again, the room seemed to get colder. He shut his eyes and snuggled down under the blankets, shutting out the room and the cold. But not the fear.

And then he heard it. A sound. A faint scraping sound, as though something heavy was being dragged along the landing. A sound that came closer and grew louder. A wet, slithering sound. And with it came a smell, a sickening smell of, oh, drains and dead leaves and decay. And the sound grew louder and he could hear breathing, harsh breathing, long choking breaths coming closer.

"Julie?" Edward said, and then he repeated it, louder. "Julie!"

But there was no answer. All he heard was the scraping, dragging sound coming closer, closer. Near his door now. Closer.

"I know it's you!" Edward shouted, and heard the fear in his voice. "You're playing ghosts again, aren't you? Aren't you?"

And then there was silence. No sound at all. Edward sat up in bed and listened. The awful slithering noise had stopped. It had gone. The ghost had gone.

He hugged himself with relief. It had been a dream, that's all. He'd imagined it. Just as Julie imagined things. Imagined ghosts.

Then he heard the breathing again. The shuddering, choking breaths. And he knew that the thing hadn't gone. That it was still there. Outside his door. Waiting. Waiting.

And Edward screamed, "Julie! Stop it! Stop it! Please stop it! I believe you! I believe in the ghost!"

The door opened. The shuddering breaths seemed to fill the room, and the smell, and the slithering wet sound of a shape, something, coming towards him, something huge and dark and –

And he screamed as the claws, yes, the claws tore at his hands, his chest, his face. And he screamed again as the darkness folded over him.

When Julie woke up and came downstairs, the ambulance had gone. Her mother was sitting alone in the kitchen, looking pale and frightened. She smiled weakly when she saw Julie, and then frowned.

"Darling," she said. "I did so hope you wouldn't wake up. I didn't want you to be frightened –"

"What's the matter, Mummy?" said Julie. "Why are you crying?"

Her mother smiled again, and drew Julie to her, folding her arms around her so that she was warm and safe. "You must be very brave, darling," she said. "Poor Edward has been hurt. We don't know what happened but he's been very badly hurt."

"Hurt? What do you mean, Mummy?"

Her mother brushed a stray curl from the little girl's face. "We don't know what happened, exactly. Something attacked him. His face –" Her voice broke then, and she looked away quickly. "He has been very badly scratched. They're not sure if his eyes –" She stopped and fumbled in her dressing-gown pocket for a tissue.

"I expect my ghost did it," Julie said smugly.

"What did you say, dear?"

Julie looked up at her mother. "My ghost did it. I told it to. I told it to hurt Edward because I hate him. The ghost hurt him. The ghost in my bedroom."

Mrs Bennett stared at Julie. "This is no time for games," she said. "We're very upset. Your father's gone to the hospital with Edward. We don't know if –" Her eyes filled with tears. "I'm in no mood for your silly stories about ghosts, Julie. Not now. I'm too upset."

"But it's true!" Julie said. "My ghost *did* do it. Because I told it to."

Mrs Bennett pushed her away and stood up. "All right, Julie, that's enough. Back to bed now. You can play your game tomorrow."

"But it's not a game," Julie persisted. "It's true! My ghost –"

And then she saw the angry expression on her mother's face, and she stopped. Instead, she snuggled up to her and whispered, "I'm sorry, Mummy. You're right. I *was* pretending.

I was only pretending about the ghost. There isn't a ghost in my room. I was making it all up. And I'm so sorry about poor Edward."

Mrs Bennett relaxed and smiled and drew Julie to her once more. "That's my baby," she said softly. "That's my sweet little girl. Of course you were only pretending. Of course there wasn't a ghost. Would I let a nasty ghost come and frighten my little girl? Would I? Would I?"

"No, Mummy," said Julie. "Of course you wouldn't."

"Off you go to bed now."

"Good night, Mummy," said Julie.

"Sleep well, my pet," said her mother.

And Julie walked out of the kitchen and into the hall and up the stairs to her bedroom. She went inside and closed the door behind her.

And the ghost came out to meet her.

"She doesn't believe me, either," Julie said. "She doesn't believe me. We'll have to show her, won't we? Just as we showed Edward."

And the ghost smiled and nodded, and they sat down together, Julie and the ghost, and decided what they would do.

A GHOST STORY

MARK TWAIN

I TOOK A LARGE ROOM, far up Broadway, in a huge old building whose upper stories had been wholly unoccupied for years until I came. The place had long been given up to dust and cobwebs, to solitude and silence. I seemed groping among the tombs and invading the privacy of the dead, that first night I climbed up to my quarters. For the first time in my life a superstitious dread came over me; and as I turned a dark angle of the stairway and an invisible cobweb swung its slazy woof in my face and clung there, I shuddered as one who had encountered a phantom.

I was glad enough when I reached my room and locked out the mould and the darkness. A cheery fire was burning in the grate, and I sat down before it with a comforting sense of relief. For two hours I sat there, thinking of bygone times; recalling old scenes, and summoning half-forgotten faces out of the mists of the past; listening, in fancy, to voices that long ago grew silent for all time, and to once familiar songs that nobody sings now. And as my reverie softened down to a sadder and sadder pathos, the shrieking of the winds outside softened to a wail, the angry beating of the rain against the panes diminished to a tranquil patter, and one by one the noises in the street subsided, until the hurrying footsteps of the last belated straggler died away in the distance and left no sound behind.

The fire had burned low. A sense of loneliness crept over me. I arose and undressed, moving on tiptoe about the room, doing stealthily what I had to do, as if I were environed by sleeping enemies whose slumbers it would be fatal to break. I covered up in bed, and lay listening to the rain and wind and the faint creaking of distant shutters, till they lulled me to sleep.

I slept profoundly, but how long I do not know. All at once I found myself awake, and filled with a shuddering expectancy. All was still. All but my own heart – I could hear it beat. Presently the bedclothes began to slip away slowly toward the foot of the bed, as if some one were pulling them! I could not stir; I could not speak. Still the blankets slipped deliberately away, till my breast was uncovered. Then with a great effort I seized them and drew them over my head. I waited, listened, waited. Once more that steady pull began, and once more I lay torpid a century of dragging seconds till my breast was naked again. At last I roused my energies and snatched the covers back to their place and held them with a strong grip. I waited. By and by I felt a faint tug, and took a fresh grip. The tug strengthened to a steady strain – it grew stronger and stronger. My hold parted, and for the third time the blankets slid away. I groaned. An answering groan came from the foot of the bed! Beaded drops of sweat stood upon my forehead. I was more dead than alive. Presently I heard a heavy footstep in my room – the step of an elephant, it seemed to me – it was not like anything human. But it was moving *from* me – there was relief in that. I heard it approach the door – pass out without moving bolt or lock – and wander away among the dismal corridors, straining the floors and joists till they creaked again as it passed – and then silence reigned once more.

When my excitement had calmed, I said to myself, "This is a dream – simply a hideous dream." And so I lay thinking it over until I convinced myself that it *was* a dream, and then a comforting laugh relaxed my lips and I was happy again. I got up and struck a light; and when I found that the locks and bolts were just as I had left them, another soothing laugh welled in my heart and rippled from my lips. I took my pipe and lit it, and was just sitting down before the fire, when – down went the pipe out of my nerveless fingers, the blood forsook my cheeks, and my placid breathing was cut short with a gasp! In the ashes on the hearth, side by side with my own bare footprint, was another, so vast that in comparison mine was but an infant's! Then I *had* had a visitor, and the elephant tread was explained.

I put out the light and returned to bed, palsied with fear. I lay a long time, peering into the darkness, and listening. Then I heard a grating noise overhead, like the dragging of a heavy body across the floor; then the throwing down of the body, and the shaking of my windows in response to the concussion. In distant parts of the building I heard the muffled slamming of doors. I heard, at intervals, stealthy footsteps creeping in and out among the corridors, and up and down the stairs. Sometimes these noises approached my door, hesitated, and went away again. I heard the clanking of chains faintly, in remote passages, and listened while the clanking grew nearer – while it wearily climbed the stairways, marking each move by the loose surplus of chain that fell with an accented rattle upon each succeeding step as the goblin that it bore advanced. I heard muttered sentences; half-uttered screams that seemed smothered violently; and the swish of invisible garments, the rush of invisible wings. Then I became conscious that my chamber was invaded – that I was not alone. I heard sighs and breathings about my bed, and mysterious whisperings. Three little spheres of soft phosphorescent light appeared on the ceiling directly over my head, clung and glowed there a moment, and then dropped – two of them upon my face and one upon the pillow. They spattered, liquidly, and felt warm. Intuition told me they had turned to gouts of blood as they fell – I needed no light to satisfy myself of that. Then I saw pallid faces, dimly luminous, and white uplifted hands, floating bodiless in the air – floating a moment and then disappearing. The whispering ceased, and the voices and the sounds, and a solemn stillness followed. I waited and listened. I felt that I must have light or die. I was weak with fear. I slowly raised myself toward a sitting posture, and my face came in contact with a clammy hand! All strength went from me apparently, and I fell back like a stricken invalid. Then I heard the rustle of a garment – it seemed to pass to the door and go out.

When everything was still once more, I crept out of bed, sick and feeble, and lit the gas with a hand that trembled as if it were aged with a hundred years. The light brought some little cheer to my spirits. I sat down and fell into a dreamy contemplation of that great footprint in the ashes. By and by its outlines began to waver and grow dim. I glanced up and the broad gas-flame was slowly wilting away. In the same moment I heard that elephantine tread again. I noted its approach, nearer and nearer, along the musty halls, and dimmer and dimmer the light waned. The tread reached my very door and paused – the light had dwindled to a sickly blue, and all things about me lay in a spectral twilight. The door did not open, and yet I felt a faint gust of air fan my cheek, and presently was conscious of a huge, cloudy presence before me. I watched it with fascinated eyes. A pale glow stole over the Thing; gradually its cloudy folds took shape – an arm appeared, then legs, then a body, and last a great sad face looked out of the vapour. Stripped of its filmy housings, naked, muscular and comely, the majestic Cardiff Giant loomed above me!

All my misery vanished – for a child might know that no harm could come with that benignant countenance. My cheerful spirits returned at once, and in sympathy with them the gas flamed up brightly again. Never a lonely outcast was so glad to welcome company as I was to greet the friendly giant. I said:

"Why, is it nobody but you? Do you know, I have been scared to death for the last two or three hours? I am most honestly glad to see you. I wish I had a chair – Here, here, don't try to sit down in that thing!"

But it was too late. He was in it before I could stop him, and down he went – I never saw a chair shivered so in my life.

"Stop, stop, you'll ruin ev–"

Too late again. There was another crash, and another chair was resolved into its original elements.

"Confound it, haven't you got any judgement at all? Do you want to ruin all the furniture on the place? Here, here, you petrified fool –"

But it was no use. Before I could arrest him he had sat down on the bed, and it was a melancholy ruin.

"Now what sort of a way is that to do? First you come lumbering about the place bringing a legion of vagabond goblins along with you to worry me to death, and then when I overlook an indelicacy of costume which would not be tolerated anywhere by cultivated people except in a respectable theatre, and not even there if the nudity were of *your* sex, you repay me by wrecking all the furniture you can find to sit down on. And why will you? You damage yourself as much as you do me. You have broken off the end of your spinal column, and littered up the floor with chips of your hams till the place looks like a marble yard. You ought to be ashamed of yourself – you are big enough to know better."

"Well, I will not break any more furniture. But what am I to do? I have not had a chance to sit down for a century." And the tears came into his eyes.

"Poor devil," I said, "I should not have been so harsh with you. And you are an orphan too, no doubt. But sit down on the floor here – nothing else can stand your weight – and besides, we cannot be sociable with you away up there above me; I want you down where I can perch on this high counting-house stool and gossip with you face to face."

So he sat down on the floor, and lit a pipe which I gave him, threw one of my red blankets over his shoulders, inverted my sitz-bath on his head, helmet fashion, and made himself picturesque and comfortable. Then he crossed his ankles, while I renewed the fire, and exposed the flat, honeycombed bottoms of his prodigious feet to the grateful warmth.

"What is the matter with the bottom of your feet and the back of your legs, that they are gouged up so?"

"Infernal chilblains – I caught them clear up to the back of my head, roosting out there under Newell's farm. But I love the

place; I love it as one loves his old home. There is no peace for me like the peace I feel when I am there."

We talked along for half an hour, and then I noticed that he looked tired, and spoke of it.

"Tired?" he said. "Well, I should think so. And now I will tell you all about it, since you have treated me so well. I am the spirit of the Petrified Man that lies across the street there in the museum. I am the ghost of the Cardiff Giant. I can have no rest, no peace, till they have given that poor body burial again. Now what was the most natural thing for me to do, to make men satisfy this wish? Terrify them into it! – haunt the place where the body lay! So I haunted the museum night after night. I even got other spirits to help me. But it did no good, for nobody ever came to the museum at midnight. Then it occurred to me to come over the way and haunt this place a little. I felt that if I ever got a hearing I must succeed, for I had the most efficient company that perdition could furnish. Night after night we have shivered around through these mildewed halls, dragging chains, groaning, whispering, tramping up and down stairs, till, to tell you the truth, I am almost worn out. But when I saw a light in your room tonight I roused my energies again and went at it with a deal of the old freshness. But I am tired out – entirely fagged out. Give me, I beseech you, give me some hope!"

I lit off my perch in a burst of excitement, and exclaimed:

"This transcends everything! Everything that ever did occur! Why you poor blundering old fossil, you have had all your trouble for nothing – you have been haunting a plaster cast of yourself – the real Cardiff Giant is in Albany!* Confound it, don't you know your own remains?"

I never saw such an eloquent look of shame, of pitiable humiliation, overspread a countenance before.

The Petrified Man rose slowly to his feet, and said:

"Honestly, *is* that true?"

---

*A fact. The original fraud was ingeniously and fraudfully duplicated, and exhibited in New York as the "only genuine" Cardiff Giant (to the unspeakable disgust of the owners of the real colossus) at the very same time that the latter was drawing crowds at a museum in Albany.—M.T.

"As true as I am sitting here."

He took the pipe from his mouth and laid it on the mantel, then stood irresolute a moment (unconsciously, from old habit, thrusting his hands where his pantaloons pockets should have been, and meditatively dropping his chin on his breast), and finally said:

"Well – I *never* felt so absurd before. The Petrified Man has sold everybody else, and now the mean fraud has ended by selling its own ghost! My son, if there is any charity left in your heart for a poor friendless phantom like me, don't let this get out. Think how *you* would feel if you had made such an ass of yourself."

I heard his stately tramp die away, step by step down the stairs and out into the deserted street, and felt sorry that he was gone, poor fellow – and sorrier still that he had carried off my red blanket and my bath-tub.

FOOTSTEPS INVISIBLE

ROBERT ARTHUR

THE NIGHT WAS DARK, and violent with storm. Rain beat down as if from an angry heaven, and beneath its force all the noises of a metropolis blended oddly, so that to Jorman they sounded like the muted grumble of the city itself.

He himself was comfortable enough, however. The little box-sized news-stand beside the subway entrance was tight against the rain.

The window that he kept open to hear prospective customers, take in change and pass out papers let in a wet chill, but a tiny oil heater in one corner gave out a glow of warmth that beat it back.

A midget radio shrilled sweetly, and Foxfire, his toy wire-haired terrier, snored at his feet.

Jorman reached up and switched the radio off. There were times when it gave him pleasure. But more often he preferred to listen to life itself, as it poured past his stand like a river.

Tonight, though, even Times Square was deserted to the storm gods. Jorman listened and could not hear a single footstep, though his inner time sense – reinforced by a radio announcement a moment before – told him it was barely half-past twelve.

He lit a pipe and puffed contentedly.

After a moment he lifted his head. Footsteps were approaching: slow, measured, familiar footsteps. They paused in front of his stand momentarily, and he smiled.

"Hello, Clancy," he greeted the cop on the beat. "A nice night for ducks."

"If I only had web feet," the big officer grumbled, "'twould suit me fine. You're a funny one, now, staying out so late on a night like this, and not a customer in sight."

"I like it," Jorman grinned. "Like to listen to the storm. Makes my imagination work."

"Mine, too," Clancy grunted. "But the only thing it can imagine is my own apartment, with a hot tub and a hot drink waitin'. Arrgh!"

He shook himself, and with a good-night tramped onward.

Jorman heard the officer's footsteps diminish. There was silence for a while, save for the rush of the rain and the occasional splashing whir of a cab sloshing past. Then he heard more steps.

This time they came towards him from the side street, and he listened intently to them, head cocked a little to one side.

They were – he searched for the right word – well, odd. *Shuffle-shuffle*, as if made by large feet encased in sneakers, and they slid along the pavement for a few inches with each step. *Shuffle-shuffle – shuffle-shuffle*, they came towards him slowly, hesitantly, as if the walker were pausing every few feet to look about him.

Jorman wondered whether the approaching man could be a cripple. A clubfoot, perhaps, dragging one foot with each step. For a moment he had the absurd thought that the sounds were made by four feet, not two; but he dismissed it with a smile and listened more closely.

The footsteps were passing him now, and though the rain made it hard to distinguish clearly, he had the impression that each shuffling step was accompanied by a slight clicking noise.

As he was trying to hear more distinctly, Foxfire woke from his slumbers. Jorman felt the little dog move at his feet, then heard the animal growling deep in its chest. He reached down and found Foxfire huddled against his shoe, tail tucked under, hair bristling.

"Quiet, boy!" he whispered. "I'm trying to hear."

Foxfire quieted. Jorman held his muzzle and listened. The footsteps of the stranger had shuffled past him to the corner. There they paused, as if in irresolution. Then they turned south on Seventh Avenue, and after a moment were engulfed in the storm noise.

Jorman released his hold on his dog and rubbed his chin perplexedly, wondering what there could have been about the pedestrian's scent to arouse Foxfire so.

For a moment Jorman sat very still, his pipe clenched in his hand. Then with a rush of relief he heard Clancy's returning tramp. The cop came up and stopped, and Jorman did not wait for him to speak. He leaned out of his little window.

"Clancy," he asked, trying to keep the excitement out of his voice, "What does that fellow look like down the block there – the one heading south on Seventh? He ought to be about in the middle of the block."

"Huh?" Clancy said. "I don't see any guy. Somebody snitch a paper?"

"No." Jorman shook his head. "I was just curious. You say there isn't anyone –"

"Not in sight," the cop told him. "Must have turned in some place. You and me have this town to ourselves tonight. Well, be good, I got to try some more doors."

He sloshed away, the rain pattering audibly off his broad, rubber-coated back, and Jorman settled back into his chair chuckling to himself. It was funny what tricks sounds played on you, especially in the rain.

He relit his dead pipe and was thinking of shutting up for the night when his last customer of the evening approached. This time he recognized the steps. It was a source of pride to him – and of revenue as well – that he could call most of his regulars by name if they came up when the street wasn't too crowded.

This one, though he didn't come often and had never come before at night, was easy. The step was a firm, decisive one. *Click* – that was the heel coming down – *slap* – that was the sole being planted firmly. *Click-slap* – the other foot. Simple. He could have distinguished it in a crowd.

"Good morning, Sir Andrew," Jorman said pleasantly as the steps came up to his stand. "*Times*?"

"Thanks." It was a typically British voice that answered. "Know me, do you?"

"Oh, yes." Jorman grinned. It was usually a source of mystification to his customers that he knew their names. But names were not too hard to learn, if the owners of them lived or worked near by. "A bellboy from your hotel was buying a paper last time you stopped. When you'd gone on, he told me who you were."

"That easy, eh?" Sir Andrew Carraden exclaimed. "Don't know as I like it so much, though, being kept track of. Prefer to lose myself these days. Had enough of notoriety in the past."

"Had plenty of it four years ago, I suppose," Jorman suggested. "I followed the newspaper accounts of your tomb-hunting expedition. Interesting work, archaeology. Always wished I could poke around in the past that way, sometime."

"Don't!" The word was sharp. "Take my advice and stay snug and cosy in the present. The past is an uncomfortable place. Sometimes you peer into it and then spend the rest of your life trying to get away from it. And – But I mustn't stop here chatting. Not in this storm. Here's your money. No, here on the counter . . ."

And then, as Jorman fumbled for and found the pennies, Sir Andrew Carraden exclaimed again.

"I say!" he said. "I'm sorry."

"Perfectly all right," Jorman told him. "It pleases me when people don't notice. A lot don't, you know, in spite of the sign."

"Blind newsdealer," Sir Andrew Carraden read the little placard tacked to the stand. "I say –"

"Wounded in the war," Jorman told him. "Sight failed progressively. Went entirely a couple of years ago. So I took this up. But I don't mind. Compensations, you know. Amazing what a lot a man can hear when he listens. But you're going to ask me how I knew you, aren't you? By your footsteps. They're very recognizable. Sort of a *click-slap, click-slap*."

His customer was silent for a moment. Jorman was about to

ask whether anything was wrong when the Englishman spoke.

"Look. I" – and his tone took on an almost hungry eagerness – "I've got to talk to somebody, or blow my top. I mean, go barmy. Completely mad. Maybe I am already, I don't know. You – you might have a few minutes to spare? You might be willing to keep me company for an hour? I – it might not be too dull."

Jorman hesitated in answering. Not because he intended to refuse – the urgency in the man's voice was unmistakable – but there was something of a hunted tone in Sir Andrew Carraden's voice that aroused Jorman's curiosity.

It was absurd – but Jorman's ears were seldom wrong. The Englishman, the archaeologist whose name had been so prominent a few years back, was a hunted man. Perhaps a desperate man. A fugitive – from what?

Jorman did not try to guess. He nodded.

"I have time," he agreed.

He bent down and picked up Foxfire, attached the leash, threw an old ulster over his shoulders and turned down his bright gasoline lantern. With Foxfire straining at the leash, he swung up his racks and padlocked the stand.

"This way," Sir Andrew Carraden said at his side. "Not half a block. Like to take my arm?"

"Thanks," Jorman touched the other's elbow. The touch told him what he remembered from photographs in the papers he had seen, years back. The Britisher was a big man. Not the kind to fear anything. Yet now he was afraid.

They bowed their heads to the somewhat lessened rain and walked the short distance to the hotel.

They turned into the lobby, their heels loud on marble. Jorman knew the place: the Hotel Russet. Respectable, but a bit run down.

As they passed the desk, a sleepy clerk called out.

"Oh, pardon me. There's a message here for you. From the manager. Relative to some work we've been doing –"

"Thanks, thanks," Jorman's companion answered impatiently, and Jorman heard paper stuffed into a pocket. "Here's the elevator. Step up just a bit."

They had been seated in easy chairs for some minutes, pipes going, hot drinks in front of them, before Sir Andrew Carraden made any further reference to the thing that was obviously on his mind.

The room they were in was fairly spacious, judging from the reverberations of their voices, and since it seemed to be a sitting-room, probably was joined to a bedroom beyond. Foxfire slumbering at Jorman's feet, they had been talking of inconsequentials – when the Englishman interrupted himself abruptly.

"Jorman," he said, "I'm a desperate man. I'm being hunted."

Jorman heard coffee splash as an unsteady hand let the cup rattle against the saucer.

"I guessed so," he confessed. "It was in your voice. The police?"

Sir Andrew Carraden laughed, a harsh, explosive sound.

"Your ears *are* sharp," he said. "The police? I wish it were! No. By a – a personal enemy."

"Then couldn't the police –" Jorman began. The other cut him short.

"No! They can't help me. Nobody in this world can help me. And God have mercy on me, nobody in the next!"

Jorman passed over the emphatic exclamation.

"But surely –"

"Take my word for it, I'm on my own," Sir Andrew Carraden told him, his voice grim. "This is a – a feud, you might say. And I'm the hunted one. I've done a lot of hunting in my day, and now I know the other side of it. It's not pleasant."

Jorman sipped at his drink.

"You – this enemy. He's been after you long?"

"Three years." The Englishman's voice was low, a bit unsteady. In his mind Jorman could see the big man leaning forward, arm braced against knee, face set in grim lines.

"It began one night in London. A rainy night like this. I was running over some clay tablets that were waiting deciphering. Part of the loot from the tomb of Tut-Ankh-Tothet. The one the stories in the papers you referred to were about.

45

"I'd been working pretty hard. I knocked off for a pipe and stood at the window looking out. Then I heard it."

"Heard it?"

"Heard him." Carraden corrected himself swiftly. "Heard *him* hunting for me. Heard his footsteps –"

"Footsteps?"

"Yes. In the pitch-black night. Heard him tramping back and forth as he tried to locate me. Then he picked up my trail and came up the garden path."

Sir Andrew paused, and Jorman heard the coffee cup being raised again.

"My dog, a Great Dane, scented him. It was frightened, poor beast, and with reason. But it tried to attack. He tore the dog to pieces on my own doorstep. I couldn't see the fight, but I could hear. The beast held him up long enough for me to run for it. Out the back door, into the storm.

"There was a stream half a mile away. I made for that, plunged into it, floated two miles down, went ashore, picked up a ride to London. Next morning I left London on a freighter for Australia before he could pick up my trail again."

Jorman heard the archaeologist draw a deep breath.

"It took him six months to get on to me again, up in the Australian gold country. Again I heard him in time. I got away on a horse as he was forcing his way into my cabin, caught a cargo plane for Melbourne, took a fast boat to Shanghai. But I didn't stay there long."

"Why not?" Jorman asked. He fancied that Carraden had shuddered slightly.

"Too much like his own country. Conditions were – favourable for him in the Orient. Unfavourable for me. I had a hunch. I hurried on to Manila and took a plane for the States there. Got a letter later from an old Chinese servant that *he* arrived the next night."

Jorman sipped slowly at his coffee, his brow knitted. He did not doubt the man's sincerity, but the story *was* a bit puzzling.

"This fellow, this enemy of yours," he commented slowly,

"you said the Orient was too much like his own country. I assume you mean Egypt."

"Yes. He comes from Egypt. I incurred his – well, his enmity there."

"He's a native then? An Egyptian native?"

Carraden hesitated, seeming to choose his words.

"Well, yes," he said finally. "In a way you might call him a native of Egypt. Though, strictly speaking, he comes from another – another country. One less well known."

"But," Jorman persisted, "I should think that you, a man of wealth, would have all kinds of recourse against a native, no matter where he might be from. After all, the man is bound to be conspicuous, and ought to be easy to pick up. I know you said the police could not help you, but have you tried? And how in the world does the fellow follow you so persistently? From London to Australia to Shanghai – that's a thin trail to run down."

"I know you're puzzled," the other told him. "But take my word for it," the police are no good. This chap – well, he just isn't conspicuous, that's all. He moves mostly by night. But even so he can go anywhere.

"He has – well, methods. And as for following me, he has his own ways of doing that, too. He's persistent. So awfully, awfully persistent. That's the horror of it: that blind, stubborn persistence with which he keeps on my trail."

Jorman was silent. Then he shook his head.

"I admit you've got me curious," he told Carraden. "I can see easily enough there are some things you don't want to tell me. I suppose the reason he's hunting you so doggedly is one of them."

"Right," the Englishman admitted. "It was while the expedition was digging out old Tut-Ankh-Tothet. It was something I did. A law I violated. A law I was aware of, but – well, I went ahead anyway.

"You see, there were some things we found buried with old Tothet the press didn't hear of. Some papyri, some clay tablets. And off the main tomb a smaller one . . .

47

"Well, I can't tell you more. I violated an ancient law, then got panicky and tried to escape the consequences. In doing so, I ran afoul of this – this fellow. And brought him down on my neck. If you don't mind –"

There was a desperate note in his host's voice. Jorman nodded.

"Certainly," he agreed. "I'll drop the subject. After all, it's your business. You've never tried to ambush the fellow and have it out with him, I suppose?"

He imagined Carraden shaking his head.

"No use," the other said shortly. "My only safety is in flight. So I've kept running. When I got to 'Frisco, I thought I was safe for a while. But this time he was on my heels almost at once. I heard him coming up the street for me late one foggy night. I got out the back door and ran for it. Got away to the Canadian plains.

"I planted myself out in the middle of nowhere, on a great, rolling grassy plain with no neighbour for miles. Where no one would even think of me, much less speak to me or utter my name. I was safe there almost a year. But in the end it was – well, almost a mistake."

Carraden put down his cup with a clatter. Jorman imagined it was because the cup had almost slipped from shaking fingers.

"You see, out there on the prairie, there were no footsteps. This time he came at night, as usual, and he was almost on me before I was aware of it. And my horse was lame. I got away. But it was a near thing. Nearer than I like to remember . . .

"So I came to New York. I've been here since, in the very heart of the city. It's the best place of all to hide. Among people. So many millions crossing and recrossing my path muddy up my trail, confuse the scent –"

"Confuse the scent?" Jorman exclaimed.

Carraden coughed. "Said more than I meant to, that time," he admitted. "Yes, it's true. He scents me out. In part, at least.

"It's hard to explain. Call it the intangible evidences of my passage."

"I see." The man's voice pleaded so for belief that Jorman nodded, though he was far from seeing.

"I've been here almost a year now," the Englishman told him. "Almost twelve months with no sign of him. I've been cautious; man, how cautious I've been! Lying in my burrow like a terrified rabbit.

"Most of that time I've been right here, close to Times Square, where a million people a day cut my trail. I've huddled in my two rooms here – there's a bedroom beyond – going out only by day. He is usually most active at night. In the day people confuse him. It's the lonely reaches of the late night hours he likes best. And it's during them I huddle here, listening wakefully . . .

"Except on stormy nights like this. Storms make his job more difficult. The rain washes away my scent, the confusion of the winds and the raging of the elements dissipate my more intangible trail. That's why I ventured out tonight.

"Some day, even here, he'll find me," Sir Andrew Carraden said continuing, his voice tight with strain. "I'm prepared. I'll hear him coming – I hope – and as he forces this door, I'll get out through the other one, the one in the bedroom, and get away. I early learned the folly of holing up in a burrow with only one exit. Now I always have at least one emergency doorway.

"Believe me, man, it's a ghastly existence. The lying awake in the quiet hours of the night, listening, listening for him; the clutch at the heart, the sitting bolt upright, the constant and continuing terror –"

Carraden did not finish his sentence. He was silent for several minutes, fighting, Jorman imagined, for self-control. Then the springs of his easy chair squeaked as he leaned forward.

"Look," the Englishman said then, in such desperate earnestness that his voice trembled a bit. "You must wonder whether I just brought you up here to tell you this tale. I didn't. I had a purpose. I told you the story to see how you reacted. And I'm satisfied. Anyway, you didn't openly disbelieve me; and if you think I'm crazy, maybe you'll humour me anyway. I have a proposition to make."

Jorman sat up a bit straighter.

"Yes?" he asked, his face expressing uncertainty. "What –"

"What kind of proposition?" Carraden finished the sentence for him. "This. That you help me out by listening for him."

Jorman jerked his head up involuntarily, so that if he had not been blind he would have been staring into the other's face.

"Listen for your enemy?"

"Yes," the Englishman told him, voice hoarse. "Listen for his approach. Like a sentinel. An outpost. Look, man, you're down there in your little stand every evening from six on, I've noticed. You stay until late at night. You're posted there not fifty yards from this hotel.

"When he comes, he'll go by you. He's bound to have to cast about a bit, to unravel the trail – double back and forth like a hunting dog, you know, until he gets it straightened out.

"He may go by three or four times before he's sure. You have a keen ear. If he goes by while you're on the job, you're bound to hear him."

Carraden's voice quickened, became desperately persuasive.

"And if you do, you can let me know. I'll instruct the doorman to come over if you signal. Or you can leave your stand and come up here; you can make it easily enough, only fifty paces. But somehow you must warn me. Say you will, man!"

Jorman hesitated in his answer. Sir Andrew mistook his silence.

"If you're frightened," he said, "there's no need to be. He won't attack you. Only me."

"That part's all right," Jorman told him honestly. "What you've told me isn't altogether clear, and – I'll be frank – I'm not absolutely sure whether you're sane or not. But I wouldn't mind listening for you. Only, don't you see, I wouldn't have any way of recognizing your enemy's step."

Carraden gave a little whistling sigh that he checked at once.

"Good man!" The exclamation was quiet, but his voice showed relief. "Just so you'll do it. That last bit is easy enough. I've heard him several times. I can imitate his step for you, I think. There's only one thing worrying me.

"He – not everyone can hear him. But I'm counting on your

50

blindness to give your ears the extra sensitivity – No matter. We have to have a go at it. Give me a moment."

Jorman sat in silence and waited. The rain, beating against the panes of two windows, was distinctly lessening. Somewhere distant a fire siren wailed, a banshee sound.

Carraden was making a few tentative scrapings, with his hands or his feet, on the floor.

"Got it!" he announced. "I've put a bedroom slipper on each hand. It's a noise like this."

With the soft-soled slippers he made a noise like the shuffle of a large bare foot – a double sound, *shuffle-shuffle*, followed by a pause, then repeated.

"If you're extra keen," he announced, "you can hear a faint click or scratch at each step. But –"

Then Jorman heard him sit up straight, knew Carraden was staring at his face.

"What is it, man?" the Englishman cried in alarm. "What's wrong?"

Jorman sat very tense, his fingers gripping the arms of his chair.

"Sir Andrew," he whispered, his lips stiff. "Sir Andrew! I've already heard those footsteps. An hour ago in the rain he went by my stand."

In the long silence that followed, Jorman could guess how the blood was draining from the other man's ruddy face, how the knuckles of his hands clenched.

"Tonight?" Carraden asked then, his voice harsh and so low that Jorman could hardly hear him. "Tonight, man?"

"Just a few minutes before you came by," Jorman blurted. "I heard footsteps – *his* steps – shuffling by. The dog woke up and whimpered. They approached me slowly, pausing, then going on."

The Englishman breathed, "Go on, man! What then?"

"They turned. He went down Seventh Avenue, going south."

Sir Andrew Carraden leaped to his feet, paced across the room, wheeled, came back.

"He's tracked me down at last!" he said in a tight voice, from which a note of hysteria was not far absent. "I've got to go. Tonight. Now. You say he turned south?"

Jorman nodded.

"But that means nothing." Carraden spoke swiftly, as if thinking out loud. "He'll find he's lost the track. He'll turn back. And since he passed, I've made a fresh trail. The rain may not have washed it quite away. He may have picked it up. He may be coming up those stairs now. Where's my bag? My passport? My money? All in my bureau. Excuse me. Sit tight."

Jorman heard a door flung open, heard the man rush into the adjoining bedroom, heard a tight bureau drawer squeal.

Then Carraden's footsteps again. A moment after, a bolt on a door pulled back. Then the door itself rattled. A pause, and it rattled again, urgently. Once again, this time violently. Jorman could hear Carraden's loud breathing in the silence that followed.

"The door won't open!" There was an edge of fear in the Englishman's voice as he called out. "There's a key or something in the lock. From the outside."

He came back into the sitting-room with a rush, paused beside Jorman.

"That message!" The words came through Carraden's teeth. "The one the bloody clerk handed me. I wonder if –"

Paper ripped, rattled. Sir Andrew Carraden began to curse.

"The fool!" he almost sobbed. "Oh, the bloody, bloody fool. 'Dear sir'" – Carraden's voice was shaking now – "'redecoration of the corridor on the north side of your suite necessitated our opening your door this afternoon to facilitate the painting of it. In closing and locking it, a key inadvertently jammed in the lock, and we could not at once extricate it. Our locksmith will repair your lock promptly in the morning. Trusting you will not be inconvenienced –'

"God deliver us from fools!" Sir Andrew gasped. "Luckily there's still time to get out this way. Come on, man, don't sit there. I'll show you down. But we must hurry, hurry."

Jorman heard the other man's teeth chattering faintly together in the excess of emotion that was shaking him, felt the muscular

52

quivering of near-panic in the big man as he put out his hand and took Sir Andrew's arm to help himself rise. And then, as he was about to lift himself, his fingers clamped tight about the Englishman's wrist.

"Carraden!" he whispered. "Carraden! *Listen!*"

The other asked no question. Jorman felt the quivering muscles beneath his fingers tense. And a silence that was like a hand squeezing them breathless seemed to envelop the room. There was not even the faint, distant sound of traffic to break it.

Then they both heard it. In the hallway, coming towards the door. The faint padding sound of shuffling footsteps . . .

It was Foxfire, whimpering piteously at their feet, that broke the spell momentarily holding them.

"He" – Carraden's word was a gasp – "he's out there!"

He left Jorman's side. Jorman heard him shoving with desperate strength at something heavy. Castors squeaked. Some piece of furniture tipped over and fell with a crash against the inside of the door.

"There!" Carraden groaned. "The desk. And the door's bolted. That'll hold him a moment. Sit tight, man. Hold the pup. He'll ignore you. It's me he wants. I've got to get that other door open before he can come through."

His footsteps raced away into the bedroom. Jorman sat where he was, Foxfire under his arm, so tense that his muscles ached from sheer fright.

In the bedroom there was a crash, as of a man plunging against a closed door that stubbornly would not give. But above the noise from the bedroom, Jorman could hear the barricaded door – the door beyond which *he* was – start to give.

Nails screamed as they came forth from wood. Hinges groaned. And the whole mass – door, lintels, desk – moved inward an inch or so. A pause, and then the terrible, inexorable pressure from the other side came again. With a vast rending the door gave way and crashed inward over the barricading furniture.

And in the echoes of the crash he heard the almost soundless *shuffle-shuffle* of feet crossing the room towards the bedroom.

In the bedroom Sir Andrew Carraden's effort to force the jammed door ceased suddenly. Then the Englishman screamed, an animal cry of pure terror from which all intelligence was gone. The window in the bedroom crashed up with a violence that shattered the glass.

After that there was silence for a moment, until Jorman's acute hearing caught, from the street outside and five floors down, the sound of an object striking the pavement.

Sir Andrew Carraden had jumped . . .

Somehow Jorman found the strength to stumble to his feet. He dashed straight forward towards the door, and fell over the wreckage of it. Hurt, but not feeling it, he scrambled up again and stumbled into the hall and down the corridor.

Somehow his questing hands found a door that was sheathed in metal, and he thrust it open. Beyond were banisters. Stairs. By the sense of feel he rushed down recklessly.

How many minutes it took to reach the lobby, to feel his way blindly past the startled desk clerk out to the street, he did not know. Or whether he had got down before *he* had.

Once outside on the wet pavement, cool night air on his cheek, he paused, his breath coming in sobbing gasps. And as he stood there, footsteps, shuffling footsteps, passed close by him from behind and turned westward.

Then Jorman heard an astounding thing. He heard Sir Andrew Carraden's footsteps also, a dozen yards distant, hurrying away from him.

Sir Andrew Carraden had leaped five floors. And still could walk . . .

No, run. For the tempo of the man's steps was increasing. He was trotting now. Now running. And behind the running footsteps of Carraden were *his* steps, moving more swiftly, too, something scratching loudly on the concrete each time he brought a foot down.

"Sir Andrew!" Jorman called loudly, senselessly, "Sir An –"

Then he stumbled and almost fell, trying to follow. Behind him the desk clerk came hurrying up. He exclaimed something in shocked tones, but Jorman did not even hear him. He was bending down, his hands exploring the object over which he had stumbled.

"Listen!" Jorman gasped with a dry mouth to the desk clerk, jittering above him. "Tell me quick! I've got to know. What did the man look like who followed me out of the hotel just now?"

"F-followed you?" the clerk stuttered. "Nobody f-followed you. Nobody but you has gone in or out in the last hu-half hour. Listen, why did he do it? Why did he jump?"

Jorman did not answer him.

"Dear God," he was whispering, and in a way it was a prayer. "Oh, dear God!"

His hand was touching the dead body of Andrew Carraden, lying broken and bloody on the pavement.

But his ears still heard those footsteps of pursued and pursuer, far down the block, racing away until not even he could make them out any longer.

THE GNOMON

JAN MARK

HANDSOME DANIEL MADDISON strolled through the hall of the Golden Wheel Guest House and chanced on a mirror that hung near the reception desk.

"Dan loves mirrors," his sister Clare had once said. "He can look at them for hours." He permitted himself a sidelong glance in passing, but halted when he heard his mother chatting in the coffee lounge with Mrs Glover, the proprietor. They were apparently discussing Daniel.

"Honestly," said Mrs Maddison, "you'd never think he was nearly sixteen."

Daniel and his reflection nodded to each other in tacit agreement. They could easily pass for eighteen, and often did.

"Sometimes he behaves like a five-year-old." Daniel scowled and moved closer to the door of the coffee lounge, the better to hear Mrs Glover's reply. Mrs Glover, schooled by years of discreet hospitality, spoke always with restraint, but it was Mrs Newcombe, a fellow guest, who answered his mother. Mrs Newcombe communicated through a built-in loud hailer.

"I'd never have suggested it, if I'd thought he'd mind," Mrs Newcombe yelled, elegantly.

"Just one afternoon he's been asked to give up, out of his

entire holiday, and he's been sulking since breakfast," said Mrs Maddison. "Still, he's not going to upset poor Susie; I'll see to that."

Daniel's afternoon, which had been scheduled to include a naughty film at the ABC in town on the strength of his easily passing for eighteen, was to be sacrificed in the interests of lolloping Susie Newcombe from Leighton Buzzard who wanted to explore certain atmospheric ruins, a squalid pile of hard core on a nearby hillside, and dignified as an ancient monument solely by the presence of a plaque erected by the Department of the Environment. Daniel's services as escort and guide had been rashly offered, and lacking his permission, by his mother who, without sharing it, liked to boast about his knowledge of archaeology. Both Maddisons and Newcombes had arrived at the Golden Wheel on the same day, but by adroit programming Daniel had avoided meeting Susie after the first confrontation at dinner on the evening of their arrival. This unfortunate introduction during which, after a day spent travelling, neither of the parties was at their best, had sealed Susie's fate as far as Daniel was concerned.

"I love old places like this," Susie had said, gesturing at the low ceilings and murky nooks of the Golden Wheel's dining-room. "I think this place is really spooky, don't you? Don't you?" Daniel remained silent and savaged his rhubarb crumble. "Don't you think it's spooky?"

"Not particularly," Daniel said. He detested words like spooky, eerie, spine-chilling; also weird, incorrectly used. "Just decrepit," he said flatly.

"But doesn't it make you *feel* weird?" Susie persisted. "I felt something, the moment I came in."

"I bet you did," Daniel mouthed, under the pretence of chewing rhubarb crumble.

"They've got a ghost," Clare chipped in. "I asked."

"I know. It's really weird how you can tell, isn't it?" Susie said. "Mrs Glover said it was a girl who crept out one day to meet her lover and he never turned up. Mrs Glover said she's still waiting."

"Has she seen her?"

58

"Nobody's seen her," Susie breathed. Crumbs flew. "Apparently you just sort of feel her, sort of waiting."

"*Weird.*"

"And you can smell roses. She was carrying roses."

"Has Mrs Glover ever smelled roses?"

"Yes. You can sometimes smell them even in winter. She said, if you ever smell roses, you'll know Maud's about – that was her name, this ghost; Maud Ibbotson."

"You'd have a job not to smell roses at this time of year," Daniel observed, looking out of the window at the July sun, low in the sky and flooding with rich colour the rose garden that lay beyond the windows.

"If I smell roses I shall *faint*," Susie remarked, allowing the skin in the jug of custard to flop like a flexible frisbee over her second helping of rhubarb crumble.

"It's really eerie, isn't it?" Clare said. "A ghost you can only smell. What happened to her, this Maud? Did she die of a broken heart, or something?"

"Oh no, I asked Mrs Glover. She said there was an accident. She had a fall, or something, while she was waiting, and when they found her it was too late to do anything, and she died."

"A fall? Out of a window?"

"I expect so. She'd be leaning out to look for him, wouldn't she? I wonder which one it was?" Susie looked round speculatively at the dining-room windows, and sniffed.

"I bet if we found it we should be able to feel something," Clare said.

Susie shuddered pleasurably. "Let's try. I've never seen a ghost, but I often *feel* things."

It was in order to commune with the past that Susie wished to explore the ruins that afternoon, in Daniel's company. Susie would feel less weird in Daniel's company, according to Daniel's mother. "I thought feeling weird was the object of the exercise," said Daniel, but to no avail. He put his head round the door of the coffee lounge and flashed a hideous smile across his face, like a neon advertisement in Piccadilly Circus.

"Where are you off to?" Mrs Maddison asked, with base suspicion.

"To wait for Susie," Daniel said, affronted. Did she really think he was such a fool as to sneak off to the cinema? "I'll be in the rose garden – will you tell her when she comes down?"

He was not lying. He fully intended to wait for Susie in the rose garden but, so far as he knew, neither Susie nor his mother was aware that at the Golden Wheel there were two rose gardens; the one at the back, beyond the dining-room, and the other one. Daniel was going to wait in the other one.

He had discovered the second garden by accident while evading, as it happened, an earlier encounter with spooky Susie and her chilly spine. The official rose garden was broad and spacious with standard trees in circular beds, a blanched statue or two, and little white iron tables and chairs disposed here and there on the clipped turf. It reminded him of a crematorium. Along one side was a low rockery hedged with conifers that had had their tops nipped off in adolescence. Resolutely squaring their shoulders they now formed an impenetrable windbreak.

"They're pleached," said Mrs Newcombe, and with her daughter's vampire ability to fasten onto a harmless word and bleed it white, she repeated it at intervals, liking the sound of it. "Pleached." It described her voice very accurately, Daniel thought. He could hear her pleaching now as he slipped away from the house, crossed the lawn beyond the dining-room windows, and sidled between the cypress boughs of the conifer hedge, into the other rose garden.

He guessed that before the conifers were planted and the rockery raised, it had been an extension of the main garden, but now the windbreak obscured it entirely. Daniel, who had originally squeezed between the trees in an effort at hasty concealment, had been amazed to find himself in an open space instead of being, as he had expected, compressed between the conifers and a wall. Today he muttered, "Open, sesame," and passed straight through to stand at the head of the second rose garden. Unlike the public part, it seemed to exist for the sole purpose of growing roses. It was narrow. Heavy banks of pink blossoms, one could scarcely call them mere flowers, overhung a trellis on either side, and shaded lush grass that had been cut, but not recently. Yellow ramblers rambled; cream climbers rioted. At the far end was a wooden rustic seat, weathered to the shade of old pewter, and at the nearer, close to where he stood, was the only other furniture, a sundial. Daniel had expected to find an inscription on its bronze plate, *Tempus fugit* perhaps, and there was one, but not *Tempus fugit*. *Time and the hour run through the roughest day*, it said in Roman letters that encircled the Roman numerals. Daniel, recognizing the quotation, took it to mean that everything must come to an end if you wait long enough. The gnomon pointed at his back as he walked down the garden to the rustic seat.

"Come into the garden, Maud," said Daniel, the scent of roses clogging his flared nostrils, and suddenly suspected that it was here, and not in the house, that Miss Ibbotson had come to her tryst. He waited for the sensation that ought to chill his spine as it certainly would have chilled Susie's. If Susie were there, would Maud Ibbotson manifest herself as she waited for her faithless lover who was now, according to Clare's researches, one hundred and twelve years overdue? He imagined her standing by the rustic seat, tall, stately, leaning several degrees from the perpendicular and counterbalanced by a bustle, like an old joke in *Punch*. She would be no joke if he did see her, but no one ever had seen her. They only smelled roses.

Daniel sat down on the rustic seat, propped his feet on the farther arm and settled back to read and yawn. Distantly, mercifully diminished by distance, Mrs Newcombe pleached on. From time to time the telephone rang in the reception hall, but in the rose garden, regardless of the sundial's admonition, time hung suspended. The roses, ripe for disintegration, nevertheless remained whole. Not a petal fell to the ground. Beyond the hedge a strident shriek, fit to chill the hardiest spine, split the gentle air.

"Danie-elll!"

He looked down discouragingly at his book.

"Danie-elll!" The voice advanced, receded, advanced again. Daniel, rather than look at the hedge in case Susie felt his penetrating gaze and discovered him, fastened his eyes upon the nearest rose, a swollen globe of lingerie pink, like something off a chorus girl's garter. He stared at it.

"Danie-el!"

Over-examined, the rose blurred and softened before his eyes, but when he refocused it was still there, and the voice, a little subdued, receded disconsolately towards the house. "Danny?" Daniel's left forefinger reached out and tipped the rose under the chin, but even now, on the point of dissolution, it remained on its stem.

"Daniel?" It was his mother's voice, sharpened by anger to Mrs Newcombe's pitch, and like a harpy echo Mrs Newcombe joined in. "Daniel?"

"I'm not here, dear," Daniel murmured. He heard their conversation in angular duet, his mother embarrassed and apologetic, Mrs Newcombe making light of things, but maternal, affronted on Susie's behalf. She and Mrs Maddison were already on Pat and Shirley terms.

"Oh Shirley, I'm *so* sorry. I can't think . . ."

"It's not *your* fault, Pat."

The telephone rang again. Daniel glanced up and saw the rose's soft sphere glowing at the very edge of his eyesight. When he reached the end of the chapter he would allow himself the pleasure of beheading that foolish, nodding flower if it did not fall before he was ready for it.

Mrs Newcombe pleached unexpectedly close to the conifer hedge. Daniel's eyes were drawn unwillingly towards it, twin lasers drilling into the back of her crimped head through the dense branches (Go away, you old bat. Hop off.) and saw, near the sundial, a rose explode silently in a shower of pink petals. Daniel stared and absorbed what he had seen. It appeared that the rose had not so much dropped as *burst*. A little closer, the same thing happened again; a second rose vanished and this time the petals did not fall down, but flew up, as if a hand had clouted the rose from below. Daniel closed his own itching forefinger against his palm and saw a third rose evaporate. At the same time he felt his trouser leg stir against his shin, a web of hair unravel across his forehead. Waiting for his own rose to drop, as it surely must now that the wind had found its way into the garden, Daniel swung his feet to the ground and felt a current of air round his ankles, too low to fell a rose; and then, on the far side of the garden, a fourth blossom erupted with such violence that the petals were knocked into the foliage and lodged there. Not one reached the grass. Three blooms in close conference on one stem were struck apart. Daniel watched the drifting confetti and pondered upon the word *struck*. It was almost, Daniel thought, as if someone were walking round the garden and striking at the roses as he went: as she went: there . . . there . . . and *there*: someone who was waiting, and had tired of waiting, tired of roses. Now a dozen died together under a downward blow that dashed them to pieces, while a lateral swipe at another spray sent petals flying against Daniel's face, three metres distant.

Now she is using both hands, Daniel thought. Left and right – oh, our patience is *exhausted*, isn't it?

There was no wind in the adjacent garden where, over the tops of the conifers, Daniel could see a crack willow weeping its burden to the ground. Just beside him, fragments of his own rose took to the air and he heard the soft thud as it broke up. It was fearfully close.

Here she comes, said Daniel, not noticing that he had closed his book and now sat on the very edge of the rustic seat, one arm flexed against the silky wood to thrust himself upright. Here she comes. Not yet impelled to run, she strode, skirt sweeping the turf, beside one trellis, across to the other, across, along, and as she went her arm swung up and *there*, another rose gone, and another, and a whole blasted bouquet there, there, and *there*.

Daniel drew in his feet as the imperious air swept by him. She was moving faster now, there, there, and *here*. Not a rose escaped that was ripe, and now she was laying into the half-blown flowers, tearing them alive from the branches, not pausing to crush them but flinging them behind her, grabbing at the next while the last was still airborne, arcing and diving. The grass was dappled all over, not only below the trellises, with pink and cream and yellow bruises. She tore at the very stems, twisting and ripping them from the briars. They were not thornless roses. Her hands were surely shredded, blood running down her scything arms to the elbow. And flayed to the bone as she must be, still she flung from one side to the other, wrenching and rending until even the buds were broken and hung down, dead before they were alive, as she cast herself from side to side, there, there and *there*.

And then she stopped, wrecked, and let her bleeding arms dangle. Daniel, straining to see the thing he must avoid, lifted himself from the seat and began to edge across the grass towards the shelter of the trellis, eyes everywhere to see where the next rose would fall. But there was no next rose. In all the garden there was not one bloom intact, no living thing left to destroy.

Except me, said Daniel, and the air struck him in the face and spun him round so that he fell back against the seat and slithered to the ground, his head aching from side to side as though it were an arm that had felled him. He saw the grass creep and gleam, under pressure, as the tempest wrapped him round, in awful, forceful silence, and dragged him to his feet.

"No!" Daniel shouted. "Not me, not me. I never kept you waiting." He wrestled with the wind that surged and sucked at him until he began to stumble down the garden towards the sundial, with cold arms about his neck, cold skirts flapping about his legs, and a frozen face against his cheek. He thought she must throw him out of her garden, neck and crop, to punish him for keeping a poor girl waiting. But he soon saw that although he and she were headed for the conifers, before them, directly in his path, stood the sundial.

"No!" he shouted again, and leaned back against the wind that all at once gathered behind him and pushed, with horrible confidence, so that the slippery soles of his shoes skated over the grass and petals towards the stone column, the bronze dial,

the shining gnomon. "No," he said, "no!" But a colder breath than his stopped the cry in his mouth, and a final thrust sent him reeling, headlong. His foot came down heavily on the greasy roses, turning his ankle, and he fell flat, on the grass, and at the same time heard a hissing whistle of breath that choked and stopped, bubbled, and died away. He lay at the foot of the sundial, one hand to his forehead where he had gashed it against the plinth, and looking up saw the gnomon pierce the cloudless sky, just where his heart would have been had his skid not thrown him to one side. It glistened wetly in the dry, still air.

After a long time he raised himself from the turf and crawled away through the conifers to the garden of the Golden Wheel, where his mother and Mrs Newcombe were spreading crockery and cakes on a little white iron table. They both turned round simultaneously and converged with shrill cries, hauling him upright.

"Where've you *been*?" his mother demanded. Daniel pointed vaguely.

"In there."

"In where?"

"There."

"What are you talking about? Oh look, Shirley, his head. Daniel, what have you done?"

"The rose garden," Daniel said. "Don't go in the rose garden."

"This is the rose garden. What is he talking about?"

"Wandering," said Mrs Newcombe, wisely, mouth pursed. "You ought to get him inside to lie down, Pat. Can't be too careful with knocks on the head, especially just there."

Mrs Glover came towards them across the starry grass.

"An accident? Oh my, what's all this?" She took Daniel by the chin and examined his forehead. "That's a nasty one. Where did you get that?"

"In the rose garden, he says. I can't imagine what happened," Mrs Maddison was saying. "We just looked round and saw him lying over there, by the rockery. I can't get any sense out of him. He just keeps saying he was in the rose garden, but he wasn't, of course. *We* were. I can't think how he got there without anyone seeing him, and I can't get him to say what hit him. It looks like something sharp – right-angled, almost. Like the corner of something."

"Not this rose garden . . . that one." He tried to raise an arm to show them, but they bore him indoors and made him lie down on the cretonne-covered settee in the coffee lounge.

"*I* thought he came out through the conifer hedge," said Mrs Newcombe.

"Oh." Mrs Glover looked so dismayed that the twittering conference fell silent. "Oh dear, *that* rose garden. Oh no, he shouldn't have gone in there.

"You mean there *is* another? Mrs Maddison rounded on Daniel. "I suppose you were trespassing."

"Not trespassing." Mrs Glover hurried to intervene. "But we don't use it any more. It gets so windy." She looked at him. "Is that what happened, dear? It got windy?"

He nodded. Mrs Newcombe swooped over him with an icy dripping flannel and swabbed his forehead.

"Oh, nonsense. There hasn't been a breath of wind all day," Mrs Maddison cried, vexed and put out. She hated scenes, especially scenes of Daniel's engineering.

"It's a funny place, that little garden," Mrs Glover said. "That's why we hedged it off. It seems to act as a kind of funnel. You get quite strong winds in there, even when it's still everywhere else." She laughed, almost apologetically. "Our little tempests, we call them."

Daniel thought of the wreckage that this little tempest had left behind it. He opened one eye and saw Mrs Glover looking at him. She telegraphed to him: *I know what you were doing in there, young man, and serve you right.*

He answered: *It's happened before, hasn't it? You ought to put up a wall.*

Mrs Newcombe was pleaching again. "He looked as if he'd seen a ghost."

"I didn't see anything," Daniel said, weakly. They came over to him and leaned down, all concern.

67

"Can you remember what happened, yet?" Mrs Maddison asked. "Did you have a fall?"

Yes, I had a fall, just like Maud. Maud had a fall, too. Do you know what she fell *on*?

"I was just reading," said Daniel, "and waiting for Susie."

"Susie was waiting for *you*," his mother retorted, asperity eroding sympathy.

"Where is she?"

"She went out with Clare, in the end. She got tired of waiting."

"She wasn't the only one," Daniel whispered, and turned his face to the cretonne back of the settee, to escape the slight smile that curled Mrs Glover's prim lips. In the end they gave up grilling him and left him to his own devices.

"A little sleep won't do any harm," said Mrs Newcombe.

When they had gone, back to their tea at the white iron table, Daniel sat up gingerly, and looked through the window towards the conifer hedge, behind which, among the scent of roses, Maud Ibbotson was still waiting, so angry, so desperate for company, her patience worn so dangerously thin.

THE HAUNTED
AND THE HAUNTERS
OR THE HOUSE AND THE BRAIN

EDWARD BULWER-LYTTON

A FRIEND OF MINE, who is a man of letters and a philosopher, said to me one day, as if between jest and earnest, "Fancy! Since we last met, I have discovered a haunted house in the midst of London."

"Really haunted? And by what? Ghosts?"

"Well, I can't answer that question; all I know is this: six weeks ago my wife and I were in search of a furnished apartment. Passing a quiet street, we saw on the window of one of the houses a sign, 'Apartments Furnished.' The situation suited us; we entered the house, liked the rooms, engaged them by the week – and left them the third day. No power on earth could have reconciled my wife to stay longer; and I don't wonder at it."

"What did you see?"

"It was not so much what we saw or heard that drove us away, as it was terror which seized both of us whenever we passed by the door of a certain unfurnished room, in which we neither saw nor heard anything. Accordingly, on the fourth morning I told the woman who kept the house that the rooms did not quite suit us, and we would not stay out our week. She said, drily, 'I know why: you have stayed longer than any other lodger. Few ever stayed a second night; none before you a third. But I take it they have been very kind to you.'

" 'They? Who?' I asked, affecting to smile.

" 'Why, they who haunt the house, whoever they are. I don't mind them; I remember them many years ago, when I lived in this house, not as a servant; but I know they will be the death of me some day. I don't care; I'm old, and must die soon anyhow. And then I shall be with them, and in this house still.' "

"You excite my curiosity," I said. "Nothing I should like better than to sleep in a haunted house. Pray give me the address of the one you left so ignominiously."

My friend gave me the address; and when we parted, I walked straight to the house. I found it shut up – no sign at the window, and no response to my knock. As I was turning away, a messenger boy said to me, "Do you want anyone at that house, sir?"

"Yes, I heard it was to be let."

"Let! Why, the woman who kept it is dead – has been dead these three weeks, and no one can be found to stay there, though Mr Jones, the owner, offered ever so much. He offered Mother, who chars for him, £1 a week just to open and shut the windows, and she would not."

"Would not! And why?"

"The house is haunted: and the old woman who kept it was found dead in her bed, with her eyes wide open. They say the devil strangled her."

"Where does the owner of the house live?"

"In Germyn Street, No 11."

"What is he – in any business?"

"No, sir, nothing particular; a single gentleman."

I was lucky enough to find Mr Jones at home. I told him my name and business. I said I heard the house was considered to be haunted; that I had a strong desire to examine it, and that I would be greatly obliged if he would allow me to hire it, though only for a night. I was willing to pay whatever he asked for that privilege.

"Sir," he said with great courtesy, "the house is at your service, for as short or as long a time as you please. Rent is out of the question. I cannot let it, for I cannot even get a servant to keep it in order or answer the door. Unluckily, the house is haunted, if I may use that expression, not only by night, but by day; though at night the disturbances are of a more unpleasant and sometimes of a more alarming character. The poor old woman who died in it three weeks ago was, in her childhood, known to some of my family and was the only person I could ever induce to remain in the house."

"How long is it since the house acquired this sinister character?" I asked.

"That I can scarcely tell you, but very many years since. The old woman I spoke of said it was haunted when she rented it between thirty and forty years ago. The fact is that my life has been spent in the East Indies, and I returned to England only last year."

"Have you never had a curiosity yourself to pass a night in that house?"

"Yes. I passed not a night, but three hours in broad daylight alone in that house. My curiosity is not satisfied, but it is quenched. I have no desire to renew the experiment. I honestly advise you not to spend a night in that house."

"My interest is exceedingly keen," said I, "and my nerves have been seasoned in such variety of danger that I have the right to rely on them – even in a haunted house."

He said very little more. He took the keys of the house out of his bureau and gave them to me. Thanking him for his frankness, I carried off my prize.

Impatient for the experiment, as soon as I reached home I summoned my servant, a young man of gay spirits, fearless temper, and as free from superstitious prejudices as anyone I could think of.

"Francis," said I, "I have heard of a house in London which is decidedly haunted. I mean to sleep there tonight. From what I hear, there is no doubt that something will allow itself to be seen or heard – something, perhaps, excessively horrible. Do you think if I take you with me, I may rely on your presence of mind, whatever may happen?"

"You may trust me, sir!" answered Francis, grinning with delight.

"Very well. Here are the keys of the house; this is the address. Go there now, and select for me any bedroom you please. Since the house has not been inhabited for weeks, make up a good fire, air the bed well, and see, of course, that there are candles as well as fuel. Take with you my revolver and my dagger – so much for my weapons – and arm yourself equally well. If we are not a match for a dozen ghosts, we shall be a sorry couple of Englishmen."

I was engaged for the rest of the day on business. I dined alone, and about half-past nine I put a book into my pocket and strolled leisurely towards the haunted house. I took with me a favourite dog – an exceedingly sharp, bold, and vigilant bull-terrier; a dog fond of prowling about strange ghostly corners and passages at night in search of rats; a dog of dogs for a ghost.

It was a summer night, but chilly, the sky gloomy and overcast. Still, there was a moon – faint and sickly, but still a moon – and if the clouds permitted, after midnight it would be brighter.

I reached the house, knocked, and my servant opened with a cheerful smile.

"All right, sir, and very comfortable."

"Oh!" said I, rather disappointed; "have you not seen nor heard anything remarkable?"

"Well, sir, I must own I have heard something queer."

"What – what?"

"The sound of feet pattering behind me; and once or twice small noises like whispers close at my ear. Nothing more."

"You are not at all frightened?"

"I! Not a bit of it, sir," and his bold look reassured me that, happen what might, he would not desert me.

We were in the hall, the street door closed, and my attention was now drawn to my dog. He had at first run in eagerly enough, but had sneaked back to the door, and was scratching and whining to get out. After being patted on the head and gently encouraged, the dog seemed to reconcile himself to the situation and followed Francis and me through the house, but keeping close at my heels instead of hurrying inquisitively in advance, which was his normal habit in all strange places.

We first visited the kitchen and the cellars, in which there were two or three bottles of wine still left in a bin, covered with cobwebs and evidently undisturbed for many years. For the rest, we discovered nothing of interest. There was a gloomy little backyard with very high walls. The stones of this yard were very damp; and what with the damp and the dust and smoke-grime on the pavement, our feet left a slight impression where we walked.

And now appeared the first strange phenomenon witnessed by myself in this strange house. I saw, just before me, the print of a foot suddenly form itself. I stopped, caught hold of my servant, and pointed to it. In advance of that footprint as suddenly dropped another. We both saw it. I went quickly to the place; the footprint kept advancing before me, a small footprint – the foot of a child. The impression was too faint to distinguish the shape, but it seemed to us both that it was the print of a naked foot. This phenomenon ceased when we arrived at the opposite wall, and it did not repeat itself as we returned.

We remounted the stairs, and entered the rooms on the ground floor, a dining parlour, a small back parlour, and a still smaller third room – all as still as death. We then visited the drawing-rooms, which seemed fresh and new. In the front room I seated myself in an armchair. Francis placed on the table the candlestick with which he had lighted us. I told him to shut the door. As we turned to do so, a chair opposite me moved from the wall quickly and noiselessly and dropped itself about a yard from my own chair, immediately in front of it.

My dog put back his head and howled.

Francis, coming back, had not observed the movement of the chair. He employed himself now in calming the dog.

I continued to gaze at the chair, and fancied I saw on it a pale blue misty outline of a human figure, but an outline so indistinct that I could only distrust my own vision. The dog was now quiet.

"Put back that chair opposite me," I said to Francis. "Put it back to the wall."

Francis obeyed. "Was that you, sir?" said he, turning abruptly.

"I! What?"

"Why, something struck me. I felt it sharply on the shoulder – just here."

"No," said I. "But we have jugglers present, and though we may not discover their tricks, we shall catch *them* before they frighten *us*."

We did not stay long in the drawing-rooms; in fact, they felt so damp and so chilly that I was glad to get to the fire upstairs. We locked the doors of the drawing-rooms – a precaution which we had taken with all the rooms we had searched below. The bedroom my servant had selected for me was the best on the floor: a large one, with two windows fronting the street. The four-posted bed, which took up much space, was opposite the fire, which burnt clear and bright. A door in the wall to the left, between the bed and the window, adjoined the room which my servant took for himself. This was a small room with a sofa-bed, and had no other door but the one leading into my bedroom. On either side of my fireplace was a cupboard, without locks, flush with the wall and covered with dull-brown paper. We examined these cupboards – only hooks to suspend dresses; nothing else. We sounded the walls – evidently solid: the outer walls of the building.

Having finished the survey of these rooms, I warmed myself a few moments and lighted my cigar. Then, still accompanied by Francis, went forth to complete my reconnoitre. In the landing-place there was another door; it was closed firmly.

"Sir," said my servant in surprise, "I unlocked this door with all the others when I first came; it cannot have got locked from the inside, for . . . "

Before he had finished his sentence, the door, which neither of

74

us then was touching, opened quietly of itself. We looked at each other. The same thought seized both of us: some human agency might be detected here. I rushed in first, my servant following. A small blank dreary room without furniture . . . a few empty boxes and hampers in a corner . . . a small window, the shutters closed . . . not even a fireplace . . . no other door than that by which we had entered . . . no carpet on the floor, and the floor seemed very old, uneven, worm-eaten, mended here and there. But no living being, and no visible place in which a living being could have hidden. As we stood gazing round, the door by which we had entered closed as quietly as it had opened. We were imprisoned.

For the first time I felt a creep of undefinable horror. Not so my servant. "Why, they don't think to trap us, sir? I could break the door with a kick of my foot."

"Try first if it will open to your hand," said I, "while I unclose the shutters and see what is outside."

I unbarred the shutters; the window looked out on the little backyard I have described. There was no ledge – nothing to break the sheer descent of the wall. No man getting out of that window would have found any footing till he had fallen on the stones below.

Francis, meanwhile, was vainly attempting to open the door. He now turned round to me and asked my permission to use force. I willingly gave him the permission he required. But though he was a remarkably strong man, the door did not even shake to his stoutest kick. Breathless and panting, he stopped. I then tried the door myself, equally in vain. As I ceased from the effort, again that creep of horror came over me; but this time it was more cold and stubborn. I felt as if some strange and ghastly vapour were rising up from the chinks of that rugged floor.

The door now very slowly and quietly opened of its own accord. We rushed out on to the landing. We both saw a large pale light – as large as the human figure but shapeless and unsubstantial – move before us, and climb the stairs that led from the landing into the attics. I followed the light, and my servant followed me. It entered a small garret, of which the door stood open. I entered in the same instant. The light then collapsed into a small globe, exceedingly brilliant and vivid; rested a moment on a bed in the corner, quivered, and vanished.

We approached the bed and examined it – a small one such as is commonly found in attics used by servants. On the chest of drawers that stood near it we saw an old faded silk scarf with the needle still left in a half-repaired tear. The scarf was covered with dust; probably it had belonged to the old woman who had last died in that house, and this might have been her bedroom. I had sufficient curiosity to open the drawers: there were a few odds and ends of female dress, and two letters tied round with a narrow ribbon of faded yellow. I took the letters.

We found nothing else in the room worth noticing, nor did the light reappear. But we distinctly heard, as we turned to go, a pattering footfall on the floor – just ahead of us. We went through the other attics (four, in all), the footfall still preceding us. Nothing to be seen – nothing but the footfall heard. I had the letters in my hand: just as I was descending the stairs I distinctly felt my wrist seized, and a faint, soft effort made to draw the letters from my clasp. I only held them the more tightly, and the effort ceased.

We returned to my room, and I then noticed that my dog had not followed us when we had left it. He was keeping close to the fire, and trembling. I was impatient to examine the letters; and while I read them, my servant opened a little box in which he had the weapons I had ordered him to bring. He took them out, placed them on a table close to my bed-head, and then occupied himself in soothing the dog, who, however, seemed to heed him very little.

The letters were short. They were dated, the dates exactly thirty-five years ago. They were evidently from a lover to his mistress, or a husband to some young wife. A reference to a voyage indicated the writer to have been a seafarer. The spelling and handwriting were those of a man poorly educated, but still the language itself was forceful. In the expressions of endearment there was a kind of rough wild love; but here and there were dark hints at some secret not of love – some secret that seemed of crime. "We ought to love each other," was one of the sentences I remember, "for how everyone else would curse us if all was known." Again: "Don't let anyone be in the same room with you at night – you talk in your sleep." And again: "What's done can't be undone; and I tell you there's nothing against us unless the dead could come to life." Here there was underlined in a better handwriting (a woman's), "They do!" At the end of the letter latest in date the same female hand had written these words: "Lost at sea the 4th of June, the same day as ———."

I put down the letters, and began to think over their contents.

Fearing, however, that the train of thought might unsteady my nerves, I determined to keep my mind in a fit state to cope with whatever the night might bring. I roused myself, laid the letters on the table, stirred up the fire, which was still bright and cheering, and opened my book. I read quietly enough till about half-past eleven. I then threw myself, dressed, upon the bed and told my servant he might retire to his own room, but must keep himself awake. I bade him leave open the door between the two rooms.

Thus alone, I kept two candles burning on the table by my bed-head. I placed my watch beside the weapons, and calmly resumed reading. Opposite me the fire burned clear; and on the hearth rug, seemingly asleep, lay the dog. In about twenty minutes I felt an exceedingly cold air pass by my cheek, like a sudden draught. I fancied the door to my right, leading to the landing-place, must have got open. But no – it was closed. I then glanced to my left, and saw the flame of the candles violently swayed as by a wind. At the same moment the watch beside the revolver softly slid from the table – softly, softly – no visible hand – it was gone.

I sprang up, seizing the revolver with one hand, the dagger with the other. I was not willing that my weapons should share the fate of the watch. Thus armed, I looked round the floor. No sign of the watch. Three slow, loud, distinct knocks were now heard at the bed-head.

My servant called out, "Is that you, sir?"

"No. Be on your guard."

The dog now roused himself and sat on his haunches, his ears moving quickly backwards and forwards. He kept his eyes fixed on me with a strange look. Slowly he rose up, all his hair bristling, and stood perfectly rigid, and with the same wild stare. I had no time, however, to examine the dog. Presently, my servant came from his room, and if ever I saw horror in the human face, it was then. I would not have recognized him had we met in the street, so altered was every line.

He passed by me quickly, saying in a whisper that seemed scarcely to come from his lips. "Run – run! It is after me!"

He gained the door to the landing, pulled it open, and rushed out. I followed him into the landing, calling him to stop; but without heeding me, he bounded down the stairs, clinging to the banisters, and taking several steps at a time. I heard the street door open – heard it again clap to. I was left alone in the haunted house.

For a brief moment I remained undecided whether or not to follow my servant. But pride and curiosity forbade a flight. I re-entered my room, closing the door after me, and went cautiously into my servant's room. I found nothing to justify his terror. I again carefully examined the walls to see if there were any concealed door. I could find no trace of one – not even a seam in the dull brown paper with which the room was hung. How, then, had the Thing, whatever it was, which had so scared him got in except through my own chamber?

I returned to my room, shut and locked the door between the rooms, and stood on the hearth, expectant and prepared. I now saw that the dog had slunk into an angle of the wall and was pressing himself close against it, as if literally striving to force his way into it. I approached the animal and spoke to it; the poor brute was beside itself with terror. It showed all its teeth, the slaver dropping from its jaws, and would certainly have bitten me if I had touched it. It did not seem to recognize me.

Finding all efforts to soothe the animal in vain, and fearing that his bite might be as poisonous in that state as in the

madness of rabies, I left it alone, placed my weapons on the table beside the fire, seated myself, and took up my book.

I soon became aware that something came between the page and the light – the page was overshadowed. I looked up, and I saw what I shall find it very difficult, perhaps impossible, to describe.

It was a Darkness shaping itself from the air in very undefined outline. I cannot say it was of a human form, and yet it was more like a human form, or rather shadow, than anything else. As it stood, wholly apart and distinct from the air and the light around it, its size seemed gigantic, the top nearly touching the ceiling.

While I gazed, a feeling of intense cold seized me. An iceberg before me could not have chilled me more. I feel convinced that it was not the cold caused by fear. As I continued to gaze, I thought – but this I cannot say exactly – that I distinguished two eyes looking down on me from the height. One moment I fancied that I saw them clearly, the next they seemed gone. But still two rays of a pale blue light frequently shot through the darkness, as from the height on which I half believed, half doubted, that I had seen the eyes.

I strove to speak – my voice utterly failed me. I could only think to myself, "Is this fear? It is *not* fear!" I strove to rise – in vain; I felt as if I were weighed down by an irresistible force – that sense of utter inadequacy to cope with a force beyond man's, which one may feel in a storm at sea.

And now, as this impression grew on me, now came, at last, horror – horror to a degree that no words can convey. Still I retained pride, if not courage; and in my own mind I said, "This is horror, but it is not fear; unless I fear I cannot be harmed; my reason rejects this thing. It is an illusion. I do not fear."

With a violent effort I succeeded at last in stretching out my hand towards the weapon on the table. As I did so, on the arm and shoulder I received a strange shock, and my arm fell to my side powerless. And now, to add to my horror, the light began slowly to wane from the candles; they were not, as it were, extinguished, but their flame seemed very gradually withdrawn; it was the same with the fire – the light went from the fuel; in a few minutes the room was in utter darkness.

The dread that came over me, to be thus in the dark with that dark Thing, brought a reaction of nerve. I found voice, though the voice was a shriek. I remember that I broke forth with words like these: "I do not fear, my soul does not fear." And at the same time I found the strength to rise. Still in that profound gloom I rushed to one of the windows, tore aside the curtain, flung open the shutters. My first thought was – LIGHT. And when I saw the moon high, clear, and calm, I felt a joy that almost drowned the previous terror. There was the moon, there was also the light from the gas-lamps in the deserted street. I turned to look back into the room; the moon presented its shadow very palely – but still there was light. The dark Thing, whatever it might be, was gone – except that I could yet see a dim shadow, which seemed the shadow of that Thing, against the opposite wall.

My eye now rested on the table, and from under it there rose a hand, visible as far as the wrist. It was the hand of an aged person – lean, wrinkled, small – a woman's hand. That hand very softly closed on the two letters lying on the table: hand and letters both vanished. There then came the same three loud measured knocks I heard at the bed-head before.

As those sounds slowly ceased, I felt the whole room vibrate; and at the far end there rose, as from the floor, sparks or globes like bubbles of light, many-coloured – green, yellow, fire red, azure. Up and down, to and fro, hither, thither, as tiny will-o'-the-wisps the sparks moved slow or swift, each at his own desire. A chair was now moved from the wall without apparent aid, and placed at the opposite side of the table.

Suddenly, from the chair, there grew a shape – a woman's shape. It was distinct as a shape of life, ghastly as a shape of death. The face was young, with a strange mournful beauty: the throat and shoulders were bare, the rest of the form in a loose robe of cloudy white. It began sleeking its long yellow hair, which fell over its shoulders; its eyes were not turned towards me, but to the door; it seemed listening, watching, waiting. The shadow of the Thing in the background grew darker; and again

81

I thought I beheld the eyes gleaming out from the top of the shadow – eyes fixed upon that shape.

As if from the door, though it did not open, there grew out another shape, equally distinct, equally ghastly – a man's shape, a young man's. It was in the dress of the last century. Just as the male shape approached the female, the dark shadow started from the wall, all three for a moment wrapped in darkness. When the pale light returned, the two phantoms were in the grasp of the Thing that towered between them. And there was a bloodstain on the breast of the female. And the phantom male was leaning on its phantom sword, and blood seemed trickling fast from the ruffles, from the lace. And the darkness of the Shadow between swallowed them up. They were gone. And again the bubbles of light shot, and sailed, growing thicker and thicker and more wildly confused in their movements.

The cupboard door to the right of the fireplace now opened, and from it there came the form of an aged woman. In her hand she held letters, the very letters over which I had seen *the* Hand close; and behind her I heard a footstep. She turned round as if to listen, and then she opened the letters and seemed to read. And over her shoulder I saw a livid face, the face of a man long drowned – bloated, bleached, seaweed tangles in its dripping hair. And at her feet lay the form of a corpse, and beside the corpse there cowered a child, a miserable squalid child with famine in its cheeks and fear in its eyes. As I looked in the old woman's face, the wrinkles and lines vanished, and it became a face of youth – hard-eyes, stony, but still youth; and the Shadow darted forth, and darkened over these phantoms as it had darkened over the last.

Nothing now was left but the Shadow, and on that my eyes were intently fixed, till again eyes grew out of the Shadow – evil, serpent eyes. And the bubbles of light again rose and fell and mingled with the wan moonlight. And now from these globes themselves, as from the shell of an egg, monstrous things burst out. The air grew filled with them: larvae so bloodless and so hideous that I can in no way describe them except to remind the reader of the swarming life which the microscope brings before his eyes in a drop of water. Things transparent, supple, agile, chasing each other, devouring each other. Forms like nothing ever seen by the naked eye.

The shapes came round me and round, thicker and faster and swifter, swarming over my head, crawling over my right arm, which was outstretched against the evil beings. Sometimes I felt myself touched, but not by them. Invisible hands touched me. Once I felt the clutch of cold soft fingers at my throat. I was still aware that if I gave way to fear I should be in bodily peril; and I concentrated all my faculties in the single focus of resisting, stubborn will. And I turned my sight from the Shadow – above all from those strange serpent eyes – eyes that had now become distinctly visible. For there, though in nothing else round me, I was aware that there was a WILL, a will of intense evil, which might crush down my own.

The pale atmosphere in the room now began to redden. The larvae grew lurid as things that live in fire. Again the room vibrated; again were heard the three measured knocks; and again all things were swallowed up in the darkness of the dark Thing, as if out of that darkness all had come, into that darkness all returned.

As the gloom retreated, the Shadow was wholly gone. Slowly as it had been withdrawn, the flame grew again into the candles on the table, again into the fuel in the grate. The whole room came once more into sight.

The two doors were still closed, the door leading to the servant's room still locked. In the corner into which he had pushed himself lay the dog. I called to him – no movement. I approached. The animal was dead. His eyes protruded, his tongue out of his mouth, the froth gathered round his jaws. I took him in my arms and brought him to the fire. I felt acute grief for the loss of my poor favourite. I imagined he had died of fright. But I found that his neck was actually broken. Had this been done in the dark? Must it not have been by a hand as human as mine? Must there not have been a living person all the while in that room? I cannot tell. I cannot do more than state the fact.

Another surprising circumstance: my watch was restored to the table from which it had been so mysteriously withdrawn. But it had stopped at the very moment it was taken, and despite all the skill of the watchmaker, it has never gone since.

Nothing more happened for the rest of the night. Nor, indeed, had I long to wait before the dawn broke. Nor till it was broad daylight did I leave the haunted house. Before I did so, I revisited the little room in which my servant and I had been for a time imprisoned. I had a strong impression that from that room had originated the phenomena which had been experienced in my chamber. And though I entered it now in the clear day, with the sun peering through the filmy window, I still felt the creep of horror which I had first experienced there the night before. I could not, indeed, bear to stay more than half a minute within those walls.

I descended the stairs, and again I heard the footsteps before me; and when I opened the street door, I thought I could distinguish a very low laugh.

I went at once to Mr Jones's house. I returned the keys to him, told him that my curiosity was gratified, and related quickly what had passed.

"What on earth can I do with the house?" he said when I had finished.

"I will tell you what I would do. I am convinced from my own feelings that the small unfurnished room at right angles to the door of the bedroom which I occupied, forms a starting point for the influences which haunt the house. I strongly advise you to have the walls opened, the floor removed – indeed, the whole room pulled down."

Mr Jones appeared to agree to my advice, and about ten days afterwards I received a letter from him saying that he had visited the house and had found the two letters I had described replaced in the drawer from which I had taken them. He had read them with misgivings like my own, and had made a cautious inquiry about the woman to whom they had been written.

It seemed that thirty-six years ago (a year before the date

of the letters) she had married, against the family's wishes, an American of very suspicious character. In fact, he was generally believed to have been a pirate. She herself was the daughter of very respectable tradespeople, and had been a nursery governess before her marriage. She had a brother, a widower, who was considerably wealthy and who had one child of about six years old. A month after the marriage, the body of this brother was found in the Thames, near London Bridge. There seemed some marks of violence about his throat, but they were not deemed sufficient to warrant any other verdict than that of "found drowned."

The American and his wife took charge of the little boy, the deceased brother having made his sister the guardian of his only child. And in the event of the child's death, the sister inherited. The child died about six months afterwards. It was supposed to have been neglected and ill-treated. The neighbours swore they heard it shriek at night. The surgeon who had examined it after death said that it was emaciated as if from lack of food, and the body was covered with bruises.

It seemed that one winter night the child had tried to escape . . . crept out into the backyard . . . tried to scale the wall . . . fell back exhausted, and had been found next morning on the stones, dying. But though there was some evidence of cruelty, there was none of murder. And the aunt and her husband had sought to excuse the cruelty by declaring the stubbornness and perversity of the child, who was said to be half-witted.

Be that as it may, at the orphan's death, his aunt inherited her brother's fortune. Before the first wedded year was out, the American left England suddenly, and never returned. He obtained a cruising vessel, which was lost in the Atlantic two years afterwards. The widow was left in wealth, but reverses of various kinds had befallen her and her money was lost. Then she entered service, sinking lower and lower, from housekeeper down to maid-of-all-work – never long retaining a place. And so she had dropped into the workhouse, from which Mr Jones had taken her, to be placed in charge of the very house which she had rented as mistress in the first year of her wedded life.

Mr Jones added that he had passed an hour alone in the unfurnished room which I had urged him to destroy, and that his impressions of dread while there were so great, though he had neither heard nor seen anything, that he was eager to have the walls bared and the floor removed as I had suggested. He had engaged men for the work, and would commence any day I named.

The date was fixed. We went into the dreary little room, took up the skirting boards, and then the floors. Under the rafters, covered with rubbish, we found a trap-door, quite large enough for a man to get through. It was closely nailed down with clamps and rivets of iron. On removing these, we descended into a room below, the existence of which had never been suspected. In this room there had been a window and a flue, but they had been bricked over evidently for many years. With the help of candles we examined the place. There was some mouldering furniture, all in the fashion of about eighty years ago. In a chest of drawers against the wall we found, half rotted away, old-fashioned articles of a man's dress, such as might have been worn eighty or a hundred years ago by a gentleman of some rank – costly steel buckles and buttons, a handsome sword. In a waistcoat which had once been rich with gold lace, but which was now blackened and foul with damp, we found five guineas, a few silver coins, and a ticket, probably for some place of entertainment long since passed away. But our main discovery was in a kind of iron safe fixed to the wall, the lock of which took much trouble to pick.

In this safe were three shelves and two small drawers. Ranged on the shelves were several small crystal bottles, sealed air-tight. They contained colourless liquids, which we discovered to be non-poisonous. There were also some very curious glass tubes and a small pointed rod of iron, with a large lump of rock-crystal and another of amber; also a magnet of great power.

In one of the drawers we found a miniature portrait set in gold, and retaining the freshness of its colours most remarkably, considering the length of time it had probably been there. The portrait was of a man who was perhaps forty-seven or forty-eight.

It was a remarkable face – a most impressive face. If you could imagine a serpent transformed into a man, you would have a better idea of that face than long descriptions can convey: the width and flatness – the tapering elegance and strength of the deadly jaw – the long, large, terrible eye, glittering and green as an emerald.

Mechanically, I turned round the miniature to examine the back of it, and on the back was engraved the date 1765. Examining still more minutely, I detected a spring; this, on being pressed, opened the back of the miniature as a lid. Inside the lid was engraved, "Marianna to thee – be faithful in life and in death to ———." Here follows a name that I will not mention, but it was familiar to me. I had heard it spoken of by old men in my childhood as the name borne by a criminal who had made a great sensation in London for a year or so, and had fled the country on the charge of a double murder within his own house: that of his mistress and his rival.

We found no difficulty in opening the first drawer within the iron safe; we found great difficulty in opening the second: it was not locked, but it resisted all efforts, till we inserted the edge of a chisel. Inside, on a small thin book, was placed a crystal saucer: this saucer was filled with a clear liquid, on which floated a kind of compass with a needle shifting rapidly round. But instead of the usual points of a compass were seven strange characters, like those used by astrologers to denote the planets.

A peculiar, but not strong nor displeasing odour came from this drawer, which was lined with hazelwood. Whatever the cause of this odour, it affected the nerves. We all felt it, even the two workmen who were in the room – a creeping, tingling sensation from the tips of the fingers to the roots of the hair. Impatient to examine the book, I removed the saucer. As I did so the needle of the compass went round and round with great swiftness, and I felt a shock that ran through my whole body, so that I dropped the saucer on the floor. The liquid was spilt; the saucer was broken; the compass rolled to the end of the room. And at that moment the walls shook to and fro, as if a giant had swayed and rocked them.

The two workmen were so frightened that they ran up the ladder by which we had descended from the trap-door; but seeing that nothing more happened, they returned.

Meanwhile I had opened the book. It was bound in plain red leather, with a silver clasp. It contained but one sheet of thick vellum, and on that sheet were inscribed words in old monkish Latin, which literally translated were: "On all that it can reach within these walls – living or dead – as moves the needle, so work my will! Accursed be the house, and restless be the dwellers therein."

We found no more. Mr Jones burnt the book and razed to the foundations the part of the building containing the secret room with the chamber over it. He had then the courage to inhabit the house himself, and a quieter, better-conditioned house could not be found in all London.

IF SHE BENDS, SHE BREAKS

JOHN GORDON

BEN HAD FELT STRANGE ever since the snow started falling. He looked out of the classroom window and saw that it had come again, sweeping across like a curtain. That was exactly what it seemed to be: a curtain. The snow had come down like a blank sheet in his mind, and he could remember nothing beyond it. He could not even remember getting up this morning or walking to school; yesterday was only a haze, and last week did not exist. And now, at this moment, he did not know whether it was morning or afternoon. He began to get to his feet, but dizziness made him sit down.

"I know it's been freezing hard." Miss Carter's voice from the front of the class seemed distant. He wanted to tell her he felt unwell, but just for the moment he did not have the energy. She had her back to the stove as usual, and the eyes behind her glasses stared like a frightened horse's as they always did when she was in a passion. "It's been freezing hard," she repeated, "but the ice is still far too dangerous, and nobody is to go anywhere near it. Do you understand?"

Tommy Drake, in the next desk to Ben, murmured something and grinned at somebody on Ben's other side. But he ignored Ben completely.

"Tommy Drake!" Miss Carter had missed nothing. "What did you say?"

"Nothing, miss."

"Then why are you grinning like a jackass? If there's a joke, we all want to hear it. On your feet."

As Tommy pushed back his chair, Ben smiled at him weakly, but Tommy seemed to be in no mood for him and winked at somebody else as though Ben himself was not there.

"Well?" Miss Carter was waiting.

Tommy stood in silence.

"Very well. If you are not going to share your thoughts with the rest of us, perhaps you will remind me of what I was saying a moment ago."

"About the ice, miss?"

"And what about the ice?"

"That it's dangerous, miss." Then Tommy, who did not lack courage, went on, "What I was saying was that you can always tell if it's safe.'

"Oh you can, can you?" Miss Carter pursed her lips, and again waited.

"If she cracks, she bears," said Tommy. "If she bends, she breaks." It was a lesson they all knew in the flat Fenland where everybody skated in winter. A solid cracking sound in the ice was better than a soft bending. But it meant nothing to Miss Carter.

"Stuff and nonsense!" she cried.

"But everybody knows it's true." Tommy had justice on his side and his round face was getting red.

"Old wives' tales!" Miss Carter was not going to listen to reason. "Sit down."

Ben saw that Tommy was going to argue, and the sudden urge to back him up made him forget his dizziness. He got to his feet. "It's quite true, miss," he said. "I've tried it out."

She paid no attention to him. She glared at Tommy. "Sit down!'

Tommy obeyed, and Miss Carter pulled her cardigan tighter over her dumpy figure.

"Listen to me, all of you." Her voice was shrill. "I don't care what anybody says in the village; I won't have any of you go anywhere near that ice. Do you hear? Nobody!" She paused, and then added softly, "You all know what can happen."

She had succeeded in silencing the classroom and, as she turned away to her own desk, she muttered something to the front row who began putting their books away. It was time for break.

Ben was still standing. In her passion she seemed not to have seen him. "What's up with her?" he said, but Tommy was on his feet and heading towards the cloakroom with the rest.

The dizziness came over Ben again. Could nobody see that he was unwell? Or was his illness something so terrible that everybody wanted to ignore it? The classroom had emptied, and Miss Carter was wiping her nose on a crumpled paper handkerchief. He would tell her how he felt, and perhaps she would get his sister to walk home with him. He watched her head swing towards him and he opened his mouth to speak, but her glance swept over him and she turned to follow the others.

A movement outside one of the classroom's tall, narrow, windows made him look out. One boy was already in the yard, and the snow was thick and inviting. Beyond the railings there was the village and, through a gap in the houses, he could see the flat fens stretching away in a desert of whiteness. He knew it all. He had not lost his memory. The stuffiness of the classroom was to blame – and outside there was delicious coolness, and space. Without bothering to follow the others to the cloakroom for his coat, he went out.

There was still only the boy in the playground; a new kid kicking up snow. He was finding the soft patches, not already trodden, and, as he ploughed into them, he made the snow smoke around his ankles so that he almost seemed to lack feet.

Ben went across to him and said, "They let you out early, did they?"

The new kid raised his head and looked at the others who were now crowding out through the door. "I reckon," he said.

"Me an' all," said Ben. It wasn't strictly true, but he didn't mind bending the truth a bit as he had been feeling ill. But not any more. "Where d'you come from?" he asked.

91

"Over yonder." The new kid nodded vaguely beyond the railings and then went back to kicking snow. "It's warm, ain't it?" he said, watching the powder drift around his knees. "When you get used to it."

"What do your dad do?"

"Horseman," said the kid, and that was enough to tell Ben where he lived and where his father worked. Only one farm for miles had working horses. Tommy's family, the Drakes, had always had horses and were rich enough to have them working alongside tractors, as a kind of hobby.

"You live along Pingle Bank, then," said Ben. The horseman had a cottage there near the edge of the big drainage canal, the Pingle, that cut a straight, deep channel across the flat fens.

"That's right," said the kid, and looked up at the sky. "More of it comin'."

The clouds had thickened over the winter sun and, in the grey light, snow had begun to fall again. The kid held his face up to it. "Best time o' the year, winter. Brings you out into the open, don't it?"

"Reckon," Ben agreed. "If them clouds was in summer we should be gettin' soaked."

"I hate gettin' wet." The kid's face was pale, and snow was resting on his eyelashes.

"Me an' all."

They stood side by side and let the snow fall on them. The kid was quite right; it seemed warm.

Then the snowball fight rolled right up to them and charging through the middle of it came Tommy, pulling Ben's sister on her sledge. Just like him to have taken over the sledge and Jenny and barge into the new kid as though he was nobody. Ben stooped, rammed snow into two hard fistfuls and hurled them with all his force at Tommy's red face. He was usually a good shot but he missed, and Tommy was yelling at Jenny as she laboured to make snowballs and pile them on the sledge.

"They ain't no good! Look, they're fallin' apart." Tommy crouched and swept them all back into the snow.

Jenny had no height but a lot of temper. She was on her feet, her face as red as his, and yanked her sledge away.

"Bring that back!" he yelled, but Ben was already charging at him.

Tommy must have been off-balance because it took no more than a touch to push him sideways and send him into the snow flat on his back.

"You want to leave my sister alone." Ben sat on his chest with his knees on Tommy's arms. "Tell her you're sorry."

He and Tommy were the same size, both strong, and sometimes they banged their heads together just to see who would be the first to back off. But this time, without any effort or even bothering to answer him, Tommy sat up and spilled Ben off his chest as though he had no weight at all. And, as he tilted back helplessly, Ben saw the new kid standing by, watching.

"Hi!" he shouted. "Snowball fight. You're on my side."

The kid looked pretty useful; pale, but solid. And Ben needed help.

"You done it wrong," the new kid said to Ben and, without hurrying, he stepped forward.

The kid reached out to where Tommy was still sitting and put a hand over his face, spreading out pale, cold fingers across his mouth and eyes. He seemed merely to stroke him, but Tommy fell backwards.

"You don't need no pressure," said the kid. "All you got to do is let 'em know you're there."

"You got him!" Ben had rolled away to let the kid tackle Tommy alone. "Show us your stuff!"

The kid seemed to be in no hurry, and Tommy lay where he was, one startled eye showing between the pallid fingers. Any second now and there would be a quick thrust of limbs and Tommy would send the kid flying. It was stupid to wait for it; Ben started forward to stop the massacre.

But then the kid looked up. The snow was still in his eyelashes, and a crust of it was at the corners of his mouth, like ice.

"Want me to do any more?' he asked.

In the rest of the playground, shouts of snowfights echoed against the high windows and dark walls of the old school building, but in this corner the grey clouds seemed to hang lower as if to deaden the kid's voice.

"I asked you," he said. "You want to see me do some more?"

Tommy stirred, gathering himself to push. In a moment the boy would pay for being so careless, unless he had some trick and was pressing on a nerve. Ben wanted to see what would happen. He nodded.

The kid did not look away from Ben, but his hand left Tommy's face. And Tommy did not get up. He simply lay there with his eyes and mouth wide open. He looked scared.

The kid, still crouching, began to stroke the snow. He curved his fingers and raked it, dusting the white powder into Tommy's hair, then over his brow and his eyes; and then the kid's hand, so pale it could not be seen in the snow, was over Tommy's lips, and snow was being thrust into the gaping mouth. The kid leant over him and Tommy was terrified. He tried to shout, but more snow was driven into his mouth. He rolled over, thrashing helplessly.

The kid paused as though waiting for instructions. But Ben, curious to see what Tommy would do, waited.

It was then that the brittle little sound of a handbell reached them. It came from the porch where Miss Carter was calling them in. But suddenly the sound ceased, and even the shouting of the snowfights died. The whole playground had seen her drop the bell.

She started forward, pushing her way through the crowds, and then, caught up in her anxiety, they came with her like black snowflakes on the wind.

It was Tommy, jerking and choking on the ground, that drew them. It was no natural fooling in the snow. He was fighting to breathe. And the new kid stood over him, looking down.

"Tommy, what have you done!" Miss Carter was stooping over him, crying out at the sight of his mouth wide open and full of whiteness. "Oh my God!"

Ben stared across her bent back at the new kid. He simply stood where he was, a sprinkle of white in the short crop of his black hair, and gazed back at him.

"Who did this to you?" Miss Carter had thrust her fingers into the snow-gape in Tommy's face, and rolled him over so that he was coughing, gasping and heaving all at once. "How did it happen?"

But he could not answer and she helped him to his feet and began walking with him.

"Who saw it? Which of you did this?" She had snow in her fur-lined boots and her grey hair was untidy. Her little red nose was sharp with the cold and she pointed it around the ring that had gathered, sniffing out the guilty one. "You?" Her eyes were on Ben but had passed by almost before he had shaken his head. "What about you?" The new kid was at the back of the crowd and did not even have to answer.

Denials came from every side, and the chattering crowd followed her into school.

Ben and the kid hung back, and were alone in the porch when the door closed and shut them out. Neither had said a word, and Ben turned towards him. The kid stood quite still gazing straight ahead as though the door was the open page of a book and he was reading it. He wore a long black jacket, and a grey scarf was wound once around his neck and hung down his back. Ben noticed for the first time that the kid's black trousers were knee-length and were tucked into long, thick socks. They looked like riding breeches, and he thought the kid must help his father with the horses. But his boots were big and clumsy, not elegant like a horseman's. There was something gawky about him; he looked poor and old-fashioned.

"You done all right," said Ben. "Tommy ain't bad in a fight."

The kid turned towards him. There was still unmelted snow on his cheeks, and his eyelashes were tinged with white. His dark eyes were liquid as though he was on the verge of crying, but that was false. They had no expression at all. "He ain't as good as he reckon," said the kid, and left it at that.

"What class you in?" Ben asked.

"Same as you."

"Didn't notice you."

"I were by the stove."

"Miss Carter always keep her bum to that, that's why it don't throw out no heat," said Ben, but the kid did not smile. He led the way inside.

They had not been missed. Miss Carter was still fussing around Tommy. She had pulled the fireguard back from the stove so that he could go to the front of the class and sit close to it. But she was still angry.

"I'm going to catch whoever did that to you, and when I do . . ." She pinched in her little mouth until it was lipless and her eyes needled around the room.

Ben had taken his usual place at the back, and suddenly he realized the new kid had wandered off. He searched, and found him. He was sitting at a desk no more than two paces from Miss Carter and Tommy. He had one arm over the desk lid, and the other resting loosely on the back of his chair. He was quite untroubled.

"Stand up, Tommy," Miss Carter ordered. "Now turn round and point out who did this terrible thing."

Tommy, a hero now, was enjoying himself. He faced the class. Ben could see the pale curve of the new kid's cheek and guessed at the deep-water look of the eyes that were turned on Tommy.

"Tommy!" said Miss Carter, and obediently Tommy looked round the room. He smirked at several people but not at Ben. He ignored him as though angry with him for what had happened yet not prepared to betray him. But there was a real risk he would get his revenge on the kid. Yet again his glance went by as though the boy's desk was empty, and he said, "Nobody done it. I just fell over, that's all."

The girl next to Ben whispered to her friend, "Maybe he had a fit. That looked like it with his mouth all white. Like he was foaming."

"Be quiet!" Miss Carter had lost her patience. "Sit down!" she ordered Tommy, and for the rest of the afternoon she was savage, even with him.

From time to time Ben looked towards the new kid, but he kept his head bowed over his work and Ben saw no more than the black bristles of his cropped hair. Nobody attempted to speak to him because whenever anybody moved, Miss Carter snapped.

The last half-hour dragged, but then, with a rattle of pencils and a banging of desk lids, the afternoon ended. The new kid wasted no time. He was out of the door ahead of everybody else, and Ben did not catch him until he was half-way across the playground.

"Where are you going?" he asked.

"The Pingle."

"We ain't supposed to. Because of the ice."

"I live there."

Then Ben remembered the horseman's cottage on the bank, but he said, "Ain't you going to hang around here a bit? We got some good slides in the yard."

"Ice is better."

The others, charging out at the door, prevented Ben saying more. Jenny, with her sledge, was being chased by Tommy. He was himself again and was telling her, "Your sledge will go great on the Pingle."

"I don't want to go," she said.

A bigger girl butted in. "You heard what Miss Carter said, Tommy Drake. Ain't you got no sense?"

Tommy paid no attention. "Come on, Jenny. I ain't got time to go home and fetch me skates, or else I would. I'll bring 'em tomorrow and you can have a go. Promise."

She was tempted, but she said, "I don't want to go there. And you know why."

"I won't take a step on it unless it's rock hard," said Tommy.

"I ain't going," said Jenny.

At the school gate, the kid moved his feet impatiently on the step. It had been cleared of snow and the metal studs on his boots rattled.

Tommy had also lost his patience. "If she cracks she bears, if she bends she breaks. Everybody know that's true, no matter what old Carter say. And I won't budge away from the bank unless it's safe."

"No," said Jenny.

Suddenly the kid kicked at the steps and made sparks fly from the sole of his boot, and Tommy looked up. The wind dived over the school roof in a howl and a plunge of snow, and the kid's voice merged with it as he yelled, "Come on!"

He and Ben ran together, and Tommy grabbed at the sledge and made for the gate. Several others came with him.

Ben and the boy kept ahead of the rest as they rounded the

corner into the lane. Traffic had failed to churn up the snow and had packed it hard, almost icy, so it would have been as good as anywhere for Jenny's sledge; but Ben ran with the boy between hedges humped and white, and the others followed.

They left the road just before it climbed to the bridge across the Pingle, and they stood at the top of the bank, looking down. They were the first to come here. The grass blades, slowly arching as the snow had added petal after petal through the day, supported an unbroken roof just clear of the ground. Below them, the straight, wide channel stretched away to left and right through the flat, white land. The water had become a frozen road, and the wind had swept it almost clear, piling the snow in an endless, smooth drift on the far side.

Tommy had come up alongside them. "You could go for miles!" he shouted.

But Jenny hung back. "I don't like it." The air was grey and cold and it almost smothered her small voice. "I want to go home."

"It ain't dark yet." His voice yelped as though it came from the lonely seagull that angled up on a frozen gust far out over the white plain. He began to move forward. "Let's get down there."

"She doesn't want to go." Ben was close to him, but Tommy paid no heed. "Nobody's going down that bank, Tommy." Ben stepped forward, blocking his way. "Nobody!"

Tommy came straight on. His eyes met Ben's but their expression did not change. His whole attention was focused on the ice below and his gaze seemed to go through Ben as though he was not there.

In a sudden cold anger Ben lowered his head and lunged with both arms. He thrust at Tommy's chest with all his force. His fingers touched, but in the instant of touching they lost their grip. He thrust with all his power, but it was air alone that slid along his arms and fingers, and Tommy was past and through and plunging down the bank.

The kid, watching him, said, "You still don't do it right."

Tommy had taken Jenny's sledge with him, and at the ice edge, he turned and shouted to them up the bank. "Come on, all of you!"

"No!" Ben stood in front of them. "Don't go!" He opened his arms, but they came in a group straight for him. "Stop!" They did not answer. Their eyes did not look directly at him. They pushed into him, like a crush of cattle, pretending he was not there. He clutched at one after another but the strange weakness he had felt earlier made him too flimsy to stop anything and they were beyond him and going down to join Tommy.

"I got to teach you a few things," said the kid.

"I don't feel too good," said Ben. "I think I ought to go home."

The boy gazed at him for a moment with eyes that again seemed to be rimmed with frost, and shook his head. "There's them down there to see to," he said.

Slowly, Ben nodded. He had to think of Jenny.

They went down together and found Tommy still on the bank. Frozen reeds stood up through the ice and there was a seepage of water at the edge that made them all hesitate. All except the new kid. He put one foot on it, testing.

"If she cracks she bears," he said.

Ben watched. The boy had plenty of courage. He was leaning forward now, putting all his weight on the ice.

"She cracks," he said.

But Ben had heard nothing. "No," he called out. "She bends."

He was too late. The boy had stepped out onto the ice. Then Ben heard the crack under his boots, and the echo of it ringing from bank to bank and away along the endless ice in thin winter music.

The boy moved out until he was a figure in black in the middle of the channel. "She bears," he called out, and Ben, who knew he could never stop the others now, stepped out to be with him.

There was no crack this time, but the ice held. He could feel the gentle pulse of it as he walked towards the middle. There was something almost like a smile on the new kid's face. "Both of us done it," he said, and Ben nodded.

On the bank there was a squabble. The big girl, protecting Jenny, was trying to pull the sledge rope from Tommy. "Let her have her sledge," she said. "You didn't ought to have brung her here."

"It's safe enough."

"I don't care whether it's safe or not, you didn't ought to have brung her. Not Jenny, of all people."

"Why all the fuss about Jenny?" said Ben to the kid. "I don't know what they're going on about."

"Don't you?" The kid's eyes, darkening as the day dwindled, rested on him. Far away along the length of the frozen channel, snow and sky and darkness joined.

"Why don't they come out here?" said Ben. "They can see us."

"We can go and fetch 'em," said the kid.

"How?"

"Get hold of that sledge. They'll follow."

Ben hesitated. Perhaps he was too weak to do even that.

The kid saw his doubt, and said, "You've pulled a sledge before, ain't you?" Ben nodded. "Well, all you got to do is remember what it feel like. That's all."

Ben had to rely on him. Everything he had tried himself had gone wrong. He walked across to where Tommy was still arguing.

"See what you done to her," the girl was saying. She had her arm around Jenny's shoulder and Jenny was crying, snuffling into her gloves. "Ain't you got no feelings, Tommy Drake?"

"Well, just because it happened once," said Tommy, "that ain't to say it's going to happen again."

"Wasn't just once! The girl thrust her head forward, accusing him. "There was another time." She lifted her arm from Jenny's shoulder and pointed up the bank behind her. "There was a boy lived up there, along Pingle Bank; he came down here and went through the ice one winter time, and they never found him till it thawed."

"That were a long time ago," said Tommy. "Years before any of us was born."

"You ought to know about that if anybody do, Tommy Drake. That boy's father worked on your farm. Everybody know about that even if it was all them years ago. His father were a horseman and lived along the bank."

"Hey!" Ben was close to Tommy. "Just like the new kid."

But even that did not make Tommy turn his way. Ben reached

101

for the sledge rope and jerked it. He felt the rope in his fingers just before it slipped through and fell, but he had tugged it from Tommy's grasp and the sledge ran out on to the ice.

"Come on, Tommy," he said. "Come with me and the new kid."

The girl was watching the sledge and accusing Tommy. "What did you want to do that for?"

"I didn't," he said.

"I did it," said Ben, but nobody looked towards him.

The girl was furious with Tommy. "Just look what you done. Now you'll have to leave it."

Tommy had put one foot on the ice, testing it. "I ain't frit," he said. "I reckon it'll hold."

"Of course it will," Ben encouraged him. "We're both out here, ain't we?" He paused and looked over his shoulder to make sure, but the kid was still there, watching. "Two of us. Me and him."

Tommy had both feet on the ice and had taken another step. "See," he called to the others on the bank. "Nothing to it."

"Don't you make a parade out there by yourself any longer, Tommy Drake." The girl pulled Jenny's face tighter into her shoulder and made an effort to muffle Jenny's ears. She leant forward as far as she could, keeping her voice low so that Jenny should not hear. "Can't you see what you're doing to her? This were just the place where Ben went through the ice last winter."

Tommy, stamping to make the ice ring beneath him, kept his back to her. "If she cracks," he said, "she bears. If she bends, she breaks."

"Can't you hear?" said the girl. "This is just the place where Ben were drowned!"

The snow came in a sudden flurry, putting a streaked curtain between Ben and the rest of them. It was then that he remembered. He remembered everything. The kid had come up to stand beside him, and they stood together and watched.

The ice under Tommy sagged as they knew it would. They heard the soft rending as it split, and they saw its broken edge rear up. They heard the yell and the slither, and remembered the cold gulp of the black water that, with years between, had swallowed each of them. But now it was somebody else who slid under.

Then Jenny's scream reached Ben through the wind that was pushing down the channel as the night came on. She should be at home; not out here watching this. He stooped to the sledge and pushed.

On the bank they saw nothing but a tight spiral of snow whipped up from the ice, but the sledge slid into the water beside Tommy and floated. He grabbed at it.

From out on the ice they saw the girl, held by the others, reach from the bank and grasp the rope, and then Tommy, soaking and freezing, crawled into the white snow and made it black. They watched as the whole group, sobbing and murmuring, climbed the bank, showed for a few moments against the darkening sky and were gone.

In the empty channel the two figures stood motionless. Their eyes gazed unblinking through the swirl as the snow came again, hissing as it blew between the frozen reeds.

ROOM 18

AIDAN CHAMBERS

I ARRIVED IN DUBLIN late one night. The boat from Holyhead had been unusually full and the crossing one of the roughest in living memory. The Irish Sea had done its worst: every soul aboard had been wretchedly sick, and we docked four hours late.

Clearing customs was more tiresome than ever. The sight of all those bilious faces, and the sour smell of sickness that hung about us as we crowded the customs shed affected even the poker-faced officers. They passed us through as quickly as a respectable show of authority would allow.

I jumped in a taxi as soon as I could, and gave the name of my usual hotel.

"You'll have trouble if you're not booked," the driver said as I sat back in my seat.

"I never have before," I replied, though not without apprehension. Taxi drivers make a habit of pessimism; but they also know what's on about town.

"And maybe you've never been in Dublin during the Festival time?"

"The Festival!"

" 'Tis plays and poetry and moving pictures, and all making

on they are Irish, though most of it comes from England and America," the driver said and laughed.

I realized then why the boat had been so crowded, and cursed myself for letting business preoccupations blind me to the doings of the rest of the world.

We drew up outside the hotel. People thronged the entrance.

"Will you wait, in case they are full?" I asked the driver.

He snugged his cloth cap and glanced over his shoulder. "It's a very good night for work," he said. "The Festival does bring in the trade, I will say that. It does indeed."

I handed him a pound note.

"I'll wait, sir," he said, "seeing you're likely to be in such difficulties!"

Before I reached the hotel door, a commissionaire barred my way as though staving off a platoon of attacking Black and Tans.

"Would you be wanting a room, sir?" he asked.

I nodded.

"Not a hope of even a chair in the lobby tonight," he said.

I got back into the taxi.

"Why sure that was mighty bad luck," said the driver brightly. "I felt in my bones you might just be in time."

"Now where?" I said, too weary and depressed to give much thought to the answer.

"That," said the driver pointedly, "is a mighty problematical question!"

The Irish Sea doing its worst had left me in no mood for Irish riddles. All I wanted was a bed for the night, and I could not have cared less at that moment where it was. Later on I was to care a good deal. I took another note from my wallet and passed it to the driver. He accepted it without a word, slipped into gear, and headed up O'Connell Street.

We drew up outside an ill-lit, ill-kempt Victorian building in a side street well away from the centre of town. It was hardly the kind of place I would normally have looked at twice, never mind asked for a room.

"I'm not promisin' anything, you understand," the driver

said, "but if they've nothing else at all, I'll lay a small wager you'll find room 18 free."

"Room 18?"

"That'll be a couple of quid on the clock, and if you don't mind, I'll not wait. My time's up for this day, and I'm more pleased than sorry about that."

I paid the fare, climbed out, and watched the taxi accelerate away as though it was my last lifeline to civilization. In the glimmer of the back-street lamps the hotel looked even gloomier than it had from inside the taxi. The downstairs rooms were dark, and only one or two windows in the upper stories were lighted. There were none of the refinements of smarter places; no bright neon signs, no canopied entrance, no commissionaires to push open the doors.

Inside, the lobby was more a passageway than a hall. The carpet was worn, and an unshaded bulb, the only source of light, hung from the ceiling above the reception desk, a mahogany affair, heavy and finger-marked like a bar in a seedy public house.

There was an old-fashioned brass handbell on the desk by the registration book, and as no one seemed to be about, I struck it. It clanged unexpectedly loud. After a moment an old chap came from a room behind the counter. His aged face was shaped so like the map of his native land, I almost laughed.

He said nothing, merely inclined the map of Ireland towards me with the kind of annoyed look people wear when they have been woken unnecessarily from a nap.

"Have you a room?" I asked, and even my anxiety to get some rest could not hide the irritation in my voice.

"In Festival time?" said the map, speaking from somewhere in the region of County Limerick.

"Nothing at all?"

A shake of the head.

"What about room 18?"

I had not expected quite the reaction I got. The old fellow's body braced, his eyebrows shot up. He stared at me with peculiar interest.

"It's not a room we usually let," he said.

Had I not been so weary, I might have asked why. But weariness kills curiosity about everything but the means of rest.

"If you have it available, I'll be glad to take it," I said. "I've had a rough crossing from England, and Dublin, as you know, is crowded. I'll settle for anything that has a bed in it."

The old chap looked at me a moment. Then he said:

"You're either exhausted, or mad, or maybe both. And then again, you might just be more brass-faced than most of your nation. But whatever it is, I'll tell you what I'll do. Pay your board for the night on the nail, and in cash, and the room is yours."

I took out my wallet. "You're not very trusting," I said.

" 'Tisn't that I don't trust you," he said, smiling, " 'Tis just the thought came to me that you might be leavin' early."

"I doubt if I shall," I said. "I'm much too tired for early rising."

"Remains to be seen," he muttered, and took the money.

The old man led me to a room on the second floor. It was at the end of a corridor, and I judged it to be at the side of the building. There, he handed me the key, without opening the door, looked at me as one might look at someone about to embark on a dangerous journey, nodded good-night, and shuffled off down the dingy passage. I could not help thinking how his slight frame and wild white hair made him look like a retreating leprechaun.

I unlocked the door and went into the room.

At this point I should say that I am not by nature either nervous or easily frightened. I do not believe in things supernatural, and have never found need for the comforts of religion. I am a scientist and a businessman, and known for my hardness of head and coolness of nerve in tight situations. All I can say is that my experiences in this room and afterwards certainly happened. Further than that I won't go. I have never tried to explain them to myself, nor to anyone else.

The air inside the room smelt dank and musty, and so, while I unpacked, I put my wristwatch between the sheets of the bed.

When I took it out, the glass was steamed up. I had learned the trick long ago as a travelling consultant, an occupation that took me around the world and into all kinds of hotel bedrooms. It was a sure way of discovering whether a bed was damp. This one certainly was: it had not been aired or slept in for weeks.

Resigned to the worst – I was too tired to waste time getting it dried out – I climbed into bed. A faint unease had settled over me since entering the room, and so for a moment as I lay there, I looked about.

There was nothing in the room that led me then to expect what happened later. A bulky and extremely ugly wardrobe stood to one side of the door, taking up what remained of the wall on that side. An ornate nineteenth-century fireplace with dull brass attachments almost covered the wall opposite the bed. The large gilt-framed looking-glass above the fireplace was pockmarked with damp, as though huge flies had blown on it. In the wall opposite the wardrobe and to my right as I lay in bed was a narrow sash window with heavy undrawn drapes hanging at either side. Beneath it stood a curious wooden chest, about six feet long and three deep, with a lid that opened upwards. Had I been less tired, I might have opened the chest and looked inside; but nothing else in the room excited even the mildest curiosity, and now that the bed was growing warm enough to bring the first drowsiness of sleep, I was only too ready to switch off the light and give myself up to it.

I woke suddenly, in a heavy sweat. The room was oppressively hot, with a dry burning heat like that from an electric fire. My face felt flushed, and the skin tingled. The wetness of my body might have been due to the dampness of the bed, but the temperature of the room I could not explain: it was a cold night outside, and the room was unheated.

I sat up, intending to throw off some bed-clothes. But as I pulled the top coverings from me, I realized that, though there was no light in the room nor any coming in from outside, I could clearly see the clothes on the bed.

I looked round. The entire room was lit by a strange

luminosity, a brightness that could come from neither sun nor moon, nor any man-made source. Every object in the room was visible, not from any light shining *on* it, but from its own incandescence. Each object glowed, as the hands of a luminous watch glow in the dark, possessing the source of light themselves. It was a greenish glister that left the walls and all the air in the room as black as impenetrable night. Half awake, I stared with puzzled incomprehension at the bed and wardrobe, the fireplace, the frame of the looking-glass, and the curious oblong box. Each one radiated the unearthly light.

I told myself it was an optical illusion, a trick of light caused, perhaps, by something I could not see outside the window.

But then something moved in the mirror. Instinctively, I looked across at it. Though the frame round the glass glowed eerily, the glass itself was dark. Dark, that is, except for the pockmarks of damp. These were visible, glowing less brightly than the objects in the room, as if they alone might be reflecting some of the green glister. And it was these spots that were moving.

I now became wide awake, sitting tense in the bed, sweating more than ever. The spots moved at first in no discernible pattern. But the movement did not seem to be without aim or purpose; rather, I felt, each point of light was *being moved*. It was as though some invisible hand guided the lights about, like pieces in a jigsaw, searching for the place into which each piece must fit. I watched, fascinated; and as I watched, the speed at which the spots were moved increased; and as the speed increased, the spots closed together, combining, adding themselves one to another, until at last there *was* a shape, a pattern I could recognize. The shape was vague at first, without details. But these were added: some lights in the pattern dimmed, others brightened, until gradually the flat, one-dimensional pattern took on form and depth, shadows and highlights.

I caught my breath, aghast at what I saw. For the form that appeared was the face of a man.

The face was caught as it might have been in a photograph – I can find no other way to describe it – not the printed positive, but the negative of a photograph: all the darks and lights reversed. Thus the irises of the eyes glowed, the whites were black, the shadows round the deep-sunk eyes shone. And the eyes were turned on me.

A cry rose in me, a cry like those that wake one from a nightmare too horrible to dream. The cry rose, but could not find voice. The oppressive heat seemed to hold me by the throat, so that the cry was strangled there, and all that escaped was a stifled, low-toned groan. Though I wished to take my eyes from the face watching me from the mirror, I could not; while every second the image grew brighter, more clearly defined, till it blazed there, a more brilliant glare than any in the room.

As I gazed, the knowledge came to me that in some unthinkable way my presence in this room had set free forces that were bringing me to the very barrier between life and death; that what I now saw formed on the surface of the mirror was the image of death. Life and death are, after all, merely reflections of something greater, more powerful than both. I do not believe in God; but that there is a force, an energy that transcends the life we know, I have no doubt. And in those confused and horrified moments, I could think only one thing: that the image on the mirror, reversed from what it would have been in life, was a sudden glimpse of death.

I have said that the image was fixed, as in a photograph. So it was, at first. Once fully formed, however, strengthened in shape and brightness, it began to move. The eyes stayed on mine, but the head nodded as if replying to my racing thoughts with an unspoken "Yes."

What little calm of reason I had left told me one thing: I must at all costs prevent the image from holding my attention. I must break myself from it. Why I should have felt that the image had a will, and that it meant to crush my own and overpower me, I do not know. But I felt this most strongly. I tried to turn my mind to other things, daily things, dreary things, anything to distract me. That ghastly crossing of the Irish Sea; the crowded Dublin streets; tomorrow's business appointment.

Sure enough, as I forced these mundane thoughts upon myself, the brilliance of the face began to fade. Encouraged by my success, I sought other topics that might rid me altogether of the awful image.

I thought of the taxi driver. The image faded more.

I thought of the bribes he had taken. The brightness dimmed again.

But thinking of the taxi driver brought another thought. How had he known about this room? How could he know it would be free?

No sooner had the questions come to me than the image brightened at once.

"Oh, no!" I tried to shout, and could not. Desperately, I pushed the thought from my mind and croaked aloud the first words that came into my head.

"The square on the hypotenuse is equal to the sum of the squares on the other two sides."

The image dimmed a little.

"I am John Randolph Taylor, of Cheyne Walk, Birmingham, England, and I have one wife, two sons, and a baby daughter."

The image faded more.

But whose is the face on the mirror?

The image brightened.

The question had slipped into my head unplanned, unwished for. But it came so strongly that it seemed to shout itself inside my brain. I struggled against it.

"I am an electronics engineer, and do not believe in the supernatural."

And who are you?

"I play golf on Sundays and whenever I can find the time."

And who are you?

"My favourite meal is lobster salad."

And who are you?

"I am forty-three and suffer from nothing but occasional indigestion."

But who are you? Who? Who?

Nothing I could do erased that question. It possessed me,

111

fascinated me. Who was this man whose image was linked in some way to myself? Deep within me, perverse and undeniable, was the desire to know the answer, no matter how appalling the horror that might attend it. Instinctively, I knew that to speak the thought aloud might release forces terrible and overwhelming, and leave me with no hope of ridding myself of the image on the mirror. Instinctively I knew this, and so drew back; only to find myself mocking my lack of courage, my weakness: urging myself to pit my disbelief of the supernatural against the fact of what my eyes could see.

At that moment the constriction in my throat eased, and I shouted firmly: "Who are you?"

I had not finished the words before the green image blazed like a protracted flash of forked lightning. The room shook, the multitude of gleaming spots broke from the mirror like sparks from an electrode. For some minutes they crackled round the room, chaotic and dazzling. Then, almost as if they had been signalled, they streamed towards a point between the bed and the fireplace, and gathered. The form they took was unshaped, a pillar of sparkling lights, each no bigger than a pinhead.

Now the light in the furniture began to shimmer; the outline blurred; and then, like iron filings to a magnet the luminosity from each object flowed towards the pillar and was absorbed by it, until the furniture was drained of light, and darkness was everywhere in the room, except for the blazing pillar of moving particles standing man-high at the foot of my bed.

It hovered there, and yet to say it was anywhere is not to speak the truth. There are no words that can tell what I saw and felt. The pillar was before my eyes; but I knew that, if I tried to touch it, my hands would pass through, feeling nothing. It was visible but had no substance. I *saw* it before me, but I *felt* enclosed by it. Nor can I tell how long this lasted. Time, like space, meant nothing now: it was endless, yet no longer than it takes to blink an eye.

Like a branch spreading from a tree trunk, a limb – no, not a limb; merely a part of it – came reaching out from the pillar towards me. I would have moved, but could not. Had hoops of steel bound me, I could not have been held more rigid. I could only sit and watch the limb of bright sparks reach out to me, pass over my face, play over my body, enfold me in green light. I felt no physical pain, no burning or piercing, no sense of being touched. But the very instant the first of those flecks of light reached me, the energy in my body began to drain away. If I were a religious man, I would say my very soul was being sucked from deep within me. But I can take no such view. All I know is that the power that makes men active, living beings – the essence of life itself – was being transfused from me by that mobile limb. And at once the pillar of light, with seeming pain and difficulty, changed into a vague, but recognizable, human figure.

Slowly the figure developed, features were moulded, again as in a photograph, though not now as a negative but as a positive; a positive printed in shimmering electric green.

When at last the limb withdrew and became itself an arm of the newborn figure, I knew the answer to the question I had shouted endless moments ago. And now a cry did break from me, for what I saw was terrifying and awful, worse – much worse – than any dream or nightmare could ever be. What I saw was a man, and that man was no stranger. He was myself.

True, he was older than I. His hair was balding, and mine – then – was thick. His face was lined with worry and pain, and mine – then – was smooth. But I knew him at once. He was myself – myself as I would be in years to come.

Even as I cried out, the spectre came towards me. Slowly. Neither walking nor moving round the bed. But straight at me it came. And as it came, it took the shape of my own fear-bristled body as I lay in the bed.

I struggled to escape the advancing figure, pushing myself up in the bed, till I was pressed against the headboard and could go no farther. There I cowered in an agony of terror. And every slightest movement of my own body I saw reflected in the body of the spectre; while the face of the advancing image showed me myself in all the ugliness of panic and fear: contorted, wild-eyed, the mouth open in a hysterical scream.

The form came within inches of my own. And suddenly I knew that above all I must prevent that other self from fusing with me: knew that this was exactly what it meant to do. I must not let that precisely similar shape meet mine, absorb me, become superimposed upon me. For that would be to join life and death, to know more than any man can know, and live.

Again I cried out loud. But this was no cry of terror: it was the roar of a man summoning up every ounce of strength he has left in a last desperate battle for survival.

That very moment, the image reached me. My body was charged as if by a massive electric shock. Violent shudders racked me. The entire room shook, and I heard a noise like that of rushing wind. I flung myself about the bed, determined to resist the fusing of the image with myself. I kicked, I thrashed my arms, I curled and uncurled my body. The heat became intense. I felt as though I wrestled with a scorching ball of fire. My heart raced and pounded, my lungs strained till I thought they must burst. And with a last supreme effort of body and will, I hurled myself from the bed.

The multitude of dazzling points of light that formed the spectre exploded wildly about the room. There was a loud noise of explosion. I was thrown against the wall so hard the breath was crushed from me.

I fell to the floor and lost consciousness.

The first light of dawn was streaming through the window when I came to, lying as I had fallen, my body stiff and painful. I stood up, trembling and groaning. Apart from the rumpled bed, everything was as it had been the night before. At first I was dazed, but gradually all that had happened came back to mind. And as it came, it brought one desire: to be gone from that hideous room.

I dressed with as much speed as my aching bones would allow, took my bags, and left without seeing anyone. The last thing I looked at in the room was the mirror above the fireplace. The pockmarks were there, as formless as when I had first noticed them.

Years have passed since that time, and in those years the horror of room 18 has dimmed. Sometimes, to entertain friends, I have told the tale, passing it off as an amusing, half-imagined party piece. Today, however, I was in my bedroom dressing for a dinner engagement. As I stood before the mirror attempting to get my tie straight, it struck me how like the face in that nightmare room my own had become. But what has caused me far more alarm is what I saw just behind the glass of the mirror.

There, newly formed, were a few tiny spots, like pockmarks of damp.

BROWNIE

R. CHETWYND-HAYES

THE HOUSE was built of grey stone, and stood on the edge of a vast moor; an awesome, desolate place, where the wind roared across a sea of heather and screamed like an army of lost souls.

Our father drove into a muddy, weed-infested drive, then braked to a halt. He smiled over his shoulder at Rodney and me, then said cheerfully: "You'll be very happy here."

We had grave doubts. On closer inspection the stonework was very dirty, the paintwork was flaking, and generally the house looked as unrelenting as the moor that lay beyond. Father opened the door and got out, his face set in that determinedly cheerful expression parents assume whenever they wish to pretend that all is well, even though appearances suggest otherwise.

"Fine people, Mr and Mrs Fairweather." He gripped Rodney's arm, then mine, and guided us up a flight of stone steps towards a vast, oak door. "You'll love 'em. Then, there are all those lovely moors for you to play on. Wish I was staying with you, instead of going back to India. But duty calls."

He was lying, we both knew it, and perhaps the knowledge made parting all the more sad. He raised a bronzed hand, but before he could grasp the knocker, the door creaked open and there stood Mrs Fairweather.

"Major Sinclair." She stood to one side for us to enter. "Come in, Sir, and the young 'uns. The wind's like a knife, and cuts a body to the bone."

The hall was large, bare, lined with age-darkened oak panels; doors broke both walls on either side of a massive staircase, and there was an old, churchy smell.

"Come into the kitchen with you," Mrs Fairweather commanded, "that being the only room that's livable in on the ground floor. The rest is locked up."

The kitchen lay behind the staircase; a grandfather of all kitchens, having a red tiled floor, a spluttering iron range that positively shone from frequent applications of black lead, and an array of gleaming copper saucepans hanging on brass hooks over the mantelpiece.

A tall, lean old man was seated behind a much-scrubbed deal table. He rose as we entered, revealing that he wore a dark-blue boiler suit and a checked cloth cap.

"Fairweather," his wife snapped, "where's yer manners? Take yer cap off."

Mr Fairweather reluctantly, or so it appeared to me, took off his cap, muttered some indistinguishable words, then sat down again. Mrs Fairweather turned to Father.

"You mustn't mind him, Sir. He's not used to company, but he's got a heart. I'll say that for him. Now, Sir, is there anything you'd like to settle with me before you leave?"

"No," Father was clearly dying to be off. "The extra sum we agreed upon will be paid by Simpson & Brown on the first of every month. The girl I engaged as governess will arrive tomorrow. Let me see," he consulted a notebook, "Miss Rose Fortesque." He put the notebook away. "I think that's all."

"Right you are, Sir," Mrs Fairweather nodded her grey head. "I expect you'll want to say a few words to the little fellows before you leave, so me and Fairweather will make ourselves scarce. Fairweather . . . " The old man raised his head. "Come on, we'll make sure the chickens are bedded down."

Mr Fairweather followed her out through the kitchen doorway, muttering bad temperedly, and we were left alone with Father, who was betraying every sign of acute discomfort.

"Well, boys," he was still determined to appear cheerful, "I guess this is good-bye. You know I'd have loved to have taken you with me, but India is no place for growing boys, and now your mother has passed on there'd be no one to look after you. You'll be comfortable enough here, and Miss Fortesque will teach you all you need to know before you go to school next autumn. OK?"

I felt like choking, but Rodney, who had a far less emotional nature, was more prepared to deal with events of the moment.

"Do we own this house, Father?"

"I own this house," Father corrected gently, "and no doubt you will one day. As I told you, Mr and Mrs Fairweather are only caretakers, and they are allowed to cultivate some of the ground for their own use. Back before the days of Henry the Eighth, the house was a monastery, but since the Reformation it's been a private house. Your great uncle Charles was the last of our family to live here. I've never found the time to bring the old place up to scratch, so it has stood empty, save for the Fairweathers, since he died."

"Pity," said Rodney.

"Quite," Father cleared his throat. "Well, I expect the old . . . Mrs Fairweather has a good hot meal waiting for you, so I'll push off." He bent down and kissed us lightly on the foreheads, then walked briskly to the kitchen door. "Mrs Fairweather, I'm off."

The speed with which the old couple reappeared suggested the chickens must be bedded down in the hall. Mr Fairweather made straight for the seat behind the table, while his wife creased her stern face into a polite smile.

"So you'll be going, Sir. I hope it won't be too long before we see you again."

"No indeed," Father shook her hand, his expression suddenly grave. "No time at all. 'Bye, boys, do what the good Mrs Fairweather tells you. Good-bye, Fairweather." He could not resist a bad joke. "Hope it keeps fine for you."

The old man half rose, grunted, then sat down again. Mrs Fairweather preceded Father into the hall. We heard the front door open, then the sound of Father's car; the crunch of gravel as he drove away. He was gone. We never saw him again. He was killed on the Indian North West Frontier fighting Afghanistan tribesmen, and, had he been consulted, I am certain that is the way he would have preferred to die. He was, above all, a soldier.

As Mrs Fairweather never failed to stress, food at Sinclair Abbey was plain, but good. We ate well, worked hard, for Mr Fairweather saw no reason why two extra pairs of hands should not be put to gainful employment, and above all, we played. An old, almost empty house is an ideal playground for two boys. The unused rooms, whenever we could persuade Mrs Fairweather to unlock the doors, were a particular joy. Dust-shrouded furniture crouched like beasts of prey against walls on which the paper had long since died. In the great dining room were traces of the old refectory where medieval monks had dined before Henry's henchmen had cast them out. One stained-glass window, depicting Abraham offering up Isaac as a sacrifice, could still be seen through a veil of cobwebs; an oak, high-backed chair, surmounted by a crucifix, suggested it had once been the property of a proud abbot. For young, inquiring eyes, remains of the old monastery could still be found.

Rose Fortesque came, as Father had promised, the day after our arrival. Had we been ten years older, doubtless we would have considered her to be a slim, extremely pretty, if somewhat retiring girl. As it was, we found her a great disappointment. Her pale, oval face, enhanced by a pair of rather sad blue eyes, gave the impression she was always on the verge of being frightened, the result possibly of being painfully shy.

Where Father had found her I have not the slightest idea. More than likely at some teachers' agency, or wherever prospective governesses parade their scholastic wares, but of a certainty, she was not equipped to deal with two high-spirited boys. It took but a single morning for us to become aware of this fact, and with the cruelty of unthinking youth, we took full advantage of the situation. She was very frightened after finding a frog in her bed, and a grass snake in her handbag, and from then onwards, she watched us with sad, reproachful eyes.

It was fully seven days after our arrival at Sinclair Abbey when we first met Brownie. Our bedroom was way up under the eaves, a long, barren room, furnished only by our two beds, a wardrobe, and two chairs, Mrs Fairweather having decided mere boys required little else. There was no electricity in that part of the house. A single candle lit us to bed, and once that was extinguished, there was only the pale rectangle of a dormer window which, in the small hours, when the sky was clear, allowed the moon to bathe the room in a soft, silver glow.

I woke suddenly, and heard the clock over the old stables strike two. It was a clear, frosty night, and a full moon stared in through the window, so that all the shadows had been chased into hiding behind the wardrobe, under the beds, and on either side of the window. Rodney was snoring, and I was just considering the possibility of throwing a boot at him, when I became aware there was a third presence in the room. I raised my head from the pillow. A man dressed in a monk's robe was sitting on the foot of my bed. The funny thing was, I couldn't feel his weight, and I should have done so, because my feet appeared to be underneath him.

I sat up, but he did not move, only continued to sit motionless, staring at the left-hand wall. The cowl of his robe was flung back to reveal a round, dark-skinned face, surmounted by a fringe of black curly hair surrounding a bald patch that I seemed to remember was called a tonsure. I was frightened, but pretended I wasn't. I whispered:

"Who are you? What do you want?"

The monk neither answered nor moved, so I tried again, this time a little louder.

"What are you doing here?"

He continued to sit like a figure in a wax museum, so I decided to wake Rodney – no mean task for he slept like Rip van

Winkle. My second shoe did the trick and he woke protesting loudly:

"Wassat? Young Harry, I'll do you."

"There's a man sitting on the foot of my bed, and he won't move."

"What!" Rodney sat up, rubbed his eyes, then stared at our silent visitor. "Who is he?"

"I don't know. I've asked him several times, but he doesn't seem to hear."

"Perhaps he's asleep."

"His eyes are open."

"Well," Rodney took a firm grip of my shoe, "we'll soon find out." And he hurled the shoe straight at the brown-clad figure.

Neither of us really believed what our eyes reported: the shoe went through the tonsured head and landed with a resounding smack on a window-pane. But still there was no response from the monk, and now I was so frightened my teeth were chattering.

"I'm going to fetch Mrs Fairweather," Rodney said after a while, "she'll know what to do."

"Rodney," I swallowed, "you're not going to leave me alone with – him, are you?"

Rodney was climbing out of the far side of the bed.

"He won't hurt you, he doesn't move, and if he does you can belt under the bed. I say, chuck the candle over, and the matches, I've got to find my way down to the next floor."

Left alone, I studied our visitor with a little more attention than formerly, for, as he appeared to be harmless, my fear was gradually subsiding.

I knew very little about monks, but this one seemed to be a shabby specimen; his gown was old, and there was even a small hole in one sleeve, as if he indulged in the bad habit of leaning his elbows on the table. Furthermore, on closer inspection – and by now I had summoned up enough courage to crawl forward a short way along the bed – he was in need of a shave. There was a distinct stubble on his chin, and one hand, that rested on his knee, had dirt under the fingernails. Altogether, I decided, this was a very scruffy monk.

Rodney had succeeded in waking the Fairweathers. The old lady could be heard protesting loudly at being disturbed, and an occasional rumble proclaimed that Mr Fairweather was not exactly singing for joy. Slippered feet came padding up the stairs, and now Mrs Fairweather's unbroken tirade took on recognizable words.

"I won't have him lurking around the place. It's more than I'm prepared to stand, though why two lumps of boys couldn't have chased him out, without waking a respectable body from her well-earned sleep, I'll never know."

"But he doesn't move," Rodney's voice intervened.

"I'll move him."

She came in through the doorway like a gust of wind, a bundle of fury wrapped in a flowered dressing gown, and in one hand she carried a striped bath towel.

"Get along with you." She might have been shooing off a stray cat. "I won't have you lurking around the house. Go on – out."

The words had no effect, but the bath towel did. Mrs Fairweather waved it in, or rather through, the apparition's face. The figure stirred, rather like a clockwork doll making a first spasmodic move, then the head turned and a look of deep distress appeared on the up to now emotionless face. The old lady continued to scold, and flapped the towel even more vigorously.

"Go on, if I've told you once, I've told you a hundred times, you're not to bother respectable folk. Go where you belong."

The monk flowed into an upright position; there is no other word to describe the action. Then he began to dance in slow motion towards the left-hand wall, Mrs Fairweather pursuing him with her flapping towel. It was a most awesome sight; first the left leg came very slowly upwards, and seemed to find some invisible foothold, then the right drifted past it, while both arms gently clawed the air. It took the monk some three minutes to reach the left-hand wall; a dreadful, slow, macabre dance, performed two feet above floor level, with an irate Mrs Fairweather urging him on with her flapping towel, reinforced by repeated instructions to go, and not come

back, while her husband, ludicrous in a white flannel nightgown, watched sardonically from the doorway.

The monk at last came to the wall. His left leg went through it, then his right arm, followed by his entire body. The last we saw of him was the heel of one sandal, which had a broken strap. Mrs Fairweather folded up her bath towel and, panting from her exertions, turned to us.

"That's got shot of him, and you won't be bothered again tonight. Next time he comes, do what I did. Flap something in his face. He doesn't like that. Nasty, dreamy creature, he is."

'But . . ." Rodney was almost jumping up and down in bed with excitement, "what . . . who is he?"

"A nasty old ghost, what did you imagine he was?" Mrs Fairweather's face expressed profound astonishment at our ignorance; "one of them old monks that used to live here, donkey's years ago."

"Gosh," Rodney eyed the wall through which the monk had vanished, "do you mean he'll come back?"

"More than likely." The old lady had rejoined her husband in the doorway. "But when he does, no waking me out of a deep sleep. Do as I say, flap something in his face, and above all, don't encourage him. Another thing," she paused and waved an admonishing finger, "there's no need to tell that Miss Fortesque about him. She looks as if she's frightened of her own shadow as it is. Now go to sleep, and no more nonsense."

It was some time before we went to sleep.

"Harry," Rodney repeated the question several times, "what is a ghost?"

I made the same answer each time.

"I dunno."

"It seems a good thing to be. I mean, being able to go through walls and dance in the air. I'd make Miss Fortesque jump out of her skin. I say, she must sleep like a log."

"Her room is some distance away," I pointed out.

"Still, all that racket I was making . . ." He yawned. "Tomorrow, we'll ask her what a ghost is."

"Mrs Fairweather said we were not to tell her about the ghost."

"There's no need to tell her we've seen one, stupid. Just ask her what it is."

Rodney tacked the question on to Henry the Eighth's wives next morning.

"Name Henry the Eighth's wives," Miss Fortesque had instructed. Rodney had hastened to oblige.

"Catherine of Aragon, Anne Boleyn, Jane Seymour, Anne of Cleeves, Catherine Howard, and Catherine Parr who survived him, but it was a near thing. Please, Miss Fortesque, what is a ghost?"

"Very good," Miss Fortesque was nodding her approval, then suddenly froze. "What!"

"What is a ghost?"

The frightened look crept back into her eyes, and I could see she suspected some horrible joke.

"Don't be silly, let's get on with the lesson."

"But I want to know," Rodney insisted, "please, what is a ghost?"

"Well," Miss Fortesque still was not happy, but clearly she considered it her duty to answer any intelligent question, "it is said, a ghost is a spirit who is doomed to walk the earth after death."

"Blimey!" Rodney scratched his head, "a ghost is dead?"

"Of course – at least, so it is said. But it is all nonsense. Ghosts do not exist."

"What!" Rodney's smile was wonderful to behold, "you mean – you don't believe ghosts exist?"

"I know they don't," Miss Fortesque was determined to leave the subject before it got out of hand. "Ghosts are the result of ignorant superstition. Now, let us get on. Harry this time. How did Henry dispose of his wives?"

I stifled a yawn.

"Catherine of Aragon divorced, Anne Boleyn beheaded, Jane Seymour died, Anne of Cleeves divorced, Catherine Howard beheaded, Catherine Parr . . ."

"I say, Harry," Rodney remarked later that day, "I bet Brownie was the odd man out."

"Who?"

"Brownie, the monk. There's always one in big establishments. You remember at prep school last year, that chap Jenkins. He was lazy, stupid, never washed. The chances are, Brownie was the odd man out among the other monks. Probably never washed or shaved unless he was chivvied by the abbot, then when he died he hadn't the sense to realize there was some other place for him to go. So, he keeps hanging about here. Yes, I guess that's it. Brownie was the stupid one."

"I don't think one should flap a towel in his face," I said, "it's not polite."

"You don't have to be polite to a ghost," Rodney scoffed, "but I agree it's senseless. Next time he comes we'll find out more about him. I mean, he's not solid, is he? You saw how the towel went right through his head."

It was several weeks before Brownie came again, and we were a little worried that Mrs Fairweather had frightened him away for good. Then one night I was awakened by Rodney. He was standing by my bed, and as I awoke he lit the candle, his hand fair shaking with excitement.

"Is he back?" I asked, not yet daring to look for myself. "Yep," Rodney nodded, "on the foot of your bed, as before. Come on, get up, we'll have some fun."

I was not entirely convinced this was going to be fun, but I obediently clambered out of bed, then with some reluctance turned my head.

He was there, in exactly the same position as before, seated sideways on the bed, the cowl slipped back on to his shoulders, and staring at the left-hand wall.

"Why does he always sit in the same place?" I asked in a whisper.

"I expect this was the room he slept in, and more than likely his bed was in the same position as yours. I say, he does look weird. Let's have a closer look."

Holding the candlestick well before him, Rodney went round the bed and peered into the monk's face. Rather fearfully, I followed him.

The face was podgy, deeply tanned, as though its owner had spent a lot of time out of doors, and the large brown eyes were dull and rather sad.

"I told you so," Rodney said with a certain amount of satisfaction, "he's stupid; spent most of his time day-dreaming while the other monks were chopping wood, getting in the harvest, or whatever things they got up to. I bet they bullied him, in a monkish sort of way."

"I feel sorry for him," I said, "he looks so sad."

"You would." Rodney put the candle down. "Let's see what he's made of. Punch your hand into his ribs."

I shook my head. "Don't want to."

"Go on, he won't hurt you. You're afraid."

"I'm not."

"Well, I'm going to have a go. Stand back, and let the dog see the rabbit."

He rolled up his pyjama sleeve, took a deep breath, then gently brought his clenched fist into contact with the brown robe.

"Can't feel a thing," he reported. "Well, here goes."

Fascinated, I saw his arm disappear into Brownie's stomach; first the fist, then the forearm, finally the elbow.

"Look round the back," Rodney ordered, "and see if my hand is sticking out of his spine."

With a cautious look at Brownie's face, which so far had displayed no signs that he resented these liberties taken with his person, I peered round the brown-covered shoulders. Sure enough, there was Rodney's hand waving at me from the middle of the monk's back.

I nodded. "I can see it."

"Feels rather cold and damp," Rodney said, and brought his arm out sideways. "As I see it, nothing disturbs him unless something is flapped in his face. I expect the monks used to flap their robes at him, when they wanted to wake him up. Now you try."

With some misgivings, I rolled up my sleeve and pushed my arm into Brownie's stomach, being careful to close my eyes first. There was an almost indefinable feeling of cold dampness, like putting my arm out of a window early on a spring morning. I heard Rodney laugh, and opened my eyes.

It is a very disturbing experience to say the least, to see your arm buried up to the elbow in a monk's stomach. I pulled it out quickly, determined to have nothing more to do with the entire business, but Rodney had only just begun.

"I'm going in head first," he announced.

Before I had time to consider what he intended to do, he plunged his head through Brownie's left ribs, and in next to no time I saw his face grinning at me from the other side. It was really quite funny and, forgetting my former squeamishness, I begged to be allowed to have a go.

"All right," Rodney agreed, "but you start from the other side."

We played happily at "going through Brownie" for the next twenty minutes. Sideways, backwards, feet first, we went in all ways – the grand climax came when Rodney took up the same position as Brownie, and literally sat inside him. But there was one lesson we learnt: Brownie was undisturbed by our efforts, as long as his head was not touched. Once Rodney tried to reach up and sort of look through the phantom's eyes. At once the blank face took on an expression of intense alarm, the eyes moved, the mouth opened, and had not Rodney instantly withdrawn, I'm certain the ghost would have started his slow . dance towards the left-hand wall.

But there is a limit to the amount of amusement one can derive from crawling through a ghost. After a while we sat down and took stock of the situation.

"I wonder if he would be disturbed if we jumped in him," Rodney inquired wistfully.

I was against any such drastic contortion. "Yes, it would be worse than flapping a towel in his face."

"I suppose so," Rodney relinquished the project with reluctance, then his face brightened. "I say, let's show him to Miss Fortesque."

"Oh no!" My heart went out to that poor, persecuted creature.

"Why not? In a way we would be doing her a service. After all, she doesn't believe in ghosts. It does people good to be proved they're wrong."

"I dunno."

"I'm going to her room," Rodney got up, his eyes alive with mischievous excitement. "I'll say there is someone in our room – no, that won't do – I'll say you've got tummy ache."

"But that's a lie," I objected.

"Well, you might have tummy ache, so it's only half a lie. You stay here, and don't frighten Brownie, in fact don't move."

Thankfully, he left me the lighted candle, having thoughtfully provided himself with a torch, for there was no moon, and being alone in the dark with Brownie was still an alarming prospect. I sat down at the phantom's feet and peered up into that blank face. Yes, it was a stupid face, but can a person be blamed for being stupid? Apart from that, his eyes were very sad, or so they appeared to me, and I began to regret the silly tricks we had played on him. Minutes passed, then footsteps were ascending the stairs; Rodney's voice could be heard stressing the gravity of my mythical stomach ache, with Miss Fortesque occasionally interposing with a soft-spoken inquiry.

Rodney came in through the doorway, his face shining with excitement. Miss Fortesque followed, her expression one of deep concern. She stopped when she saw Brownie. Her face turned, if possible, a shade paler, and for a moment I thought she would faint.

"Who . . . ?" she began.

"Brownie," Rodney announced. "He's a ghost."

"Don't talk such nonsense. Who is this man?"

"A ghost," Rodney's voice rose. "He is one of the monks who lived here ages ago. Look."

He ran forward, stationed himself before the still figure and plunged his arm into its chest. Miss Fortesque gasped: "Oh," just once before she sank down on to the bed and closed her eyes. The grin died on Rodney's face, to be replaced by a look of alarmed concern.

130

"Please," he begged, "don't be frightened, he won't hurt you, honestly. Harry and I think he's lost. Too stupid to find his way to . . ." he paused, "to wherever he ought to go."

Miss Fortesque opened her eyes and took a deep breath. Though I was very young, I admired the way she conquered her fear, more, her abject terror, and rose unsteadily to her feet. She moved very slowly to where Brownie sat, then stared intently at the blank face.

"You have done a dreadful thing," she said at last, "to mock this poor creature. I am frightened, very frightened, but I must help him. Somehow, I must help him."

"How?" inquired Rodney.

"I don't know." She moved nearer and peered into the unblinking eyes. "He looks like someone who is sleep-walking. How do you rouse him?"

"Touch his head. Mrs Fairweather flaps a towel in his face."

Miss Fortesque raised one trembling hand and waved it gently before Brownie's face. He stirred uneasily, his eyes blinked, then, as the hand was waved again, flowed slowly upwards. Miss Fortesque gave a little cry and retreated a few steps.

"No." She spoke in a voice only just above a whisper. "Please, please listen."

Brownie was already two feet above floor level, but he paused and looked back over one shoulder, while a look of almost comical astonishment appeared on his face.

"Please listen," Miss Fortesque repeated, "you can hear me, can't you?"

A leg drifted downwards, then he rotated so that he was facing the young woman, only he apparently forgot to descend to floor level. There was the faintest suggestion of a nod.

"You shouldn't be here," Miss Fortesque continued. "You, and . . . all your friends, died a long time ago. You ought to be . . . somewhere else."

The expression was now one of bewilderment and Brownie looked helplessly round the room; his unspoken question was clear.

"Not in this house," she shook her head, "perhaps in heaven, I don't know, but certainly in the place where one goes to after death. Can't you try to find it?"

The shoulders came up into an expressive shrug, and Rodney snorted.

"I told you, he's too stupid."

"Will you be quiet," Miss Fortesque snapped, "how can you be so cruel?" She turned to Brownie again. "Forgive them, they are only children. Surely the other monks taught you about . . . Perhaps you did not understand. But you must leave this house. Go –" she gave a little cry of excitement. "Go upwards! I'm sure that's right. Go up into the blue sky, away from this world; out among the stars, there you'll find the place. Now, I'm absolutely certain. Go out to the stars."

Brownie was still poised in the air; his poor stupid face wore a perplexed frown as he pondered on Miss Fortesque's theory. Then, like the sun appearing from behind a cloud, a smile was born. A slow, rather jolly smile, accompanied by a nod, as though Brownie had at last remembered something important he had no business to have forgotten.

He straightened his legs, put both arms down flat with his hips, and drifted upwards, all the while smiling that jolly, idiotic grin, and nodding. His head disappeared into the ceiling, followed by his shoulders and then his hips. The last we saw were those two worn sandals. Miss Fortesque gave a loud gasp, then burst into tears. I did my best to comfort her.

"I'm sure you sent him in the right direction," I said, "he looked very pleased."

"I bet he finishes up on the wrong star," Rodney commented dourly. I turned on him.

"He won't, I just know he won't. He wasn't so dumb. Once Miss Fortesque sort of jolted his memory he was off like a shot."

"Now, boys," Miss Fortesque dried her eyes on her dressing-gown sleeve, "to bed. Tomorrow we must pretend this never happened. In fact," she shuddered, "I'd like you to promise me you'll never mention the matter again – ever. Is that understood?"

We said, "Yes," and Rodney added, "I think you're quite brave, honestly."

She blushed, kissed us both quickly on our foreheads, then departed. Just before I drifted into sleep, I heard Rodney say:

"I wouldn't mind being a ghost. Imagine being able to drift up through the ceiling, and flying out to the stars. I can't wait to be dead."

Miss Fortesque's theory must have been right. We never saw Brownie again.

THE LAMP

AGATHA CHRISTIE

IT WAS UNDOUBTEDLY AN OLD HOUSE. The whole square was old, with that disapproving dignified old age often met with in a cathedral town. But No 19 gave the impression of an elder among elders; it had a veritable patriarchal solemnity; it towered greyest of the grey, haughtiest of the haughty, chillest of the chill. Austere, forbidding, and stamped with that particular desolation attaching to all houses that have been long untenanted, it reigned above the other dwellings.

In any other town it would have been freely labelled "haunted", but Weyminster was averse from ghosts and considered them hardly respectable except as the appanage of a "county family". So No 19 was never alluded to as a haunted house; but nevertheless it remained, year after year, "To be Let or Sold".

Mrs Lancaster looked at the house with approval as she drove up with the talkative house agent, who was in an unusually hilarious mood at the idea of getting No 19 off his books. He inserted the key in the door without ceasing his appreciative comments.

"How long has the house been empty?" inquired Mrs

Lancaster, cutting short his flow of language rather brusquely.

Mr Raddish (of Raddish & Foplow) became slightly confused.

"Er – er – some time," he remarked blandly.

"So I should think," said Mrs Lancaster drily.

The dimly lighted hall was chill with a sinister chill. A more imaginative woman might have shivered, but this woman happened to be eminently practical. She was tall with much dark brown hair just tinged with grey and rather cold blue eyes.

She went over the house from attic to cellar, asking a pertinent question from time to time. The inspection over, she came back into one of the front rooms looking out on the square and faced the agent with a resolute mien.

"What is the matter with the house?"

Mr Raddish was taken by surprise.

"Of course, an unfurnished house is always a little gloomy," he parried feebly.

"Nonsense," said Mrs Lancaster. "The rent is ridiculously low for such a house – purely nominal. There must be some reason for it. I suppose the house is haunted?"

Mr Raddish gave a nervous little start but said nothing.

Mrs Lancaster eyed him keenly. After a few moments she spoke again.

"Of course that is all nonsense. I don't believe in ghosts or anything of that sort, and personally it is no deterrent to my taking the house; but servants, unfortunately, are very credulous and easily frightened. It would be kind of you to tell me exactly what – what thing *is* supposed to haunt this place."

"I – er – really don't know," stammered the house agent.

"I am sure you must," said the lady quietly. "I cannot take the house without knowing. What was it? A murder?"

"Oh! no," cried Mr Raddish, shocked by the idea of anything so alien to the respectability of the square. "It's – it's – only a child."

"A child?"

"Yes."

"I don't know the story exactly," he continued reluctantly. "Of course, there are all kinds of different versions, but I believe that

135

about thirty years ago a man going by the name of Williams took No 19. Nothing was known of him; he kept no servants; he had no friends; he seldom went out in the daytime. He had one child, a little boy. After he had been there about two months, he went up to London, and had barely set foot in the metropolis before he was recognized as being a man 'wanted' by the police on some charge – exactly what, I do not know. But it must have been a grave one, because, sooner than give himself up, he shot himself. Meanwhile, the child lived on here, alone in the house. He had food for a little time, and he waited day after day for his father's return. Unfortunately, it had been impressed upon him that he was never under any circumstances to go out of the house or to speak to anyone. He was a weak, ailing, little creature, and did not dream of disobeying this command. In the night, the neighbours, not knowing that his father had gone away, often heard him sobbing in the awful loneliness and desolation of the empty house."

Mr Raddish paused.

"And – er – the child starved to death," he concluded, in the same tones as he might have announced that it had just begun to rain.

"And it is the child's ghost that is supposed to haunt the place?" asked Mrs Lancaster.

"It is nothing of consequence really," Mr Raddish hastened to assure her. "There's nothing *seen*, not *seen*, only people say, ridiculous, of course, but they do say they hear – the child – crying, you know."

Mrs Lancaster moved towards the front door.

"I like the house very much," she said. "I shall get nothing as good for the price. I will think it over and let you know."

"It really looks very cheerful, doesn't it, Papa?"

Mrs Lancaster surveyed her new domain with approval. Gay rugs, well-polished furniture, and many knick-knacks, had quite transformed the gloomy aspect of No 19.

She spoke to a thin, bent old man with stooping shoulders and a delicate mystical face. Mr Winburn did not resemble his daughter; indeed no greater contrast could be imagined than that presented by her resolute practicalness and his dreamy abstraction.

"Yes," he answered with a smile, "no one would dream the house was haunted."

"Papa, don't talk nonsense! On our first day too."

Mr Winburn smiled.

"Very well, my dear, we will agree that there are no such things as ghosts."

"And please," continued Mrs Lancaster, "don't say a word before Geoff. He's so imaginative."

Geoff was Mrs Lancaster's little boy. The family consisted of Mr Winburn, his widowed daughter, and Geoffrey.

Rain had begun to beat against the window – pitter-patter, pitter-patter.

"Listen," said Mr Winburn. "Is it not like little footsteps?"

"It's more like rain," said Mrs Lancaster, with a smile.

"But *that, that* is a footstep," cried her father, bending forward to listen.

Mrs Lancaster laughed outright.

"That's Geoff coming downstairs."

Mr Winburn was obliged to laugh too. They were having tea in the hall, and he had been sitting with his back to the staircase. He now turned his chair round to face it.

Little Geoffrey was coming down, rather slowly and sedately, with a child's awe of a strange place. The stairs were of polished oak, uncarpeted. He came across and stood by his mother. Mr Winburn gave a slight start. As the child was crossing the floor, he distinctly heard another pair of footsteps on the stairs, as of someone following Geoffrey. Dragging footsteps, curiously painful they were. Then he shrugged his shoulders incredulously. "The rain, no doubt," he thought.

"I'm looking at the spongecakes," remarked Geoff with the admirably detached air of one who points out an interesting fact.

His mother hastened to comply with the hint.

"Well, Sonny, how do you like your new home?" she asked.

"Lots," replied Geoffrey with his mouth generously filled. "Pounds and pounds and pounds." After this last assertion, which was evidently expressive of the deepest contentment, he relapsed into silence, only anxious to remove the spongecake from the sight of man in the least time possible.

Having bolted the last mouthful, he burst forth into speech.

"Oh! Mummy, there's attics here, Jane says; and can I go at once and *egg*zplore them? And there might be a secret door. Jane says there isn't, but I think there must be, and, anyhow, I know there'll be *pipes, water pipes* (with a face full of ecstasy) and can I play with them, and oh! can I go and see the boi-i-ler?" He spun out the last word with such evident rapture that his grandfather felt ashamed to reflect that this peerless delight of childhood only conjured up to his imagination the picture of hot water that wasn't hot, and heavy and numerous plumber's bills.

'We'll see about the attics tomorrow, darling," said Mrs Lancaster. "Suppose you fetch your bricks and build a nice house, or an engine."

"Don't want to build an 'ouse."

"*H*ouse."

"House, or h'engine h'either."

"Build a boiler," suggested his grandfather.

Geoffrey brightened.

"With pipes?"

"Yes, lots of pipes."

Geoffrey ran away happily to fetch his bricks.

The rain was still falling. Mr Winburn listened. Yes, it must have been the rain he had heard; but it did sound like footsteps.

He had a queer dream that night.

He dreamt that he was walking through a town, a great city it seemed to him. But it was a children's city; there were no grown-up people there, nothing but children, crowds of them. In his dream they all rushed to the stranger crying: "Have you brought him?" It seemed that he understood what they meant and shook his head sadly. When they saw this, the children turned away and began to cry, sobbing bitterly.

The city and the children faded away and he awoke to find

himself in bed, but the sobbing was still in his ears. Though wide awake, he heard it distinctly; and he remembered that Geoffrey slept on the floor below, while this sound of a child's sorrow descended from above. He sat up and struck a match. Instantly the sobbing ceased.

Mr Winburn did not tell his daughter of the dream or its sequel. That it was no trick of his imagination, he was convinced; indeed soon afterwards he heard it again in the daytime. The wind was howling in the chimney, but *this* was a separate sound – distinct, unmistakable: pitiful little heartbroken sobs.

He found out too that he was not the only one to hear them. He overheard the housemaid saying to the parlourmaid that she "didn't think as that there nurse was kind to Master Geoffrey. She'd 'eard 'im crying 'is little 'eart out only that very morning." Geoffrey had come down to breakfast and lunch beaming with health and happiness; and Mr Winburn knew that it was not Geoff who had been crying, but that other child whose dragging footsteps had startled him more than once.

Mrs Lancaster alone never heard anything. Her ears were not perhaps attuned to catch sounds from another world.

Yet one day she also received a shock.

"Mummy," said Geoffrey plaintively. "I wish you'd let me play with that little boy."

Mrs Lancaster looked up from her writing table with a smile.

"What little boy, dear?"

"I don't know his name. He was in an attic, sitting on the floor crying, but he ran away when he saw me. I suppose he was *shy* (with slight contempt), not like a *big* boy, and then, when I was in the nursery building, I saw him standing in the door watching me build, and he looked so awful lonely and as though he wanted to play wiv me. I said: 'Come and build a h'engine,' but he didn't say nothing, just looked as – as though he saw a lot of chocolates, and his mummy had told him not to touch them." Geoff sighed, sad personal reminiscences evidently recurring to him. "But when I asked Jane who he was and told her I wanted to play wiv him, she said there wasn't no little boy in the 'ouse and not to tell naughty stories. I don't love Jane at all."

Mrs Lancaster got up.

"Jane was right. There was no little boy."

"But I saw him. Oh! Mummy, do let me play wiv him, he did look so awful lonely and unhappy. I *do* want to do something to 'make him better'."

Mrs Lancaster was about to speak again, but her father shook his head.

"Geoff," he said very gently, "that poor little boy *is* lonely, and perhaps you may do something to comfort him; but you must find out how by yourself – like a puzzle – do you see?"

"Is it because I am getting *big* I must do it all my lone?"

"Yes, because you are getting big."

As the boy left the room, Mrs Lancaster turned to her father impatiently.

"Papa, this is absurd. To encourage the boy to believe the servants' idle tales!"

"No servant has told the child anything," said the old man gently. "He's seen – what I *hear*, what I could see perhaps if I were his age."

"But it's such nonsense! Why don't I see it or hear it?"

Mr Winburn smiled, a curiously tired smile, but did not reply.

"Why?" repeated his daughter. "And why did you tell him he could help the – the – thing? It's – it's all so impossible."

The old man looked at her with his thoughtful glance.

"Why not?" he said. "Do you remember these words:

> What Lamp has Destiny to guide
> Her little Children stumbling in the Dark?
> 'A Blind Understanding,' Heaven replied.

"Geoffrey has that – a blind understanding. All children possess it. It is only as we grow older that we lose it, that we cast it away from us. Sometimes, when we are quite old, a faint gleam comes back to us, but the Lamp burns brightest in childhood. That is why I think Geoffrey may help."

"I don't understand," murmured Mrs Lancaster feebly.

"No more do I. That – that child is in trouble and wants – to be set free. But how? I do not know, but – it's awful to think of it – sobbing its heart out – a *child*."

A month after this conversation Geoffrey fell very ill. The east wind had been severe, and he was not a strong child. The doctor shook his head and said that it was a grave case. To Mr Winburn he divulged more and confessed that the case was quite hopeless. "The child would never have lived to grow up, under any circumstances," he added. "There has been serious lung trouble for a long time."

It was when nursing Geoff that Mrs Lancaster became aware of that – other child. At first the sobs were an indistinguishable part of the wind, but gradually they became more distinct, more unmistakable. Finally she heard them in moments of dead calm: a child's sobs – dull, hopeless, heartbroken.

Geoff grew steadily worse and in his delirium he spoke of the "little boy" again and again. "I do want to help him get away, I do!" he cried.

Succeeding the delirium there came a state of lethargy. Geoffrey lay very still, hardly breathing, sunk in oblivion. There was nothing to do but wait and watch. Then there came a still night, clear and calm, without one breath of wind.

Suddenly the child stirred. His eyes opened. He looked past his mother towards the open door. He tried to speak and she bent down to catch the half-breathed words.

"All right, I'm comin'," he whispered; then he sank back.

The mother felt suddenly terrified; she crossed the room to her father. Somewhere near them the other child was laughing. Joyful, contented, triumphant, the silvery laughter echoed through the room.

"I'm frightened; I'm frightened," she moaned.

He put his arm round her protectingly. A sudden gust of wind made them both start, but it passed swiftly and left the air quiet as before.

The laughter had ceased and there crept to them a faint sound, so faint as hardly to be heard, but growing louder till they could distinguish it. Footsteps – light footsteps, swiftly departing.

Pitter-patter, pitter-patter, they ran – those well-known halting little feet. Yet – surely – now *other* footsteps suddenly mingled with them, moving with a quicker and a lighter tread.

With one accord they hastened to the door.

Down, down, down, past the door, close to them, pitter-patter, pitter-patter, went the unseen feet of the little children *together*.

Mrs Lancaster looked up wildly.

"There are *two* of them – *two!*"

Grey with sudden fear, she turned towards the cot in the corner, but her father restrained her gently, and pointed away.

"There," he said simply.

Pitter-patter, pitter-patter – fainter and fainter.

And then – silence.

THE HAUNTING OF
CHAS McGILL

ROBERT WESTALL

T HE DAY WAR BROKE OUT, Chas McGill went up in the world. What a Sunday morning! Clustering round the radio at eleven o'clock, all hollow-bellied like the end of an England–Australia Test. Only this was the England–Germany Test. He had his score-cards all ready, pinned on his bedroom wall; number of German tanks destroyed; number of German planes shot down; number of German ships sunk.

The Prime Minister's voice, finally crackling over the air, seemed to Chas a total disaster. Mr Chamberlain *regretted* that a state of war now existed between England and Germany. Worse, he bleated like a sheep; or the sort of kid who, challenged in the playground, backs into a corner with his hands in front of his face and threatens to tell his dad on you. Why didn't he threaten to kick Hitler's teeth in? Chas hoped Hitler wasn't listening, or there'd soon be trouble . . .

Immediately, the air-raid sirens went.

German bombers. Chas closed his eyes and remembered the cinema newsreels from Spain. Skies thick with black crosses, from which endless streams of tiny bombs fell. Endless as the streams of refugee women scurrying through the shattered houses, all wearing head-scarves and ankle-socks. Rows of dead children laid out on the shattered brickwork like broken-stick dolls with glass eyes. (He had always shut his eyes at that point, but *had* to peep.) And the German bomber-pilots, hardly human in tight black leather flying-helmets, laughing and slapping each other on the back and busting open bottles of champagne and spraying each other.

He opened his eyes again. Through his bedroom window the grass of the square still dreamed in sunlight. Happy ignorant sparrows, excused the war, were busy pecking their breakfast from the steaming pile of manure left by the Co-op milk-horse. The sky remained clear and blue; not a Spitfire in sight.

Chas wondered what he ought to *do*? Turn off the gas and electric? With Mam in the middle of Sunday dinner, that'd be more dangerous than any air-raid. His eye fell on his teddy-bear, sitting on top of a pile of toys in the corner. He hadn't given Ted a glance in years. Now, Ted stared at him appealingly. There'd been teddy-bears in the Spanish newsreels too; the newsreels were particularly keen on teddy-bears split from chin to crotch, with all their stuffing spilling out. Headless teddy-bears, legless teddy-bears . . . Making sure no one was watching, he grabbed Ted and shoved him under the bed to safety.

Not a moment too soon. Mam came in, drying sudsy hands.

"Anything happening out front? Nothing happening out the back." She made it sound like they were waiting for a carnival with a brass band, or something. She peered intently out of the window.

"There's an air-raid warden."

"It's only old Jimmy Green."

"*Mr* Green to you. Well, he wrote to the Air Raid Precautions yesterday, offering his services, so I expect he thinks he's got to do his bit."

Jimmy was wearing his best blue suit; though whether in honour of the war, or only because it was Sunday, Chas couldn't tell. But he was wearing all his medals from the Great War, and his gas-mask in a cardboard box, hanging on a piece of string across his chest. His chest was pushed well out, and he was marching round the square, swinging his arms like the Coldstream guardsman he'd once been.

"I'll bet he's got Hitler scared stiff."

"If he sounds his rattle," said Mam, "put your gas-mask on."

"He hasn't *got* a rattle."

"Well, that's what it says in the papers. An' if he blows his whistle, we have to go down the air-raid shelter."

Chas bleakly surveyed the Anderson shelter, lying in pieces all over the front lawn, where it had been dumped by council workmen yesterday. It might do the worms a bit of good . . .

"Who's that?"

Jimmy had been joined by a more important air-raid warden. So important he actually had a black steel helmet with a white "W" on the front. Jimmy pointed to a mad happy dog who, finding the empty world much to his liking, was chasing his tail all over the square. The important warden consulted a little brown book, and obviously decided the dog was a threat to national security. They made a prolonged and helpless attempt to catch the dog, who loved it.

"The Germans are dropping them Alsatians by parachute," said Chas. "To annoy the wardens."

That earned a clout. "Stop spreading rumours and causing despondency. They can put you in prison for that!"

Chas wondered about prison; prisons had thick walls and concrete ceilings, at least in the movies. Definitely bomb-proof . . .

But a third figure had emerged into the square. An immensely stocky lady in a flowered hat. A cigarette thrust from her mouth and two laden shopping-bags hung from each hand. She was moving fast, and panting through her cigarette; the effect was of a small but powerful steam-locomotive. The very sight of her convinced Chas that the newsreels from Spain were no more real than Marlene Dietrich in *Destry Rides Again*. Ridiculous.

She made the wardens look pretty ridiculous, too, as they ran one each side of her, gesticulating fiercely.

"Get out of me way, Arthur Dunhill, an' tek' that bleddy silly hat off. Ye look like something out of a carnival. Aah divvent care if they hev made ye Chief Warden. Aah remember ye as a snotty-nosed kid being dragged up twelve-in-two-rooms in Back Brannen Street. If ye think that snivelling gyet Hitler can stop me performin' me natural functions on a Sunday morning ye're very much mistaken . . ."

"It's your Nana," said Mam, superfluously but with much relief. Next minute, Nana was sitting in the kitchen, sweating cobs and securely entrenched among her many shopping-bags.

"Let me get me breath. Well, she's done it now. Tempy. She's *really* done it."

"It wasn't Tempy," said Chas. "It was Hitler."

"Aah'll cross his bridge when Aah come to it. You know what Tempy's done? Evaccyated all her school to Keswick, and we've all got to go and live at 'The Elms' as caretakers."

Chas gave an inward screech of agony. Tempy gone to Keswick meant the loss of ten shillings a term. Thirty bob a year. How many Dinky Toys would that buy?

War might be hell, but thirty shillings was serious.

The siren suddenly sounded the all-clear.

Mam let Chas go out and watch for the taxi in the blackout. The blackout was a flop. It just wasn't black. True, the street-lamps weren't lit, and every house-window carefully curtained. But the longer he stood there, the lighter the sky grew, until it seemed as bright as day.

He'd hauled the two big suitcases out of the house, with a lot of sweat. He stood between them, ready to duck in case a low-flying Messerschmitt 109 took advantage of the lack of blackout to strafe the square. Machine-gun bullets throwing up mounds of earth, like in *Hell's Angels* starring Ben Lyon. He wondered if the suitcases would stop a bullet. They seemed full of insurance books and all fifteen pairs of Mam's apricot-coloured knickers. Still, in war, one had to take risks . . .

The taxi jerked into the square at ten miles an hour, and pulled up some distance away.

"Number eighteen?" shouted the driver querulously. "Can't see a bloody thing." No wonder. He had covered his windscreen with crosses of sticky-tape to protect it against bomb-blast, and peered through like a spider out of its web.

"Get on, ye daft bugger," shouted Nana from the back. "Aah cud drive better wi' me backside." Granda, totally buried beside her in a mound of blankets, travelling rugs, overcoats and mufflers for his chest, coughed prolonged agreement.

It was a strange journey to "The Elms". Chas had to sit on the suitcases, with what felt like Nana's washday-mangle sticking in his ribs.

"I shouldn't have left the house empty like that," wailed Mam. "There'll be burglars an' who's going to water the tomatoes?"

"You coulda left a note asking the burglars to do it," said Chas. It was too dark and jam-packed in the taxi for any danger of a clout.

"Ye'll be safer at 'The Elms', hinny," said Nana. "Now ye haven't got a man to put a steadyin' hand to you."

"She's got *me*," said Chas.

"God love yer – a real grown man. 'Spect ye'll be j'ining up in the Army soon as ye're twelve."

"Aah j'ined up at fourteen," said Granda. "To fight the Boers. Fourteen years, seven months, six days. Aah gave a false birthday."

"Much good it's done you since," said Nana, "wi' that gassing they gave you at Wipers."

"That wasn't the Boers," said Chas helpfully, "that was the Germans."

Granda embarked on a bout of coughing, longer and more complicated than "God Save the King", that silenced all opposition for two miles.

"It'll be safer for the bairn," added Nana finally. "Good as evaccyating him. Hitler won't bomb Preston nor 'The Elms'. He's got more respec' for his betters . . . besides, ye had to come, hinny. I can't manage that great spooky place on my own – not wi' yer Granda an' his chest."

"Spooky?" asked Chas.

"Don't mind me," said Nana hastily. "That's just me manner of speakin'."

Just then, the taxi turned a corner too sharply; outside there was a thump, and the crunch of breaking glass. "Ah well," said Nana philosophically, "we won't be needing them street-lamps for the duration. Reckon it'll be all over by Christmas, once the Navy's cut off Hitler's vitals . . ."

"Painful," said Chas.

"Aah owe it to Tempy," concluded Nana. "Many a job she's pushed my way, ower the years, when yer Granda's had his chest . . ."

Chas pushed his nose against the steamed-up window of the taxi, feeling as caged as a budgie. He watched the outskirts of Garmouth fall away; a few fields, then the taxi turned wildly into the private road where the roofs of great houses peeped secretly over shrubbery and hedge and tree, and at the end was "The Elms", Miss Temple's ancestral home and late private school and biggest of them all.

So by bedtime, on the third of September 1939, Chas had risen very high in the world indeed. A third-floor attic, with the wind humming in the wireless-aerial that stretched between the great chimneys, and ivy leaves tapping on his window, so it sounded as if it was raining. Granda's old army greatcoat had been hung over the window, for lack of curtains.

Chas didn't like it at all, even if he did have candle and matches, a rather dim torch, a book called *Deeds That Have Won the VC* and six toy pistols under his pillow. You couldn't shoot spooks with a toy pistol, he didn't feel like winning the VC, and he wanted the lav, bad.

There was a great cold white chamber-pot under the narrow servant's bed, but he'd no intention of using it. Mam would be sure to inspect the contents in the morning, and tell everyone at breakfast how his kidneys were functioning. Mam feared malfunctioning kidneys more than Stuka divebombers.

Finally, he gathered his courage, a pistol, his torch and his too-short dressing-gown around him, and set out to seek relief.

The dark was a trackless desert, beyond his dim torch. The wind, finding its way up through the floorboards, ballooned-up the worn passage-carpet like shifting sand-dunes. The only oases were the light switches, and most of them didn't work, so they were, strictly speaking, mirages. Down one narrow stair . . .

The servant's lav was tall and gaunt, like a gallows; its rusting chain hung like a hangman's noose, swaying in the draught. The seat was icy and unfriendly.

Afterwards, reluctant to go back upstairs, he pressed on. A slightly open door, a shaft of golden light, the sweet smell of old age and illness. Granda's cough was like a blessing in the strangeness.

But he didn't go in. He didn't dislike Granda, but he didn't like him either. Granda's chest made him as strange as the pyramids of Egypt. Granda's chest was the centre of the family, around which everything else revolved. As constant as the moon. He had his good spells and his bad. His good spells, when he turned over a bit of his garden, or hung a picture on the wall, grew no better. His bad spells grew no worse.

Chas passed on, noiselessly, down another flight of stairs.

He knew where he was, now. A great oak hall, with a landing running round three sides, and a broad open staircase leading down into a dim red light. Miss Temple's study was on the right.

Miss Temple, headmistress, magistrate, city councillor of Newcastle. He knew her highly polished shoes well; her legs, solid as table-legs in their pale silk stockings, her black headmistress's gown or her dark fur coat. He had never seen her face. It was always too high above him, too awesome. God must look like Miss Temple.

At the end of every term, ever since he had started school, Nana had taken him to see Miss Temple at "The Elms". With his school report clutched in his hand. They were shown in by a housemaid called Claire, neat in black frock, white lace hat and apron. Up to Miss Temple's study. There, the polished black shoes would be waiting, standing four-square on the Turkey carpet, the pale solid legs above them.

A sallow plump soft hand, with dark hairs on the back,

would descend into his line of vision. He would put the school report into it. Hand and report would ascend out of sight. There would be a long silence, like the Last Judgement. Then Miss Temple's voice would come floating down, deep as an angel's trumpet.

"Excellent, Charles . . . excellent." Then she would ask him what he was going to be when he grew up; but he could never answer. The plump hand would descend again, with the report and something brown that crackled enticingly.

A ten-bob note. He would mumble thanks that didn't make sense even to himself. Then the tiny silver watch that slightly pinched the dark plump wrist would be consulted, and a gardener-chauffeur called Holmes would be summoned, to drive Miss Temple in state to Newcastle, for dinner or a meeting of the full council, or some other god-like occasion.

It never varied. He never really breathed till he was outside again, and the air smelled of trees and grass, and not of polish and Miss Temple. Sometimes, hesitating, he would ask Nana why Miss Temple was not like anybody else. Nana always said it was because she had never married; because of something that happened in the Great War.

And now there was another war, and Miss Temple fled to Keswick with all her pupils, and her study door locked, and outside Hitler and a great wind were loose in the world.

He crept on, past the grandfather clock on the landing that ticked on, as indifferent to him as Holmes the chauffeur in his shiny leather gaiters. Prowled out to the back wing, where the girls' classrooms were. Searched their empty desks by torchlight, exulting spitefully over the spelling mistakes in an abandoned exercise-book. There was a knicker-blue shoe-bag hanging on the back of one classroom door. He put his hand inside with a guilty thrill, but it only contained one worn white plimsoll.

Downstairs, he got into a panic before he found the light-proof baize-covered kitchen-door; thought he was cut off in the whole empty windy house, with only Granda above, immobilized and coughing.

He pushed the baize door open an inch. Cosy warmth streamed out. A roaring fire in the kitchen range. Nana, in flowered pinny, pouring tea. Mam, still worrying on about burglars, peeling potatoes. Claire the housemaid, raffish without her lace hat, legs crossed, arms crossed, fag in her mouth, eyes squinting up against the smoke.

"Shan't be here to bother you much longer. Off to South Wales next week, working on munitions. They pay twice as much as *she* does. Holmes? Just waiting for his call-up papers, for the Army. Reckon's he'll spend a cushy war, driving Lord Gort about."

Chas was tempted to go in; he loved tea and gossip. Hated the idea of the long climb back to the moaning wireless-aerial and ivy-tapping windows. But Mam would only be angry . . .

He climbed. At the turn of the last stair, a landing window gave him a view of the roof and the chimneys and the row of attic windows. Six attic windows. His was the fourth . . . no the fifth, it must be, because the fifth was dimly candlelit. Oh God, he'd left his candle burning, and Granda's greatcoat was useless as blackout, and soon there'd be an air-raid warden shouting "Put that bloody light out."

He ran, suddenly panting. Burst into his room.

It was in darkness, of course. He'd never lit his candle. And his was the fourth room in the corridor, the fourth shabby white door.

He ran back to the landing window. There was candlelight in the fifth window, the room next to his own. It moved, as if someone were moving about, inside the room.

Who?

Holmes, of course. Snooty Holmes. Well, Holmes's flipping blackout was Holmes's flipping business . . . Chas got back into his ice-cold bed, keeping his dressing-gown on for warmth. Put his ear to the wall. He could hear Holmes moving about, restlessly; big leather boots on uncarpeted floorboards, and a kind of continuous mournful low whistling. Miserable stuck-up bugger . . .

On that thought, he fell asleep.

Next morning, before going to the lav, he peered round his door in the direction of Holmes. He dreaded the sneer that would cross Holmes's face if he saw a tousle-haired kid running about in pyjamas. Nana said Holmes had once been a gentleman's gentleman, and it showed.

But there was no sign of Holmes. In fact, the whole width of the corridor, just beyond Chas's room, was blocked off by a dirty white door, unnoticed in the blackout last night. It looked like a cupboard door, too, with a keyhole high up.

Chas investigated. It *was* a cupboard; contained nothing but a worn-out broom and a battered blue tin dustpan. Then Chas forgot all about Holmes; because the inside of the cupboard was papered over with old newspapers. Adverts for ladies' corsets, stiffened with the finest whalebone and fitted with the latest all-rubber suspenders. All for three shillings and elevenpence threefarthings! Better still, photographs of soldiers, mud and great howitzers. And headlines.

NEW OFFENSIVE MOUNTED AT CAMBRAI
MILE OF GERMAN FIRST-LINE TRENCH TAKEN
NEW 'TANKS' IN ACTION

Chas read on, enthralled and shivering, till Nana shouted up the stairs to ask if they were all dead up there?

As he was hurling himself into his clothes, a new thought struck him. All those old newspapers seemed to be from 1917 . . . if the cupboard had been there since then, how on earth did Holmes get into his room? He went back and rapped violently all over the inside of the cupboard. The sides were solid plaster; the plaster of the corridor walls. The back boomed hollowly, as if the corridor went on beyond it. But there was no secret door at the back; the pasted-on newspapers were intact: not a torn place anywhere.

"Are ye doing an impersonation o' a death-watch beetle? Cos they only eat wood, an' in that case aah'm going to throw your breakfast away."

Even though he knew it was Nana's voice, he still nearly jumped a yard in the air.

"There's newspapers here, with pictures of the Great War."

"Ye've got war on the bleddy brain," said Nana. "Isn't one war enough for ye? Ye'll have a war on yer hands in the kitchen too, if ye don't come for breakfast. Yer Mam's just heard on the radio that school's been abolished for the duration, an' it's raining. Aah don't know what we're going to do wi' you. Wi' all the bairns driving their mams mad, gettin' under their feet, Hitler's goin' to have a walkover."

But Chas was surprisingly good, all day. He did demand his mac and wellies, and walked round the house no less than fourteen times, staring up at the windows and counting compulsively, and getting himself soaked.

"He'll catch his death, out there," wailed Mam.

"He'll catch my hand on his lug if he comes bothering us in here. Let him bide while we're busy," said Nana, her mouth full of pins from the blackout curtains she was sewing.

Then he came in and had his hair rubbed with a towel by Nana, till he thought his ears were being screwed off. Then he scrounged a baking-board and four drawing-pins, a sheet of shelf-lining paper, and Mam's tape-measure, and did a carefully measured plan of the whole kitchen, which everyone agreed was very fine.

"What's that great fat round thing by the kitchen sink?" asked Nana.

"You, doing the washing-up," said Chas, already ducking so her hand missed his head by inches; she'd a heavy hand, Nana. Then, sitting up, he announced, "I'm going to do something to help the war effort."

"Aye," said Nana. "Ye're running down to the shop for another packet of pins for me."

"No, besides that. I'm going to make a plan of the whole house, to help the Fire Brigade in case we get hit by an incendiary-bomb . . ."

"Ye're a proper little ray o' sunshine . . ."

"Can I go into all the rooms and measure them?"

"No," said Mam. "Miss Temple wouldn't like it."

"Can I, Nana," said Chas blatantly.

"What Tempy's eyes don't see, her heart won't grieve. Let the bairn be, while he's good," said Nana, reaching her whole bunch of keys from her pocket.

So, in between running down to the shop for pins, and running back to the kitchen every time there was a news broadcast, Chas roamed the veriest depths of the house.

Looking for the backstair leading up to Holmes's room.

Looking for the hidden stair leading up to Holmes's room.

Looking for the secret stair leading up to Holmes's room . . .

He searched and measured till he was blue in the face. Went outside and counted windows over and over and got himself soaked again.

No way was there a secret stair up to Holmes's room. He was pretty hungry when he came back in for tea.

Nana switched off the radio with a sniff. "The Archbishop of Canterberry has called for a National Day of Prayer for Poland. God help the bleddy Poles, if it's come to *that*."

"Nana," said Chas, "where does Holmes live?"

"*Mr* Holmes, to you," said Mam in a desperate voice. At which Holmes himself, the sneaky sod, rose in all the glory of his chauffeur's uniform and shiny leggings from the depths of the wing-chair by the fire, where he'd been downing a pint mug of tea.

"And why do you want to know that, my little man?" Holmes said, with a know-all smirk on his face. Chas blushed from head to foot.

"Because you're in the room next to mine, an' I can't see how you get up there." He wouldn't have blurted it out, if he hadn't been so startled.

"Well, that's where you're wrong, my little man," said Holmes. "I have a spacious home above the stables, with my good wife and Nancy Jane, aged nine. You must come and have tea with Nancy Jane, before I go off to serve my king and country. She'd like that. But why on earth did you think I had a room up in the attics?"

"Because someone was moving last night, an' whistling . . ."

155

Holmes looked merely baffled; so did young Claire. Mam was blushing for his manners, like a beetroot. But Chas thought Nana turned as white as a sheet.

"It's only the wind in that bleddy wireless-aerial. Get on wi' yer tea and stop annoying your elders an' betters . . ."

Next evening Chas pushed open the door of Granda's room, cautiously. The old man lay still, propped up on pillows, arms lying parallel on top of the bedclothes. He looked as if he was staring out of the window, but he might be asleep. That was one of the strange things about Granda, the amount of staring out of windows he did, when he was having one of his bad spells; and the way you could never tell if he was staring or asleep. Also the fact that his hair didn't look like hair, and his whiskers didn't look like whiskers. They looked like strange grey plants, growing out of his purply-grey skin. Or the thin roots that grow out of a turnip . . .

"Granda?"

The head turned; the eyes came back from somewhere. They tried to summon up a smile, but Chas's eyes ducked down before they managed it.

"Granda – can I borrow your brace-and-bit?"

"Aye, lad, if ye tek care of it . . . it's in the bottom drawer, wi' the rest o' my gear . . ." The old head turned away again, eyes on a red sunset. Chas pulled out the drawer, and there was Granda's gear. Granda's gear was the one thing Chas really loved about Granda; the old man could never bear to throw things away. Everything might come in useful . . . the drawer was full of odd brass taps, bundles of wire neatly tied up, tin toffee-boxes full of rusty screws and nails, a huge bayonet in its scabbard that Granda only used for cutting his endless supplies of hairy white string. There was the brace-and-bit, huge and lightly oiled, sweet-smelling. He pulled it out, and a hank of wire came with it, and leaping from the wire on to the floor, a small silver badge he hadn't seen before.

"What's that, Granda?"

"That's me honourable discharge medal, that Aah got after

Aah was gassed. Ye had to hev one o' those, or you got no peace in Blighty, if you weren't in uniform. Women giving ye the white feather, making out ye were a coward, not being at the Front. The military after ye, for being a deserter. Ye had to wear that, an' carry yer discharge-papers or ye didn't get a moment's peace, worse nor being at the Front, fightin' Jerry . . . Put it back safe, there's a good lad . . ." Granda's voice, vivid with memory for a moment, faded somewhere else again. Chas took the brace-and-bit, and fled.

Up to the corridor-cupboard by his bedroom. Soon the brace-and-bit were turning in his hands, tearing the pasted newspapers (in a boring bit, advocating Senna Pods for Constipation). Then came the curling shavings of yellow pine, smelling sweetly. After a long while, he felt the tip of the bit crunch through the last of the pine, and out into the open air behind the cupboard. He withdrew it, twisting the bit in reverse as Dad had once shown him, and put his eye to the hole.

He saw more corridor, just like the corridor he was standing in. Ending in a blank wall, ten yards on. A green, blistered door lay on the left, but no secret stair. No possible place the top of a secret stair could be. The green door was slightly ajar, inwards, but he could see nothing. The only window, in the right-hand wall, was thick with cobwebs; years of cobwebs. There was a little mat on the floor of the corridor, kicked up as if somebody had rushed past heedlessly and not bothered to replace it; many, many years ago. The air in that corridor, the kicked mat, were the air and the mat of 1917. It was like opening a box full of 1917 . . .

Then a bedspring creaked; footsteps moved on boards, more footsteps returning, a sigh, and then the bedspring creaked again. Then came the sound of tuneless, doleful whistling, and a squeaking, like cloth polishing metal . . .

Chas slammed the cupboard door and ran through the gathering gloom for the kitchen. He didn't realize he still had the brace-and-bit in his hands till he burst in on the family, gathered round the tea-table.

There were toasted teacakes for tea, dripping melted butter.

And on the news, the announcer said the Navy had boarded and captured ten more German merchant-ships; they were being brought under escort into Allied ports. Slowly, Chas shook off the memory of the noises in the attic. Bedtime was far off yet. He dug into another teacake to console himself, and Nana loudly admired his appetite.

"Got a job for you after tea, our Chas. We've finished all the blackout curtains. When it's really dark, ye can go all round the outside o' the house, an' if ye spot a chink of light, ye can shout 'Put that light out' just like a real air-raid warden."

"That was no chink you saw in my bedroom last night," said Holmes in a girlish simpering voice, "that was an officer of the Imperial Japanese Navy . . ."

Mam didn't half give him a look, for talking smut in front of a child. Which was a laugh, because Chas had told Holmes that joke just an hour ago; he was working hard, softening Holmes up; know your enemy!

Chas was really enjoying himself, out there in the dark garden. He was again half-soaked, through walking into dripping bushes; he had trodden in something left behind by Miss Temple's dog, but such were the fortunes of war.

A little light glowed in the drawing-room window, where the blackout had sagged away from its frame. He banged on the window sharply, indicating where the light-leak was, and inside, invisible, Nana's hand pressed the curtain into place. The little glow vanished.

"OK," shouted Chas, "that's all the ground floor."

"Let me draw breath and climb upstairs," came Nana's voice back faintly.

Chas paced back across the wet lawn; the grass squeaked under his wellies, and he practised making the squeaking louder. Then he glanced up at the towering bulk of "The Elms". The blackouts on the first floor looked pretty good, though he wasn't going to let Nana get away with anything; it was a matter of national security . . .

Reluctantly, his eyes flicked upwards . . . Granda's room was

OK. There was no point to looking at the attics. There was only his own room, and there was no electric light in there, and his candle wasn't lit . . .

He looked up at the attics, and moaned.

The fifth window from the right was gently lit with candlelight again. And there was the distinct outline of a man's head and shoulders, looking out of that window. He could only see the close-cropped hair, and the ears sticking out. But he knew the man was looking at him; he *felt* him looking, felt the caressing of his eyes. Then the man raised a hand and waved it in faint shy greeting. It was not the way Holmes would have waved a hand . . . or was Holmes taking the mickey out of him?

Suddenly, beside himself with rage, Chas shouted, at the dark, shy invisible face, "Put that bloody light out; put that bloody light out!"

He was still shouting hysterically when Nana came out and fetched him in.

"There's a face in that window next to mine," shouted Chas. "There *is*. Look!"

He pointed a trembling finger.

But when he dared to look again himself, there was nothing but the faint reflection of drifting clouds, moving across the dim shine of the glass.

Nevertheless, when Nana picked him up bodily and carried him inside, as she often had when he was a little boy (she was a strong woman), Chas thought that she was trembling too.

He was given an extra drink, and set by the fire. "Drink your tea as hot as you can," said Nana. It was her remedy for all ills, from lumbago to Monday wash-day misery.

Nana and Mam went on with the washing-up. They kept their voices low, but Chas still caught phrases. "Highly strung" and "over-active brain". Then Nana said, "We'll move him down next to his Granda afore tomorrow night." When Mam objected, Nana said sharply, "Don't you remember? It was all in the papers. Course you'd only be a young lass at the time . . ." The whispering went on, but now they had lowered their voices so much, Chas couldn't hear a thing.

He wakened again in the dark. The luminous hands on his Mickey Mouse clock only said two o'clock. That meant he'd woken up four times in four hours. It had never happened to him in his life before. He listened. Horrible total silence; not even the wind sighing in the wireless-aerial. Then, glad as a beacon on a headland to a lost ship, came the racking sound of Granda's cough downstairs.

It gave Chas courage; enough courage to put his ear to the wall of the room next door. And again he heard it; the creak of bedsprings, the endless tuneless whistling. Did he never stop? Granda's cough again. Then whistle, whistle, whistle. Fury seized Chas. He hammered on the wall with his fist, like Dad did at home when the neighbours played the wireless too loud.

Then he wished he hadn't. Because the wall did not sound solid brick like most walls. It trembled like cardboard under his fist, and gave off a hollow sound. And, at the same time, there was a noise of little things falling under his bed; little things like stones. He bent under the bed with his torch, without getting outside the bedclothes. A lump of the wall had cracked and fallen out. Plaster lay all over the bare floorboards, leaving exposed what looked like thin wooden slats. Perhaps there was a hole he could peep through . . . He put on his dressing-gown and crawled under the bed, and squinted at the place where the plaster had fallen off.

There seemed to be a thin glim of golden candlelight . . . Suddenly Chas knew there was no more sleep for him. He had a choice. The indignity of running down to Mam's room, like a baby with toothache. Or finding out just what the hell was going on behind that wall.

Downstairs, Granda coughed again.

Chas took hold of the first slat, and pulled towards him. There was a sharp crack of dry wood, and the stick came out, pulling more plaster with it.

After that, he made a big hole, quite quickly. But the wall had *two* thin skins of slats and plaster. And the far one was still intact except for a long thin crack of golden light he couldn't see through. He'd just make a peephole, no bigger than a mousehole . . .

He waited again, for the support of Granda's cough, then he pushed at the far slats.

Horror of horrors, they resisted stoutly for a moment, then gave way with a rush. The hole on the far side was as big as the hole this side. He could put his head and shoulders through it; if he dared. He just lay, paralysed, listening. The man next door *must* have heard him; couldn't *not* have heard him.

Silence. Then a voice said, "Come on in, if you're coming." A Geordie voice, with a hint of a laugh in it. Not a voice to be afraid of.

He wriggled through, only embarrassed now, like Granda had caught him playing with his watch.

It was a soldier, sitting on a bed very like his own. A sergeant, for his tunic with three white stripes hung on a nail by his head. He was at ease, with his boots off and his braces dangling, polishing the badge of his peaked cap, with a yellow duster in his hand. A tin bottle of Brasso stood open on a wooden chair beside him; the sharp smell came clearly to Chas's nostrils. He was a ginger man, with close-cropped ginger hair, the tips of which glinted in the candlelight. And a long sad ginger moustache. Chas thought he looked a bit old to be a soldier . . . or old-fashioned, somehow. Maybe that was because he was a sergeant . . .

"What you doing here?" Chas asked; then felt terribly rude.

But the soldier went on gently polishing his cap-badge.

"Aah'm on leave. From the Front."

"Oh," said Chas. "I mean, what you doing *here*?"

"Aah met the girl downstairs. She knew Aah needed a billet, so she fetched me up here."

"Oh, Claire?"

The man didn't answer, merely went on polishing, whistling gently that same old tune.

"Do you stay up here all the time? Must be a bit boring, when you're on leave?"

The man sighed, and held his badge up to the candle, to see if it were polished enough. Then, still with his head on one side, he said mildly, "You can do wi' a bit o' boredom, after what we've been through."

162

"At the Front?"

"Aye, at the Front."

"With the British Expeditionary Force?"

"Aye, wi' the British Expeditionary Force."

"But the BEF's not done anything yet. The war's just started."

"They'll tell you people on the home front anything. Aah've just started to realize that. Why, we've marched up to Mons, and we fought the Germans at Mons, and beat 'em. Then we had to retreat from Mons, shelled all the way, and didn't even have time to bury our mates . . ."

"What's the worst thing? The German tanks?"

"Aah hevvn't seen no German tanks, though Aah've seen a few of ours, lately. No, the worst things is mud and rats and trench-foot."

"What's trench-foot?"

The man beckoned him over, and took off his grey woollen sock. Up between his toes grew a blue mould like the mould on cheese. The stink was appalling. Chas wrinkled his nose.

"It comes from standing all day in muddy water. First your boots gan rotten, then your feet. Aah'm lucky – they caught mine in time. Aah've known fellers lose a whole foot, wi' gangrene." He put back his sock, and the smell stopped.

"Is that why you're up here, all day – cos you got trench-foot? You ought to be going out with girls – enjoying yourself. After all, you are home on leave . . . aren't you?"

The man turned and looked straight at him. His eyes . . . his eyes were sunk right back in his head. There were terrible, unmentionable things in those eyes. Then he said, "Can yer keep a secret, Sunny Jim? Aah came home on leave, all right. That was my big mistake. Aah knew Aah shuddn't. Aah didn't for three whole years . . . got a medal for my devotion to duty. Got made sergeant. Then they offered me a fortnight in Blighty, an' Aah was tempted. The moment Aah got home, an' saw the bonny-faced lasses, an' the green fields an' trees an' the rabbits playing, Aah knew Aah cud never gan back. So when me leave was up, the girl here . . . she's a bit sweet on me . . . she hid me up here. She feeds me what scraps she can . . ." He kicked an enamel plate on the floor, with a few crusts on it. "Ye can get used to being in Hell, when you've forgotten there's owt else in the world, but when ye come home, an' realize that Heaven's still there . . . well, ye cannot bring yourself to go back to Hell."

"You've got no guts," said Chas angrily. "You're a *deserter*."

"Aye, Aah'm a deserter all right. They'll probably shoot me if they catch me . . . but Aah tell ye, Aah had plenty guts at the start. We used to be gamekeepers afore the war, Manny Craggs an' me. They found us very useful at the front. We could creep out into No Man's Land wi'out making a sound, and bring back a brace of young Jerries, alive an' kicking an' ready for interrogation afore breakfast. It was good fun, at first. Till Manny copped it, on the Marne. It wes a bad time that, wi' the mud, an' Jerry so close we could hear him whispering in his own trench, and their big guns shelling our communication trench. We couldn't get Manny's body clear, so in the end we buried him respectful as we could, in the front wall o' our trench. Only the rain beat us. We got awake next morning, an' the trench-wall had part-collapsed, and there was his hand sticking out, only his hand. An' no way could we get the earth to cover it again. Can ye think what that was like, passing that hand twenty times a day? But every time the lads came past, they would shake hands wi' old Manny, an' wish him good morning like a gentleman. It kept you sane. Till the rats got to the hand; it was bare bone by the next morning, and gone the morning after. Aah didn't have much *guts* left after that . . . but Aah cudda hung on, till Aah made the mistake of coming on leave . . . now Aah'm stuck here, and there's neither forward nor backward for me . . . just polishing me brasses to look forward to. You won't shop me, mate? Promise?"

"Oh, it's nothing to do with me," said Chas haughtily. The man was a coward, and nothing to be afraid of. He must have run away the moment he got to France; if he'd ever been to France at all . . . the war had only been on three days. Making up these stupid stories to fool me cos he thinks I'm just an ignorant kid . . . "I won't give you away."

And with that, he wriggled back through the hole in the wall, and pushed his trunkful of toys against the hole, and went to bed and fast asleep. To show how much he despised a common deserter.

The following morning, when he woke up, he was quite sure he'd dreamt the whole thing. Until he peeped under his bed and saw the trunk pushed against the wall, and plaster all over the floor. He pulled the trunk back, and shouted "Hallo" through the hole. There was no reply, or any other sound. Puzzled, he shoved his head through the hole. The room next door was empty. Except for the bed with its mattress, and the wooden chair, lying on its side in a corner. Something made him look up to the ceiling above where the chair lay; there was a big rusty hook up there driven into the main roofbeam. The hook fascinated him; he couldn't seem to take his eyes off it. You could hang big things from that; like sides of bacon. He didn't stay long, though; the room felt so very *sad*. Maybe it was just the dimness of the light from the cobwebbed windows. He wriggled back through the hole, pushed back the trunk to cover it, and cleaned up the fallen plaster into the chamber-pot and took it outside before Mam could spot it.

Anyway, the whole business was over; either the man had scarpered, or he'd dreamt the whole thing. People could walk in their sleep; why couldn't they knock holes in walls in their sleep too? He giggled at the thought. Just then, Mam came in, looking very brisk for business. He was to be moved downstairs immediately, next to Granda.

Suddenly, perversely, he didn't *want* to be moved. But Mam was adamant, almost hit him.

"What's the matter? What's got into you?" he shouted. But Mam, tight-lipped and pale-faced, just said, "The very idea of putting you up here . . . get that map down off the wall, quick!"

It was his war-map of Europe, with all the fronts marked with little Union Jacks and swastikas, and Hammer-and-sickles. He began pulling the Union Jack pins out of the Belgian border with France. Then he paused. There, right in the middle of neutral

Belgium, where no British soldier could possibly be, was the town of Mons. And there was a river called the Marne . . .

"Granda?"

The old, faded grey eyes turned from the window; from the scenes he would never talk about.

"Aye, son?"

"In the last war, was there a battle of Mons?"

"Aye, and a retreat from Mons, an' that was a bleddy sight worse. Shelled all the way, and no time to stop and bury your mates . . ."

"And was there a battle of the Marne . . . very rainy and muddy?"

"Aye. Never seen such mud . . . till the Somme."

Then Chas knew he'd been talking to a ghost.

Oddly enough, he wasn't at all scared; instead, he was both excited and indignant. With hardly a minute's hesitation, he said, "Thanks, Granda," and turned and left the room and walked up the stairs; though he began to go faster and faster, in case his courage should run out before he got there. He wasn't sure about this courage he'd suddenly acquired; it wasn't the kind of courage you needed for a fight in the playground. It might leave him as suddenly as it had come. He pulled aside the trunk of toys, and went through the hole like a minor avalanche of plaster.

The sergeant was there, looking up from where he sat on the bed, still cleaning his cap-badge, like he'd been last night. The pair of them looked at each other.

"You're a ghost," said Chas abruptly.

"I am *not*," said the sergeant. "I'm living flesh and blood. Though for how much longer, I don't know, if I have to go on sitting in this place, with nothing to do but polish this cap-badge."

His eyes strayed upwards, to the big rusty hook in the ceiling, then flinched away; with a sour grimace of the mouth. "I *am* flesh and blood, and that's a fact. Feel me." And he held out a large hand, with little ginger hairs and freckles all over the back. His expression was so harmless and friendly that, after a long hesitation, Chas shook hands with him. The freckled hand, indeed, was warm, solid and human.

"I don't understand this," said Chas, outraged. "I don't understand this at *all*."

"No more do I," said the sergeant. "I'd ha' thought I imagined you, if it hadn't been for that great hole in the wall. Wi' your funny cap an' funny short trousers an' socks an' shoes. An' your not giving me away to the folks down below. Where are you from?"

"I think it's rather a case of *when* am I from," said Chas, wrinkling up his brow. "My date is the sixth of September, 1939."

"Aah *am* dreamin'?" said the sergeant. "Today's the sixth of September, 1917. Unless Aah'm out in me reckoning . . . he nodded at the wall, where marks had been scrawled on the plaster with a stub of pencil. Six upright marks, each time, then a diagonal mark across them, making the whole group look like a gate or a fence. "Eight weeks Aah been in this hole . . ."

"Why don't you get out of it?"

"Aye," said the sergeant. "That'd be nice. Down into Shropshire, somewhere, where me old Da sent me to be made a good gamekeeper. They'll be wantin' help wi' the harvest, now, wi' all the lads bein' away. Then I'll lose meself into the green woods. Hole up in some cave in Wenlock Edge for winter, an' watch the rabbits an' foxes, and start to forget."

He screwed his eyes up tightly, as if shutting something out. "That is, if God gave a man the power to forget. Aah don't need me sins forgiven; Aah need the memories forgiven." He opened his blue eyes again. "A nice dream, Sunny Jim, but it wouldn't work. Wi'out civvy clothes an' discharge-papers, I wouldn't get as far as Newcastle . . ." Again, that glance up at the hook in the ceiling . . .

"I'll try and help," said Chas.

"How?" The sergeant looked at him, nearly as trusting as a little kid.

"Well, look," said Chas. He took off his school-cap and gave it to the man. "Put it on!"

The sergeant put it on with a laugh, and made himself go cross-eyed and put out his tongue. "Thanks for the offer, but Aah'd not get far in a bairn's cap . . ."

Chas snatched it back, satisfied. "Wait and see."

He had to wait a long time, before Nana was busy hanging out the washing, and Mam holding the peg-basket, and Granda was asleep. Then he moved in quick, to the drawer where Granda kept his treasures. The honourable-discharge badge, and the discharge-papers were easy enough to find. Though he made a noise shutting the door, Granda didn't waken. The wardrobe-door creaked too, but his luck held. He dug deep into the smelly dark, full of the scents of Granda, tobacco, Nana, fox-furs, dust and old age. He took Granda's oldest overcoat, the tweed one he'd used when he last worked as a stevedore, with the long oilstains and two buttons missing. And an oily old cap. They would have to do. He pushed the wardrobe-door to, getting a glimpse of sleeping Granda in the mirror. Then he was off, upstairs.

He had a job getting the overcoat through the hole. When he finally managed it, he found the room was bare, cold and empty. The chair was back in the corner, kicked away from under the rusty iron hook. The sight filled him with despair; the whole room filled him with despair. But he laid the overcoat neatly on the bare mattress, and the cap on top, and the badge, and the discharge-papers. Then, with a last look round, and a shudder at the cold misery of the place, he wriggled out. At least he'd kept his word.

He haunted that room for a fortnight, more faithfully than any ghost. Perhaps I have become the ghost, he thought, with an enjoyable shudder.

The coat and cap remained exactly where they were. He tried to imagine that the papers had moved a little, but he knew he was kidding himself.

Then came the night of the raid. The siren went at ten, while they were still eating their supper. Rather disbelievingly, they took cover in the cellars. Perhaps it was as well they did. The lone German bomber, faced with more searchlights and guns on the river than took its fancy, jettisoned its bombs on Preston. Three of the great houses fell in bitter ruin. A stick of incendiaries fell into the conservatory at "The Elms", turning it into a stinking ruin of magnesium-smoke and frying green things.

Nana surveyed it in the dawn; and pronounced, "That won't suit Tempy. And it's back home for you, my lad. This place is more dangerous than the bleddy docks, and yer Mam's still worrying about those bleddy tomato-plants . . ."

Chas packed, slowly and tiredly. Folded up his war-map of Europe. Thought he might as well get back Granda's badge and coat from upstairs.

But when he wriggled through, they weren't on the bed . . .

Who'd moved them, Nana or Mam? Why hadn't they *said* anything?

And the chair was upright by the empty bed, not kicked away in the corner. And on it, shining bright, something winked at Chas.

A soldier's cap-badge, as bright as if polished that very day. And on the plaster by the chair was scrawled a message, with a stub of pencil.

THANKS, SON. THEY FIT A TREAT. SHAN'T WANT BADGE NO MORE – FAIR EXCHANGE NO ROBBERY. YOUR GRANDFATHER'S A BRAVE MAN – KEPT RIGHT ON TO THE END OF THE ROAD – MORE THAN I WILL DO, NOW. RESPECTFULLY YOURS, 1001923 MELBOURNE, W.J., SGT.

Chas stood hugging himself, and the cap-badge, with glee. He had played a trick on time itself . . .

But time, once interfered with, had a few tricks up its sleeve too. The next few minutes were the weirdest he'd ever known.

Brisk footsteps banged along the corridor. Stopped outside his room next door, looked in, saw he wasn't there, swept on . . .

Swept on straight through where the corridor-cupboard was . . . or should be. The door of the soldier's room began to open. Chas could have screamed. The door had no right to open. It was fastened away, inaccessible behind the corridor-cupboard . . .

But there was no point in screaming, because it was only Nana standing there, large as life. "There you are, you little monkey. Aah knew ye'd be here, when Aah saw that bleddy great hole in the wall . . . ye shouldn't be in this room."

"Why not?"

"Because a poor feller hanged himself in this room – a soldier who couldn't face the trenches. Hanged himself from that very hook in the ceiling, standing on this very chair . . ." She looked up; Chas looked up.

There was no longer any hook in the beam. There had been one, but it had been neatly sawn off with a hacksaw. Years ago, because the sawn edge was red with rust.

Nan passed a hand over her pale weary face. "At least . . . Aah *think* Aah heard that poor feller hanged himself . . . they blocked off this room wi' a broom-cupboard."

She peered round the door, puzzled. So did Chas. There was no broom-cupboard now. Nor any mark where a broom-cupboard might have been. The corridor ran sheer and uninterrupted, from one end to the other.

"Eeh," said Nana, "your memory plays you some funny tricks when you get to my age. Aah could ha' sworn . . . Anyway, what's Melly going to say when I tell her ye made a bleddy great hole in her wall? I expect you want me to blame it on Hitler and the Jarmans?"

"Who's Melly? You mean Tempy?" said Chas, grasping at straws in his enormous confusion.

"What d'you mean, who's Melly? Only Mrs Melbourne who owns this house, and runs the school, and has given ye more ten-bob notes than I care to remember."

Chas wrinkled up his face. Was it Miss Temple, shoes, legs and gown, who gave him ten-bob notes . . . or was it Mrs Melbourne, who sat kindly in a chair and smiled at him. Who when he was

170

smaller had sometimes taken him down to the kitchen for a dish of jelly and ice-cream from her wonderful new-fangled refrigerator? He had a funny idea they were one and the same person, only different. Then time itself, with a last whisk of its tail, whipped all memory of Miss Temple from his mind; and his mind was the last place on earth in which Miss Temple had ever existed.

"I don't know what the hell you made that hole in wall for," said Nana. "You could just as easily have walked in through the door; it's never been locked."

Chas could no longer remember himself, as he tucked the shining cap-badge in his pocket, and gave Nana a hand to take his belongings down to the taxi.

"Why did I think a feller hanged himself in that room," repeated Nana. "Must be getting morbid in me old age . . ."

"Yeah," said Chas, squinting at the cap-badge surreptitiously.

THE TELL-TALE HEART

EDGAR ALLAN POE

TRUE! nervous, very, very dreadfully nervous I had been and am; but why *will* you say that I am mad? The disease had sharpened my senses, not destroyed, not dulled them. Above all was the sense of hearing acute. I heard all things in the heaven and in the earth. I heard many things in hell. How, then, am I mad? Hearken! and observe how healthy – how calmly I can tell you the whole story.

It is impossible to say how first the idea entered my brain; but once conceived, it haunted me day and night. Object there was none. Passion there was none. I loved the old man. He had never wronged me. He had never given me insult. For his gold I had no desire. I think it was his eye! yes, it was this! One of his eyes resembled that of a vulture – a pale blue eye, with a film over it. Whenever it fell upon me, my blood ran cold; and so by degrees, very gradually, I made up my mind to take the life of the old man, and thus rid myself of the eye for ever.

Now this is the point. You fancy me mad. Madmen know nothing. But you should have seen *me*. You should have seen how wisely I proceeded – with what caution – with what foresight, with what dissimulation, I went to work. I was never kinder to the old man than during the whole week before I killed him. And every night, about midnight, I turned the latch of his door and opened it – oh, so gently! And then, when I had made an opening sufficient for my head, I put in a dark green lantern, all closed, closed, so that no light shone out, and then I thrust in my head. Oh, you would have laughed to see how cunningly I thrust it in! I moved it slowly, very, very slowly, so that I might not disturb the old man's sleep. It took me an hour to place my whole head within the opening so far that I could see him as he lay upon his bed. Ha! would a madman have been so wise as this? And then, when my head was well in the room, I undid the lantern cautiously – oh, so cautiously (for the hinges creaked), I undid it just so much that a single thin ray fell upon the vulture eye. And this I did for seven long nights, every night just at midnight, but I found the eye always closed, and so it was impossible to do the work; for it was not the old man who vexed me, but his Evil Eye. And every morning, when the day broke, I went boldly into the chamber, and spoke courageously to him, calling him by name in a hearty tone, and inquiring how he had passed the night. So you see he would have been a very profound old man, indeed, to suspect that every night, just at twelve, I looked in upon him while he slept.

Upon the eighth night I was more than usually cautious in opening the door. A watch's minute hand moves more quickly than did mine. Never before that night had I *felt* the extent of my own powers, of my own sagacity. I could scarcely contain my feelings of triumph. To think that there I was opening the door, little by little, and he not even to dream of my secret deeds or thoughts. I fairly chuckled at the idea; and perhaps he heard me; for he moved on the bed suddenly, as if startled. Now you may think that I drew back – but no. His room was as black as pitch with the thick darkness (for the shutters were close fastened through fear of robbers), and so I knew that he could not see the opening of the door, and I kept pushing it on steadily, steadily.

I had my head in, and was about to open the lantern, when my thumb slipped upon the tin fastening, and the old man sprang up in the bed, crying out, "Who's there?"

I kept quite still and said nothing. For a whole hour I did not move a muscle, and in the meantime I did not hear him lie down. He was still sitting up in the bed listening; just as I have done, night after night, hearkening to the death watches in the wall.

Presently I heard a slight groan, and I knew it was the groan of mortal terror. It was not a groan of pain or grief – oh no! it was the low stifled sound that arises from the bottom of the soul when overcharged with awe. I knew the sound well. Many a night, just at midnight, when all the world slept, it has welled up from my own bosom, deepening, with its dreadful echo, the terrors that distracted me. I say I knew it well. I knew what the old man felt, and pitied him, although I chuckled at heart. I knew that he had been lying awake ever since the first slight noise, when he had turned in the bed. His fears had been ever since growing upon him. He had been trying to fancy them causeless, but could not. He had been saying to himself, "It is nothing but the wind in the chimney, it is only a mouse crossing the floor," or "It is merely a cricket which has made a single chirp." Yes, he had been trying to comfort himself with these suppositions; but he had found all in vain. *All in vain*; because Death, in approaching him, had stalked with his black shadow before him, and enveloped the victim. And it was the mournful influence of the unperceived shadow that caused him to feel, although he neither saw nor heard, to *feel* the presence of my head within the room.

When I had waited a long time, very patiently, without hearing him lie down, I resolved to open a little – a very, very little crevice in the lantern. So I opened it – you cannot imagine how stealthily, stealthily – until at length, a single dim ray, like the thread of a spider, shot out from the crevice and fell upon the vulture eye.

It was open – wide, wide open – and I grew furious as I gazed upon it. I saw it with perfect distinctness – all a dull blue, with a hideous veil over it that chilled the very marrow in my bones; but I could see nothing else of the old man's face or person: for I had directed the ray as if by instinct, precisely upon the damned spot.

And now have I not told you that what you mistake for madness is but over-acuteness of the senses? Now, I say, there came to my ears a low, dull, quick sound, such as a watch makes when enveloped in cotton. I knew *that* sound well, too. It was the beating of the old man's heart. It increased my fury, as the beating of a drum stimulates the soldier into courage.

But even yet I refrained and kept still. I scarcely breathed. I held the lantern motionless. I tried how steadily I could maintain the ray upon the eye. Meantime the hellish tattoo of the heart increased. It grew quicker and quicker, and louder and louder every instant. The old man's terror *must* have been extreme! It grew louder, I say, louder every moment! – do you mark me well? I have told you that I am nervous: so I am. And now at the dead hour of the night, amid the dreadful silence of that old house, so strange a noise as this excited me to uncontrollable terror. Yet, for some minutes longer I refrained and stood still. But the beating grew louder, louder! I thought the heart must burst. And now a new anxiety seized me – the sound would be heard by a neighbour! The old man's hour had come! With a loud yell, I threw open the lantern and leaped into the room. He shrieked once – once only. In an instant I dragged him to the floor, and pulled the heavy bed over him. I then smiled gaily, to find the deed so far done. But, for many minutes, the heart beat on with a muffled sound. This, however, did not vex me; it would not be heard through the wall. At length it ceased. The old man was dead. I removed the bed and examined the corpse. Yes, he was stone, stone dead. I placed my hand upon the heart and held it there many minutes. There was no pulsation. He was stone dead. His eye would trouble me no more.

If you still think me mad, you will think so no longer when I describe the wise precautions I took for the concealment of the body. The night waned, and I worked hastily, but in silence. First of all I dismembered the corpse. I cut off the head and the arms and the legs.

I then took up three planks from the flooring of the chamber, and deposited all between the scantlings. I then replaced the boards so cleverly, so cunningly, that no human eye – not even *his* – could have detected anything wrong. There was nothing to wash out – no stain of any kind – no bloodspot whatever. I had been too wary for that. A tub had caught all – ha! ha!

When I had made an end of these labours, it was four o'clock – still dark as midnight. As the bell sounded the hour, there came a knocking at the street door. I went down to open it with a light heart, for what had I *now* to fear? There entered three men, who introduced themselves, with perfect suavity, as officers of the police. A shriek had been heard by a neighbour during the night: suspicion of foul play had been aroused: information had been lodged at the police office, and they (the officers) had been deputed to search the premises.

I smiled – for *what* had I to fear? I bade the gentlemen welcome. The shriek, I said, was my own in a dream. The old man, I mentioned, was absent in the country. I took my visitors all over the house. I bade them search – search *well*. I led them, at length, to *his* chamber. I showed them his treasures, secure, undisturbed. In the enthusiasm of my confidence, I brought chairs into the room, and desired them *here* to rest from their fatigues, while I myself, in the wild audacity of my perfect triumph, placed my own seat upon the very spot beneath which reposed the corpse of the victim.

The officers were satisfied. My *manner* had convinced them. I was singularly at ease. They sat, and while I answered cheerily, they chatted of familiar things. But, ere long, I felt myself getting pale and wished them gone. My head ached, and I fancied a ringing in my ears: but still they sat and still chatted. The ringing became more distinct; it continued and became more distinct; I talked more freely to get rid of the feeling; but it continued and gained definitiveness – until at length, I found that the noise was *not* within my ears.

No doubt I now grew *very* pale – but I talked more fluently, and with a heightened voice. Yet the sound increased – and what could I do? *It was a low, dull, quick sound – much such a sound as a watch makes when enveloped in cotton.* I gasped for breath – and yet the officers heard it not. I talked more quickly – more vehemently; but the noise steadily increased. I arose and argued about trifles, in a high key and with violent gesticulations, but the noise steadily increased. Why *would* they not be gone? I paced the floor to and fro with heavy strides, as if excited to fury by the observation of the men – but the noise steadily increased. Oh God! what *could* I do? I foamed – I raved – I swore! I swung the chair upon which I had been sitting, and grated it upon the boards, but the noise arose over all and continually increased. It grew louder – louder – *louder*! And still the men chatted pleasantly and smiled. Was it possible they heard not? Almighty God! – no, no! They heard – they suspected! – they *knew*! – they were making a *mockery* of my horror! – this I thought, and this I think. But anything was better than this agony! Anything was more tolerable than this derision! I could bear those hypocritical smiles no longer! I felt that I must scream or die! – and now – again! – hark! louder! louder! *louder* –

"Villains!" I shrieked, "dissemble no more! I admit the deed! – tear up the planks! – here, here! – it is the beating of his hideous heart!"

THE DEATH OF
PEGGY MORRISSEY

WILLIAM TREVOR

L IKE ALL CHILDREN, I led a double life. There was the
ordinariness of dressing in the morning, putting on shoes
and combing hair, stirring a spoon through porridge I
didn't want, and going at ten to nine to the nuns' elementary
school. And there was a world in which only the events I wished
for happened, where boredom was not permitted and of which
I was both God and King.

In my ordinary life I was the only child of parents who years
before my birth had given up hope of ever having me.
I remember them best as being different from other parents: they
were elderly, it seemed to me, two greyly fussing people with
grey hair and faces, in grey clothes, with spectacles. "Oh, no,
no," they murmured regularly, rejecting on my behalf an
invitation to tea or to play with some other child. They feared on
my behalf the rain and the sea, and walls that might be walked
along, and grass because grass was always damp. They rarely
missed a service at the Church of the Holy Assumption.

In the town where we lived, a seaside town thirty miles from
Cork, my father was employed as a senior clerk in the offices of
Devereux and O'Brien, Solicitors and Commissioners for Oaths.

With him on one side of me and my mother on the other, we walked up and down the brief promenade in winter, while the seagulls shrieked and my father worried in case it was going to rain. We never went for walks through fields or through the heathery wastelands that sloped gently upwards behind the town, or by the river where people said Sir Walter Raleigh had fished. In summer, when the visitors from Cork came, my mother didn't like to let me near the sands because the sands, she said, were full of fleas. In summer we didn't walk on the promenade but out along the main Cork road instead, past a house that appeared to me to move. It disappeared for several minutes as we approached it, a trick of nature, I afterwards discovered, caused by the undulations of the landscape. Every July, for a fortnight, we went to stay in Montenotte, high up above Cork city, in a boarding-house run by my mother's sister, my Aunt Isabella. She, too, had a grey look about her and was religious.

It was here, in my Aunt Isabella's Montenotte boarding-house, that this story begins: in the summer of 1936, when I was seven. It was a much larger house than the one we lived in ourselves, which was small and narrow and in a terrace. My Aunt Isabella's was rather grand in its way, a dark place with little unexpected half-landings, and badly lit corridors. It smelt of floor polish and of a mustiness that I have since associated with the religious life, a smell of old cassocks. Everywhere there were statues of the Virgin, and votive lights and black-framed pictures of the Holy Child. The residents were all priests, old and middle-aged and young, eleven of them usually, which was all the house would hold. A few were always away on their holidays when we stayed there in the summer.

In the summer of 1936 we left our own house in the usual way, my father fastening all the windows and the front and back doors and then examining the house from the outside to make sure he'd done the fastening and the locking properly. We walked to the railway station, each of us carrying something, my mother a brown cardboard suitcase and my father a larger one of the same kind. I carried the sandwiches we were to have on the train, and a flask of carefully made tea and three apples, all packed into a sixpenny fish basket.

In the house in Montenotte my Aunt Isabella told us that Canon Maguire and Father Quinn were on holiday, one in Tralee, the other in Galway. She led us to their rooms, Canon Maguire's for my father and Father Quinn's for my mother and myself. The familiar trestle-bed was erected at the foot of the bed in my mother's room. During the course of the year a curate called Father Ryan had repaired it, my aunt said, after it had been used by Canon Maguire's brother from America, who'd proved too much for the canvas.

"Ah, aren't you looking well, Mr Mahon!" the red-faced and jolly Father Smith said to my father in the dining-room that evening. "And isn't our friend here getting big for himself? He laughed loudly, gripping a portion of the back of my neck between a finger and a thumb. Did I know my catechism? he asked me. Was I being good with the nuns in the elementary school? "Are you in health yourself, Mrs Mahon?" he inquired of my mother.

My mother said she was, and the red-faced priest went to join the other priests at the main dining-table. He left behind him a smell that was different from the smell of the house, and I noticed that he had difficulty in pulling the chair out from the table when he was about to sit down. He had to be assisted in this by a new young curate, a Father Parsloe. Father Smith had been drinking stout again, I said to myself.

Sometimes in my aunt's house there was nothing to do except to watch and to listen. Father Smith used to drink too much stout; Father Maginnis, who was so thin you could hardly bear to look at him and whose flesh was the colour of whitewash, was not long for this world; Father Riordon would be a bishop if only he could have tidied himself up a bit; Canon Maguire had once refused to baptize a child; young Father Ryan was going places. For hours on end my Aunt Isabella would murmur to my parents about the priests, telling about the fate of one who had left the boarding-house during the year or supplying background information about a new one. My parents, so faultlessly regular

in their church attendance and interested in all religious matters, were naturally pleased to listen. God and the organization of His Church were far more important than my father's duties in Devereux and O'Brien, or my mother's housework, or my own desire to go walking through heathery wastelands that sloped gently upwards behind our town. God and the priests in my Aunt Isabella's house, and the nuns of the convent elementary school and the priests of the Church of the Holy Assumption, were at the centre of everything. "Maybe it'll appeal to our friend," Father Smith had once said in the dining-room, and I knew that he meant that maybe one day I might be attracted towards the priesthood. My parents had not said anything in reply, but as we ate our tea of sausages and potato-cakes I could feel them thinking that nothing would please them better.

Every year when we stayed with my aunt there was an afternoon when I was left in charge of whichever priests happened to be in, while my parents and my aunt made the journey across the city to visit my father's brother, who was a priest himself. There was some difficulty about bringing me: I had apparently gone to my uncle's house as a baby, when my presence had upset him. Years later I overheard my mother whispering to Father Riordon about this, suggesting – or so it seemed – that my father had once been intent on the priestly life but had at the last moment withdrawn. That he should afterwards have fathered a child was apparently an offence to his brother's feeling of propriety. I had the impression that my uncle was a severe man, who looked severely on my father and my mother and my Aunt Isabella on these visits, and was respected by them for being as he was. All three came back subdued, and that night my mother always prayed for much longer by the side of her bed.

"Father Parsloe's going to take you for a walk," my Aunt Isabella said on the morning of the 1936 visit. "He wants to get to know you."

You walked all the way down from Montenotte, past the docks, over the river and into the city. The first few times it could have been interesting, but after that it was worse than walking on the concrete promenade at home. I'd have far preferred to have played by myself in my aunt's overgrown back garden, pretending to be grown up, talking to myself in a secret way, having wicked thoughts. At home and in my aunt's garden I became a man my father had read about in a newspaper and whom, he'd said, we must all pray for, a thief who broke the windows of jewellers' shops and lifted out watches and rings. I became Father Smith, drinking too much stout and missing the steps of the stairs. I became Father Maginnis and would lie on the weeds at the bottom of the garden or under a table, confessing to gruesome crimes at the moment of death. In my mind I mocked the holiness of my parents and imitated their voices; I mocked the holiness of my Aunt Isabella; I talked back to my parents in a way I never would; I laughed and said disgraceful things about God and the religious life. Blasphemy was exciting.

"Are you ready so?" Father Parsloe asked when my parents and my aunt had left for the visit to my uncle. "Will we take a bus?"

"A bus?"

"Down to the town."

I'd never in my life done that before. The buses were for going longer distances in. It seemed extraordinary not to walk, the whole point of a walk was to walk.

"I haven't any money for the bus," I said, and Father Parsloe laughed. On the upper deck he lit a cigarette. He was a slight young man, by far the youngest of the priests in my aunt's house, with reddish hair and a face that seemed to be on a slant. "Will we have tea in Thompson's?" he said. "Would that be a good thing to do?"

We had tea in Thompson's café, with buns and cakes and huge meringues such as I'd never tasted before. Father Parsloe smoked fourteen cigarettes and drank all the tea himself. I had three bottles of fizzy orangeade. "Will we go to the pictures?" Father Parsloe said when he'd paid the bill at the cash desk. "Will we chance the Pavilion?"

I had never, of course, been to the pictures before. My mother said that Horgan's Picture-House, which was the only one in our town, was full of fleas.

"One and a half," Father Parsloe said at the cash desk in the

Pavilion and we were led away into the darkness. THE END, it announced on the screen, and when I saw it I thought we were too late. "Ah, aren't we in lovely time?" Father Parsloe said.

I didn't understand the film. It was about grown-ups kissing one another, and about an earthquake, and then a motor-car accident in which a woman who'd been kissed a lot was killed. The man who'd kissed her was married to another woman, and when the film ended he was sitting in a room with his wife, looking at her. She kept saying it was all right.

"God, wasn't that great?" Father Parsloe said as we stood in the lavatory of the Pavilion, the kind of lavatory where you stand up, like I'd never been in before. "Wasn't it a good story?"

All the way back to Montenotte I kept remembering it. I kept seeing the face of the woman who'd been killed, and all the bodies lying on the streets after the earthquake, and the man at the end, sitting in a room with his wife. The swaying of the bus made me feel queasy because of the meringues and the orangeade, but I didn't care.

"Did you enjoy the afternoon?" Father Parsloe asked, and I told him I'd never enjoyed anything better. I asked him if the pictures were always as good. He assured me they were.

My parents, however, didn't seem pleased. My father got hold of a *Cork Examiner* and looked up the film that was on at the Pavilion and reported that it wasn't suitable for a child. My mother gave me a bath and examined my clothes for fleas. When Father Parsloe winked at me in the dining-room my parents pretended not to notice him.

That night my mother prayed for her extra long period, after the visit to my uncle. I lay in the dimly lit room, aware that she was kneeling there, but thinking of the film and the way the people had kissed, not like my parents ever kissed. At the convent elementary school there were girls in the higher classes who were pretty, far prettier than my mother. There was one called Claire, with fair hair and a softly freckled face, and another called Peggy Morrissey, who was younger and black-haired. I had picked them out because they had spoken to me, asking me my name. I thought them very nice.

I opened my eyes and saw that my mother was rising from her knees. She stood for a moment, at the edge of her bed, not smiling, her lips still moving, continuing her prayer. Then she got into bed and put out the light.

I listened to her breathing and heard it become the breathing which people have when they're asleep, but I couldn't sleep myself. I lay there, still remembering the film and remembering being in Thompson's and seeing Father Parsloe lighting one cigarette after another. For some reason, I began to imagine that I was in Thompson's with Father Parsloe and the two girls from the convent, and that we all went off to the Pavilion together, swinging along the street. "Ah, isn't this the life for us?" Father Parsloe said as he led us into the darkness, and I told the girls I'd been to the Pavilion before and they said they never had.

I heard eleven o'clock chiming from a nearby church. I heard a stumbling on the stairs and then the laughter of Father Smith, and Father Riordon telling him to be quiet. I heard twelve chiming and half-past twelve, and a quarter to one, and one.

After that I didn't want to sleep. I was standing in a classroom of the convent and Claire was smiling at me. It was nice being with her. I felt warm all over, and happy.

And then I was walking on the sands with Peggy Morrissey. We ran, playing a game she'd made up, and then we walked again. She asked if I'd like to go on a picnic with her, next week perhaps.

I didn't know what to do. I wanted one of the girls to be my friend. I wanted to love one of them, like the people had loved in the film. I wanted to kiss one and be with one, just the two of us. In the darkness of the bedroom they both seemed close and real, closer than my mother, even though I could hear my mother breathing. "Come on," Peggy Morrissey whispered, and then Claire whispered also, saying we'd always be best friends, saying we might run away. It was all wrong that there were two of them, yet both vividly remained. "Tuesday," Peggy Morrissey said. "We'll have the picnic on Tuesday."

Her father drove us in his car, away from the town, out beyond the heathery wastelands, towards a hillside that was even nicer. But a door of the car, the back door against which Peggy Morrissey was leaning, suddenly gave way. On the dust of the road she was as dead as the woman in the film.

"Poor Peggy," Claire said at some later time, even though she hadn't known Peggy Morrissey very well. "Poor little Peggy." And then she smiled and took my hand and we walked together through the heathery wastelands, in love with one another.

A few days later we left my Aunt Isabella's house in Montenotte and returned on the train to our seaside town. And a week after that a new term began at the convent elementary school. Peggy Morrissey was dead, the Reverend Mother told us, all of us assembled together. She added that there was diptheria in the town.

I didn't think about it at first; and I didn't connect the reality of the death with a fantasy that had been caused by my first visit to a cinema. Some part of my mind may passingly have paused over the coincidence, but that was all. There was the visit to the Pavilion itself to talk about in the convent, and the description of the film, and Father Parsloe's conversation and the way he'd smoked fourteen cigarettes in Thompson's. Diptheria was a terrible disease, my mother said when I told her, and naturally we must all pray for the soul of poor Peggy Morrissey.

But as weeks and months went by, I found myself increasingly remembering the story I had told myself on the night of the film, and remembering particularly how Peggy Morrissey had fallen from the car, and how she'd looked when she was dead. I said to myself that that had been my wickedest thought, worse than my blasphemies and yet somehow part of them. At night I lay in bed, unable to sleep, trying hopelessly to pray for forgiveness. But no forgiveness came, for there was no respite to the images that recurred, her face in life and then in death, like the face of the woman in the film.

A year later, while lying awake in the same room in my aunt's boarding-house, I saw her. In the darkness there was a sudden patch of light and in the centre of it she was wearing a sailor-suit that I remembered. Her black plaits hung down her back. She smiled at me and went away. I knew instinctively then, as I watched her and after she'd gone, that the fantasy and the reality were part and parcel: I had caused this death to occur.

Looking back on it now, I can see, of course, that that feeling was a childish one. It was a childish fear, a superstition that occurring to an adult would cause only a shiver of horror. But, as a child, with no one to consult about the matter, I lived with the thought that my will was more potent than I knew. In stories I had learnt of witches and spells and evil spirits, and power locked up in people. In my games I had wickedly denied the religious life and goodness, and holiness. In my games I had mocked Father Smith, I had pretended that the dying Father Maginnis was a criminal. I had pretended to be a criminal myself, a man who broke jewellers' windows. I had imitated my parents when it said you should honour your father and your mother. I had mocked the holiness of my Aunt Isabella. I had murdered Peggy Morrissey because there wasn't room for her in the story I was telling myself. I was possessed and evil: the nuns had told us about people being like that.

I thought at first I might seek advice from Father Parsloe. I thought of asking him if he remembered the day we'd gone on our outing, and then telling him how, in a story I was telling myself, I'd caused Peggy Morrissey to be killed in a car accident like the woman in the film, and how she'd died in reality, of diptheria. But Father Parsloe had an impatient kind of look about him this year, as if he had worries of his own. So I didn't tell him and I didn't tell anyone. I hoped that when we returned to our own house at the end of the stay in Montenotte I wouldn't see her again, but the very first day we were back I saw her at four o'clock in the afternoon, in the kitchen.

After that she came irregularly, sometimes not for a month and once not for a year. She continued to appear in the sudden way but in different clothes, and growing up as I was growing up. Once, after I'd left the convent and gone on to the Christian Brothers, she appeared in the classroom, smiling near the blackboard.

She never spoke. Whether she appeared on the promenade or at school or in my aunt's house or our house, close to me or at a distance, she communicated only with her smile and with her eyes: I was possessed of the Devil, she came herself from God. In her eyes and her smile there was that simple message, a message which said also that my thoughts were always wicked, that I had never believed properly in God or the Virgin or Jesus who died for us.

I tried to pray. Like my mother, kneeling beside my bed. Like my aunt and her houseful of priests. Like the nuns and Christian Brothers, and other boys and girls of the town. But prayer would not come to me, and I realized that it never had. I had always pretended, going down on my knees at Mass, laughing and blaspheming in my mind. I hated the very thought of prayer. I hated my parents in an unnatural manner, and my Aunt Isabella and the priests in her house. But the dead Peggy Morrissey, fresh from God's heaven, was all forgiveness in her patch of light, smiling to rid me of my evil spirit.

She was there at my mother's funeral, and later at my father's. Claire, whom I had destroyed her for, married a man employed in the courthouse and became a Mrs Madden, prematurely fat. I naturally didn't marry anyone myself.

I am forty-six years old now and I live alone in the same seaside town. No one in the town knows why I am solitary. No one could guess that I have lived with a child's obsession for half a lifetime. Being no longer a child, I naturally no longer believe that I was responsible for the death. In my passing, careless fantasy I wished for it and she, already dead, picked up my living thoughts. I should not have wished for it because in middle age she is a beautiful creature now, more beautiful by far than fat Mrs Madden.

And that is all there is. At forty-six I walk alone on the brief promenade, or by the edge of the sea or on the road to Cork, where the moving house is. I work, as my father worked, in the offices of Devereux and O'Brien. I cook my own food. I sleep alone in a bed that has an iron bedstead. On Sundays I go hypocritically to Mass in the Church of the Holy Assumption; I go to Confession and do not properly confess; I go to Men's Confraternity, and to Communion. And all the time she is there, appearing in her patch of light to remind me that she never leaves me. And all the time, on my knees at Mass, or receiving the Body and the Blood, or in my iron bed, I desire her. In the offices of Devereux and O'Brien I dream of her nakedness. When we are old I shall desire her, too, with my shrunken, evil body.

In the town I am a solitary, peculiar man. I have been rendered so, people probably say, by my cloistered upbringing, and probably add that such an upbringing would naturally cultivate a morbid imagination. That may be so, and it doesn't really matter how things have come about. All I know is that she is more real for me than anything else is in this seaside town or beyond it. I live for her, living hopelessly, for I know I can never possess her as I wish to. I have a carnal desire for a shadow, which in turn is His mockery of me: His fitting punishment for my wickedest thought of all.

CHRISTMAS IN THE RECTORY

CATHERINE STORR

IT WAS MY GREAT-AUNT who told me this story. She had known the people concerned, though I think she had never visited the rectory itself. It is a very old story. It took place more than a hundred years ago.

My great-aunt's especial friend was Kate, who, when she was a nearly grown-up young lady, had gone with her sister Elspeth to stay with their brother and his family in Cornwall for Christmas. William was a parson; a month or so earlier, he had taken charge of a small parish near the sea. Kate and Elspeth had never been to Cornwall, but they had heard that it was a wild sort of country, with a great bare moor in the middle, and all around high cliffs and jagged rocks and roaring seas. So they were surprised to find their brother's rectory a solid grey granite box of a house, more suitable to a city terrace than to remote country, standing alone in a small valley, well planted with trees and shrubs. They could see, from the bent and twisted trees, how strong the blustering winds could be on that coast; but on the day they arrived, though it was the middle of December, the air was still and vaporous under a leaden sky.

This much, and the glossy leaves of the massive rhododendron bushes surrounding the house like a green tide

191

which threatened to engulf the lower windows, was all that the sisters could make out in the fading light of a winter afternoon, as William drove them up to the front door. While he took the pony and chaise round to the stables, his wife, Fanny, welcomed the girls and proposed to show them the room they were to occupy, and then the rest of the house. The two small children at first followed their mother silently, staring at their young aunts with solemn eyes; but soon they remembered that Kate and Elspeth had been welcome playmates not so very long ago, and they began to chatter and to take their part in the guided tour of the house, showing their own particular possessions. "That's my chair, and that's Emmy's." "This is my best dolly." "Here's my horse, his tail is made of real hair." "That's my bed, that's nurse's." This was Emmy in the night-nursery.

"Hugh is such a big boy now, he sleeps in the other nursery by himself," Fanny said, and Kate thought there was a note of reassurance in her voice as if Hugh perhaps needed consolation for having had to leave the comfort of sharing a night-nursery with nurse and Emmy. But he seemed pleased to show them his new bed, looking very small in a corner of the large day nursery, which, in spite of the fire flickering in the grate and the closely pulled curtains, felt chilly. Yes, Fanny agreed in answer to Elspeth's inquiry, it was a difficult house to keep warm. Even now, when the weather was so unseasonably mild, there were cold draughts in the rooms and passages, and an all-pervading odour of damp. William was sure it was nothing but the sea air that she was smelling, and perhaps he was right. It was true, before their arrival, the house had been standing empty for some months.

"And you've been here such a short time! When you've lived here for longer it will dry out and feel different," Elspeth said.

"I hope so," was Fanny's only reply, and it seemed to Kate that it was spoken without conviction. But they had come now to the head of the stairs, and Fanny, going ahead with Emmy, was saying, "Now we'll show you the little sitting room where we're all going to have tea."

Hugh put a hand confidingly in Kate's and they followed

Fanny downstairs. On the half landing Kate noticed a door which Fanny hadn't opened for them on their way up and asked, "Where does that lead to?"

Hugh didn't answer. Instead he pulled her towards the lower flight, as if in a hurry to gain the hall. Kate allowed herself to be led, but asked again, "What's behind that door?"

Fanny turned to answer over her shoulder. "It isn't a proper room. It's a sort of half-finished attic over William's study. I keep the door locked because . . ." She broke off to say gently to Hugh, who was preparing for a tremendous spring down the last four steps, "Gently, Hugh. You mustn't interrupt Mamma." Then she went on. "It's very dark. There aren't any windows, and the roof comes down so low you can't stand upright. There's a trap-door in the floor, too, and I don't want one of the children getting it open and falling through."

Hugh's leap having been accomplished and duly admired, Fanny opened the door into a small room where tea things were laid in front of a comfortable-looking fire. "Come in and get warm. The children are going to have tea with us for a treat."

Certainly Hugh and Emmy did justice to the toast and tea and seedcake. But Kate, remembering that convulsive clutch of her hand on the stairs, observed Hugh and thought that he was still uneasy. He seemed to her to be looking frequently towards the room door, and sure enough, before the children's nurse had appeared there to carry them off to bed, he had disappeared, and did not show himself when called.

Fanny found him, crouching between the end of the sofa and the wall.

"Bedtime, Hugh. Go upstairs with Agnes," she said.

"No. Won't! Don't want to!"

"Hugh! You know what Papa said?"

Whatever William had said, it was enough to bring Hugh out of hiding, and to make him follow Agnes very slowly towards the door, the corners of his mouth drooping.

"You come up to see me in bed, Mamma?"

"Yes. I'll come and say good night to you when you're safe in bed."

"I don't remember Hugh being difficult about going to bed last year," Kate said when the children had left the room.

"He isn't used to the house yet," Fanny said. She began to put the tea things together.

"Won't one of the maids do that?" Elspeth asked.

"The maids don't stay here at night. They are all village girls and they go home to sleep," Fanny said.

"Nurse too?"

"No, Agnes doesn't come from the neighbourhood. She came down here with us. The children are very fond of her. We shall miss her dreadfully when she goes."

"Why is she leaving?" Kate asked.

Fanny corrected herself. "I should have said *if* she goes. She hasn't really settled here yet and she talks of finding another place. But I hope I shall be able to persuade her to stay." Fanny carried the tray out of the room and put an end to the conversation.

"Do you think Fanny's happy here?" Kate asked her sister, as they were changing their dress before supper.

"Why shouldn't she be?"

"I'm not sure. There's something . . . It's not just the house being damp or not having any servants in the evenings. She keeps on looking at the children . . ."

"You're imagining things. Like that time we went to see all those big stones on top of a hill somewhere. You said you felt they were evil. Remember?" Elspeth said. She opened the door of their bedroom and went out, calling back, "Hurry up! You'll be late for supper. We're having it in William's study, remember."

Supper, eaten by a good fire in the long, low study, might have reassured Kate, if she had seen that Fanny was relaxed as she surely had been when the sisters had stayed with the family before. There were occasions when Fanny appeared not to have heard remarks addressed to her. She was preoccupied, almost as if she were listening for some expected sound outside the room. Half-way through the meal, she abruptly got up and left the room; they heard her hasty steps on the stairs and, through the open door, the sound of a child crying. William made a sound of annoyance.

"Hugh again!" he said.

"What's the matter? Can't he sleep?" Kate asked.

"He has got into a bad habit of crying out after he has been put to bed. I have told Fanny that he must not be indulged. He must learn to control himself," William said.

"But if he's really frightened?" Kate said.

"There is nothing for him to be frightened of. I have asked him what makes him cry out and he cannot explain. Fanny allows him to leave his bedroom door open and she leaves a candle burning in the passage, though I have told her I think this is giving in to weakness. He should fight his fear. If he is afraid," William said.

When Fanny reappeared she reported that she had left Hugh calmer. It had been another of his bad dreams, he had woken up screaming and terrified. Now Agnes was sitting with him till he should go to sleep.

"He shouldn't be allowed to form the habit of having someone stay with him all evening," William said.

"He can't be left alone in that state," Fanny said.

"He calls out to you to draw attention to himself," William said.

"No, William, it's not that. You've seen him when he wakes up like this. He's wild with terror. He has real, horrible nightmares."

"What does he dream about?" Elspeth asked. Neither William nor Fanny answered. Kate saw them glance at each other and she knew that some unspoken message, which she and Elspeth did not understand, was passing between husband and wife.

Both sisters slept soundly that night, a heavy, dreamless sleep from which they woke with difficulty. But in the daylight of the next morning, Kate began to think that she must have been over-tired and fanciful the night before. Fanny seemed less anxious, and Hugh was triumphant and apparently carefree, leading his aunts down to visit "his" beach, to watch him trying to make a great crab emerge from under its protective overhang of rock, and showing how well he could negotiate the long tongues of black spiked rocks which ran out into the ocean. The only disappointment was that there was still no wind. The sea lay smooth and white under the low, overcast sky, and the shore was silent, except for the whisper and the suck of the water where it met the sand, like the murmur of a conspiracy, a secret, not to be overheard.

In the afternoon, William walked the sisters to the village, a huddle of cottages and an inn near the squat grey tower of the church. There wasn't much to admire inside the building. Kate and Elspeth walked round, looking at the old-fashioned high box pews, reading the memorial tablets on the walls and sympathizing with William's regrets that there was not enough money to put the place into good order. Leaving their brother to discuss the music for the Christmas services with the church harmonium player, they wandered out into the churchyard, where a fine thin rain was shrouding the trees and hedges in a white veil. An elderly man, sweeping up dead leaves from between the neglected graves, stopped his work and stared curiously at them as they approached.

"Good day!" Elspeth called as they approached him.

He eyed them curiously. "You be Parson's sisters?"

"Yes, we are. We've come to spend Christmas with him," Elspeth said.

"Haven't been here before, have you?"

"No, this is our first time . . ."

"That's what I reckoned," the man said.

"But we'll be coming back again. In the summer, when the weather's better."

The man shook his head. "Parson won't stay that long," he said.

"Of course he will! He's only been here two months."

"He won't, though. They don't stay," the man said.

"Who don't stay?"

The man leant his broom against a mausoleum with a large urn on its massive lid. "Did you see that tablet in church? List of all the parsons that's ever been here?"

"I saw it, but I didn't read all the names," Elspeth said.

"If you had, you'd ha'seen. Not a one of them stopped out the year. Not since *he* was here, and that's more'n seventy years gone."

"Who was *he*?"

"I'm not speaking his name. You won't find it up on that tablet, either. A real bad one he was, according to what they say. But for all that, he was parson here. Twenty-five years he was here. Terrible years they was, too."

"What did he do? What happened to him?" Elspeth asked, fearfully.

"Hanged hisself, didn't he? In his own house. Over the room he was building where Parson has his study," the man said, with a ghoulish pleasure in shocking.

"*Hanged* himself?"

"Or his Master did it for him, more like. My father used to say he'd sold hisself to . . ." He stopped abruptly as William's voice came across the churchyard. "Elspeth! Kate! We should be getting back before the dark."

"What did your father say he'd done?" Elspeth asked quickly, but the man had turned away. Over his shoulder, he said, "Nothing. And don't you go telling Parson I said anything. It's only a pack of silly stories. Some folk'd believe anything." He picked up his broom and shuffled off as William appeared at the end of the path.

"You're cold! I shouldn't have let you stay out in this damp spot for so long," he said. As they turned in the direction of the Rectory, he said, "I saw you talking to old Johnstone. What was he telling you?"

"We were telling him we'd love to see this place in the summer. If you're still here," Elspeth said before Kate could answer.

"Why shouldn't I still be here?" William asked.

"He seemed to think you wouldn't be staying for long. He didn't explain why."

"I see no reason why he should think that. I have no intention of leaving."

They walked on in silence. Kate was aware that William was

displeased, but she could think of nothing to say to improve the situation. Presently William said, "Perhaps one of the village girls who work in the house has heard Fanny talking about the children's health, and spread the story that I may not be staying here."

"Are the children not well?" Kate asked.

"They are perfectly well. Fanny is apt to be nervous about them. I am hoping that she will see there is nothing in this place to give her any anxiety when . . ." Kate had thought he was going to say, ". . . when the better weather comes." But instead, he said, ". . . when the nights are shorter." A curious way of putting it, she thought.

She remembered this conversation later in the day, when she again noticed Hugh's behaviour as bedtime approached. For more than an hour before Nurse was due to fetch him and Emmy upstairs, he was uneasy, alternating between long silences and frantic gaiety. When Agnes announced that his bath was ready, Kate offered to go upstairs with him, and half an hour later she was sitting on the side of the bed, looking at his trembling lip and sure that William was wrong. This was a very frightened child.

Fanny came in from the night-nursery and bent to kiss Hugh good night."

"Sleep well, my darling. And Hugh! Don't call out tonight. You know it annoys Papa."

"But Mamma . . ."

"I'll come and look at you before I go to bed to make sure you are all right.

Hugh lay still. But, as Kate and Fanny moved towards the door, he cried out desperately. "Don't shut the door, Mamma! Don't shut the door!"

"I'm not going to, my dear. Look! I'll leave it like this, so you can see the light from the passage."

That evening Hugh did not call out for his mamma. But, in the middle of the night, Kate was woken by the screams of a younger child. She opened her room door and saw Fanny coming from the night-nursery, with Emmy in her arms. "A nightmare. I'm taking her back to my room," Fanny said, trying to reassure. But, back in bed beside Elspeth who had hardly stirred, Kate lay awake, with that small face, contorted with terror before her mind's eye; while in the quiet room the shadows from the dying fire reached out like fingers, advancing and retreating, advancing and retreating, never quite reaching where she lay.

"Do both the children have nightmares?" she asked Fanny the next day.

"They don't sleep as well here as they did in Coombe. They may be better when the weather improves and they can go out and get more fresh air," Fanny said.

"But Fanny, these dreams . . ."

Fanny stopped her. "Dear Kate, don't ask me any more. William is sure I am anxious about nothing. He thinks it is my nervousness which infects the children and induces them to sleep badly. I expect he is right. I ought to have more faith, and to believe that if he has been called to this place, nothing can really go wrong with any of us."

Kate was still puzzled. But this was the day before Christmas, and there was too much for everyone to do to leave time for fancy or speculation. The children were excited, naughty, charming, in all the places where they were supposed not to be, and never there when they were wanted. They were sufficiently exalted by the mystery of Christmas to go to bed with a fairly good grace; they hung their stockings on the nursery mantelpiece, listened to the Christmas story from their father and were safely tucked up by seven o'clock. Supper was undisturbed by either child's dreams and, soon after ten o'clock, William and Fanny were persuaded by the two sisters to leave the rest of the preparations to them.

"There's not so much to do. The holly garlands, and I must finish the red frock for Emmy's doll," Kate said.

"Very well, if you are sure you don't mind. But don't stay up too late! Remember we are all going to have a long, tiring day tomorrow," Fanny said, as she gratefully took her bedroom candle and left the study. William, five minutes later, repeated the injunction. "Don't stay up late."

It was very quiet in the study after Fanny and William had gone. No child cried out tonight. The only sounds were the crackling of the glowing fire, the soft tap of the rhododendron leaves against the windows, and the regular tick of the big grandfather clock in the hall outside. The sisters hardly spoke, both intent on their work. The clock struck eleven, and still they hadn't finished. It was nearly an hour later when Kate put the finishing stitches to the doll's frock, and was just about to ask Elspeth how her work was getting on, when she heard the footsteps.

They were outside the room. At first she thought they were coming down the stairs. Then she realized that they were overhead, in the attic space above the study. She looked across at Elspeth, who had laid down the garland of holly on which she'd been pricking her fingers for the last hour and a half.

"Who?" Kate breathed. But as she spoke, she heard the whine of rusty hinges and from where she sat near the fire, she could see the trap-door in the ceiling of the room slowly lifted.

"It's William! He's come to scold us for being so long down here," Elspeth said, and without moving, she called out. "Yes, William, we're just going up. We'll be very quiet, we won't disturb you."

There was a long silence. No rebuke for their tardiness. No friendly good night. Instead a long blast of cold air swept down from the trap-door. Then the hinges creaked again and the trap was dropped. They heard slow, heavy footsteps pass over their heads. Then silence again.

"Let's go to bed. Quickly," Elspeth said, and Kate noticed, as they climbed the stairs, their candles shedding small pools of light before them, that Elspeth more than once looked back over her shoulder. Almost as if she was afraid of the dark, which lay like a great ocean behind them. At the last step, a croak and a rattle down below made her cry out, "What's that?"

"It's the clock clearing its throat before it strikes. There! Midnight! Come *on*," said Kate.

"You're cold," said Elspeth, as they lay side by side in the large bed.

"It was chilly down there in the study," Kate said. But, as she felt her sister's hand, she knew that it hadn't been the perpetual damp of the great grey house which had chilled them both that night.

They woke to shouts from the nursery, the scampering of small bare feet along the corridor, and the morning was taken up with church-going, present-giving, the preparation, and later the eating, of the Christmas feast. The holly garlands were admired, the doll's frock a perfect fit, William and Fanny were delighted with the gifts the sisters had brought from the rest of the family, Kate and Elspeth were touched and pleased with the presents Fanny had devised for the children to give them. In the general bustle and excitement of the day, they forgot the events of the night before until late in the evening, when, the children safely in bed, tired out with pleasure and feasting, William rose from his easy chair, deciding that he, at least, must go early to bed.

"And you mustn't be late either. You both stayed up late enough last night, working for today," Fanny said to the two girls.

"We weren't so very late. We went upstairs directly after William called down to us," Elspeth said.

"I called down to you? What do you mean?" William asked.

"You opened the trap-door up there and told us to go to bed."

"I certainly did not . . ."

"No, it wasn't you that called out. It was Elspeth. She called out to you that we were just coming," Kate said.

"It was just before twelve o'clock. The grandfather in the hall struck as we went up the stairs," Elspeth said.

"William was asleep before eleven last night," Fanny said.

"It must have been some other sound you heard. That trap hasn't been opened since we came to the house," William said.

"We heard your footsteps over the study. Walking along the floor up there. Then the trap-door opened and we thought it must be you, William . . ."

Fanny was very pale. She said, "William!", imploring him. Kate said, "Then there really is something . . . ?" but she didn't finish the sentence. Suddenly she began to understand. The children's fear of the dark. Fanny's nervousness. The refusal of the village girls to spend the night in the house. The half-told tale of the sexton the day before. The cold damp that hung around the rooms in spite of the generous fires. And, as the explanation crept into her mind and illuminated everything she had found mysterious before, she heard William's voice, cracking in its intensity as he asked, "Kate! Elspeth! When the trap opened . . . you didn't look up, did you? For God's sake, tell me you didn't look up?"

THE CANTERVILLE GHOST

OSCAR WILDE

1

WHEN MR HIRAM B OTIS, the American Ambassador, bought Canterville Chase, everyone told him he was doing a very foolish thing, as there was no doubt at all that the place was haunted. Indeed, Lord Canterville himself had felt it his duty to mention the fact to Mr Otis, when they came to discuss terms.

"We have not cared to live in the place ourselves," said Lord Canterville, "since my grand-aunt, the Dowager Duchess of Bolton, was frightened into a fit, from which she never really recovered, by two skeleton hands being placed on her shoulders as she was dressing for dinner, and I feel bound to tell you, Mr Otis, that the ghost has been seen by several living members of my family, as well as by the rector of the parish, the Rev Augustus Dampier. After the unfortunate accident to the Duchess, none of our younger servants would stay with us, and Lady Canterville often got very little sleep at nights in consequence of the mysterious noises that came from the corridor and the library."

"My lord," answered the Ambassador, "I will take the furniture and the ghost at a valuation. I come from a modern country, where we have everything that money can buy, and I reckon that if there were such a thing as a ghost in Europe, we'd have it at home in a very short time in one of our museums."

"I fear that the ghost exists," said Lord Canterville, smiling. "It has been well known for three centuries, since 1584 in fact, and always makes its appearance before the death of any member of our family."

"Well, so does the family doctor for that matter, Lord Canterville. But there is no such thing, sir, as a ghost, and I guess the laws of nature are not going to be suspended for the British aristocracy."

A few weeks after this, the purchase was completed, and at the close of the season the Ambassador and his family went down to Canterville Chase. Mrs Otis was a very handsome middle-aged woman, with fine eyes and a superb profile. Her eldest son, christened Washington by his parents in a moment of patriotism, which he never ceased to regret, was a fair-haired, rather good-looking young man, and in London was well known as an excellent dancer. Miss Virginia E Otis was a girl of fifteen, lithe and lovely as a fawn, and with a fine freedom in her large blue eyes. After Virginia came the twins, who were usually called "The Stars and Stripes" as they were always being caned. They were delightful boys, and with the exception of the worthy Ambassador the only true republicans of the family.

As Canterville Chase is seven miles from Ascot, the nearest railway station, Mr Otis had telegraphed for a carriage to meet them, and they started on their drive in high spirits. It was a lovely July evening, and the air was delicate with the scent of the pinewoods. Now and then they heard a wood pigeon or saw, deep in the rustling fern, the burnished breast of the pheasant. Little squirrels peered at them from the beech-trees as they went by, and the rabbits scudded away through the brushwood and over the mossy knolls, with their white tails in the air. As they entered the avenue of Canterville Chase, however, the sky became suddenly overcast with clouds, a curious stillness seemed to hold the atmosphere, a great flight of rooks passed silently over their heads, and, before they reached the house, some big drops of rain had fallen.

Standing on the steps to receive them was an old woman, neatly dressed in black silk, with a white cap and apron. This was Mrs Umney, the housekeeper. She made them each a low curtsey as they alighted, and said in a quaint, old-fashioned manner, "I bid you welcome to Canterville Chase." Following her, they passed through the fine Tudor hall into the library, a long, low room, panelled in black oak, at the end of which was a large stained-glass window. Here they found tea laid out for them, and, after taking off their wraps, they sat down and began to look round, while Mrs Umney waited on them.

Suddenly Mrs Otis caught sight of a dull red stain on the floor just by the fireplace and, quite unconscious of what it really signified, said to Mrs Umney, "I am afraid something has been spilt there."

"Yes, madam," replied the old housekeeper in a low voice, "blood has been spilt on that spot."

"How horrid," cried Mrs Otis; "I don't at all care for bloodstains in a sitting-room. It must be removed at once."

The old woman smiled, and answered in the same low, mysterious voice, "It is the blood of Lady Eleanore de Canterville, who was murdered on that very spot by her own husband, Sir Simon de Canterville in 1575. Sir Simon survived her by nine years, and disappeared suddenly under very mysterious circumstances. His body has never been discovered, but his guilty spirit still haunts the Chase. The bloodstain has been much admired by tourists and others, and cannot be removed."

"That is all nonsense," cried Washington Otis; "Pinkerton's Champion Stain Remover and Paragon Detergent will clean it up in no time," and before the terrified housekeeper could interfere he had fallen upon his knees, and was rapidly scouring the floor with a small stick of what looked like a black cosmetic. In a few moments no trace of the bloodstain could be seen.

"I knew Pinkerton would do it," he exclaimed triumphantly, as he looked round at his admiring family; but no sooner had he said these words than a terrible flash of lightning lit up the sombre room, a fearful peal of thunder made them all start to their feet, and Mrs Umney fainted.

"What a monstrous climate!" said the American Ambassador calmly, as he lit a long cheroot. "I guess the old country is so overpopulated that they have not enough decent weather for everybody."

"My dear Hiram," cried Mrs Otis, "what can we do with a woman who faints?"

"Charge it to her like breakages," answered the Ambassador; "she won't faint after that"; and in a few moments Mrs Umney certainly came to. There was no doubt, however, that she was extremely upset, and she sternly warned Mr Otis to beware of some trouble coming to the house.

"I have seen things with my own eyes, sir," she said, "that would make any Christian's hair stand on end, and many and many a night I have not closed my eyes in sleep for the awful things that are done here." Mr Otis, however, and his wife warmly assured the honest soul that they were not afraid of ghosts, and, after invoking the blessings of Providence on her new master and mistress, and making arrangements for an increase of salary, the old housekeeper tottered off to her own room.

2

The storm raged fiercely all that night, but nothing of particular note occurred. The next morning, however, when they came down to breakfast, they found the terrible stain of blood once again on the floor.

"I don't think it can be the fault of the Paragon Detergent," said Washington, "for I have tried it with everything. It must be the ghost." He accordingly rubbed out the stain a second time, but the second morning it appeared again. The third morning also it was there, though the library had been locked up at night by Mr Otis himself, and the key carried upstairs. The whole family were now quite interested. Mr Otis began to suspect that he had been too dogmatic in his denial of the existence of ghosts, and that night all his doubts about them were removed for ever.

The day had been warm and sunny; and, in the cool of the evening, the whole family went out for a drive. They did not return home till nine o'clock, when they had a light supper. The conversation in no way turned upon ghosts, nor was Sir Simon de Canterville alluded to at all. At eleven o'clock the family retired and by half-past all the lights were out.

Some time after, Mr Otis was awakened by a curious noise in the corridor, outside his room. It sounded like a clank of metal, and seemed to be coming nearer every moment. He got up at once, struck a match, and looked at the time. It was exactly one o'clock. He was quite calm, and felt his pulse, which was not at all feverish. The strange noise still continued, and with it he heard distinctly the sound of footsteps. He put on his slippers, took a small oblong phial out of his dressing-case, and opened the door. Right in front of him he saw, in the warm moonlight, an old man of terrible aspect. His eyes were as red as burning coals; long grey hair fell over his shoulders in matted coils; his garments, which were of antique cut, were soiled and ragged, and from his wrists and ankles hung heavy manacles and rusty chains.

"My dear sir," said Mr Otis, "I really must insist on your oiling those chains, and have brought you for that purpose a small bottle of the Tammany Rising Sun Lubricator. It is said to be completely efficacious upon one application, and there are several testimonials to that effect on the wrapper. I shall leave it here for you by the bedroom candles, and will be happy to supply you with more, should you require it." With these words the United States Ambassador laid the bottle down on a marble table, and, closing his door, retired to rest.

For a moment the Canterville ghost stood quite motionless in natural indignation; then, dashing the bottle violently upon the polished floor, he fled down the corridor, uttering hollow groans, and emitting a ghastly green light. Just, however, as he reached the top of the great oak staircase, a door was flung open, two little white-robed figures appeared, and a large pillow whizzed past his head! There was evidently no time to be lost, so, as a means of escape, he vanished through the wainscoting, and the house became quite quiet.

On reaching a small secret chamber in the left wing, the ghost leaned up against a moonbeam to recover his breath, and began to try and realize his position. Never, in a brilliant and uninterrupted career of three hundred years, had he been so grossly insulted. He thought of the Dowager Duchess, whom he had frightened into a fit as she stood before the glass in her lace and diamonds; and of the four housemaids, who had gone off into hysterics when he merely grinned at them through the curtains of one of the spare bedrooms. He remembered the terrible night when the wicked Lord Canterville was found choking in his room, with the knave of diamonds half-way down his throat, and confessed, just before he died, that he had cheated Charles James Fox out of £50,000 by means of that very card, and swore that the ghost had made him swallow it. And the butler who had shot himself in the pantry because he had seen a green hand tapping at the window pane. He went over his most celebrated performances, and smiled bitterly to himself as he recalled to mind his last appearance as "Gaunt Gibeon, the Blood-sucker of Bexley Moor", and the excitement he had caused one lonely June evening by playing ninepins with his own bones upon the lawn tennis court. And after all this, some wretched modern Americans were to come and offer him the Rising Sun Lubricator, and throw pillows at his head! It was quite unbearable. Besides, no ghosts in history had ever been treated in this manner. Accordingly, he determined to have vengeance, and remained till daylight in an attitude of deep thought.

3

The next morning when the Otis family met at breakfast, they discussed the ghost at some length. The United States Ambassador was naturally a little annoyed to find that his present had not been accepted. "I have no wish," he said, "to do the ghost any personal injury, and I must say that, considering the length of time he has been in the house, I don't think it is at all polite to throw pillows at him" – a very just remark, at which the twins burst into shouts of laughter. "On the other hand," he continued, "if he really declines to use the Rising Sun Lubricator, we shall have to take his chains from him. It would be quite impossible to sleep, with such a noise going on outside the bedrooms."

For the rest of the week, however, they were undisturbed, the only thing that excited any attention being the continual renewal of the bloodstain on the library floor. This certainly was very strange, as the door was always locked at night by Mr Otis, and the windows kept closely barred. The colour of the stain also excited a good deal of comment. Some mornings it was a dull red, then it would be vermilion, then a rich purple, and once when they came down, they found it a bright emerald-green. These changes naturally amused the party very much, and bets on the subject were freely made every evening. The only person who did not enter into the joke was Virginia, who, for some unexplained reason, was always a good deal distressed at the sight of the bloodstain, and very nearly cried the morning it was emerald-green.

The second appearance of the ghost was on Sunday night. Shortly after they had gone to bed they were suddenly alarmed by a fearful crash in the hall. Rushing downstairs, they found that a large suit of old armour had become detached from its stand, and had fallen on the stone floor, while, seated in a high-backed chair, was the Canterville ghost, rubbing his knees with an expression of acute agony on his face. The twins, having brought their peashooters with them, at once discharged two pellets at him, while the United States Ambassador covered him with his revolver, and called upon him to hold up his hands! The ghost started up with a wild shriek of rage, and swept through them like a mist, extinguishing Washington Otis's candle as he passed, and so leaving them all in total darkness. On reaching the top of the staircase, he recovered himself, and determined to give his celebrated peal of demoniac laughter. This he had on more than one occasion found extremely useful: and it was said to have turned Lord Raker's wig grey in a single night.

He accordingly laughed his most horrible laugh, till the old vaulted roof rang and rang again, but hardly had the fearful echo died away when a door opened, and Mrs Otis came out in a light blue dressing-gown.

"I am afraid you are far from well," she said, "and have brought you a bottle of Dr Dobell's tincture. If it is indigestion you will find it a most excellent remedy."

The ghost glared at her in fury, and began at once to make preparations for turning himself into a large black dog, an accomplishment for which he was justly renowned, when the sound of approaching footsteps made him hesitate. So he contented himself with becoming faintly phosphorescent, and vanished with a deep church-yard groan, just as the twins had come up to him.

On reaching his room he entirely broke down, and for some days was extremely ill, hardly stirring out of his room at all, except to keep the bloodstain in proper repair. However, by taking great care of himself, he recovered, and resolved to make a third attempt to frighten the United States Ambassador and his family. He selected Friday, the 17th of August, for his appearance, and spent most of that day in looking over his wardrobe, ultimately deciding in favour of a large slouched hat with a red feather, a winding-sheet frilled at the wrists and neck, and a rusty dagger. Towards evening a violent storm of rain came on, and the wind was so high that all the windows and doors in the old house shook and rattled. In fact, it was just such weather as he loved.

His plan of action was this. He was to make his way quietly to Washington Otis's room, gibber at him from the foot of the bed, and stab himself three times in the throat to the sound of slow music. He bore Washington a special grudge, being quite aware that it was he who was in the habit of removing the famous Canterville bloodstain by means of Pinkerton's Paragon Detergent.

Having reduced the reckless and foolhardy youth to a condition of abject terror, he was then to proceed to the room occupied by the United States Ambassador and his wife, and there to place a clammy hand on Mrs Otis's forehead, while he hissed into her trembling husband's ear the awful secrets of the charnel-house.

With regard to Virginia, he had not quite made up his mind. She had never insulted him in any way, and was pretty and gentle. A few hollow groans from the wardrobe, he thought, would be more than sufficient, or, if that failed to wake her, he might grabble at the counterpane with palsy-twitching fingers.

As for the twins, he was quite determined to teach them a lesson. The first thing to be done was, of course, to sit upon their chests, so as to produce the stifling sensation of nightmare. Then, as their beds were quite close to each other, to stand between them in the form of a green, icy-cold corpse, till they became paralysed with fear, and finally, to throw off the winding-sheet, and crawl round the room, with white bleached bones and one rolling eyeball, in the character of "Dumb Daniel, or the Suicide's Skeleton".

At half-past ten he heard the family going to bed, and by quarter-past eleven all was still. As midnight sounded, the ghost sallied forth. The owl beat against the window panes, the raven croaked from the old yew-tree, and the wind wandered moaning round the house like a lost soul; but the Otis family slept unconscious of their doom, and high above the rain and storm he could hear the steady snoring of the Ambassador.

The ghost stepped stealthily out of the wainscoting, with an evil smile on his cruel, wrinkled mouth, and the moon hid her face in a cloud as he stole past the great stained-glass window, where his own coat of arms and those of his murdered wife were blazoned in azure and gold. On and on he glided, like an evil shadow, the very darkness seeming to loathe him as he passed. Once he thought he heard something call, and stopped; but it was only the baying of a dog from the Red Farm, and he went on, muttering strange sixteenth-century curses, and brandishing the rusty dagger in the midnight air. Finally he reached the corner of the passage that led to luckless Washington's room. For a moment he paused there, the wind blowing his long grey locks about his head, and twisting into grotesque and fantastic folds the nameless horror of the dead man's shroud. Then the clock struck the quarter hour, and he felt the time was come.

The ghost chuckled to himself, and turned the corner; but no sooner had he done so, than, with a piteous wail of terror, he fell back, and hid his white face in his long, bony hands. Right in front of him was standing a horrible spectre, motionless as a carven image, and monstrous as a madman's dream! Its head was bald and burnished; its face round, and fat, and white; and hideous laughter seemed to have writhed its features into an eternal grin. From the eyes streamed rays of scarlet light, the mouth was a wide well of fire, and a hideous garment, like his own, swathed its silent form. On its breast was a placard with strange writing: some scroll of shame it seemed, some record of wild sins, some awful calendar of crime, and, with its right hand, it bore aloft a sword of gleaming steel.

Never having seen a ghost before, he naturally was terribly frightened, and, after a second hasty glance at the awful phantom, he fled back to his room, tripping up in his long winding-sheet as he sped down the corridor, and finally dropping the rusty dagger into the Ambassador's boots, where it was found in the morning by the butler. Once in the privacy of his own apartment, he flung himself down on a small pallet-bed and hid his face under the clothes. After a time, however, the brave old Canterville spirit asserted itself, and he determined to go and speak to the other ghost as soon as it was daylight.

Accordingly, just as the dawn was touching the hills with silver, he returned towards the spot where he had first laid eyes on the grisly phantom, feeling that, after all, two ghosts were better than one, and that, by the aid of his new friend, he might safely grapple with the twins. On reaching the spot, however, a terrible sight met his gaze. Something had evidently happened to the spectre, for the light had entirely faded from its hollow eyes, and the sword had fallen from its hand, and it was leaning up against the wall in a strained and uncomfortable attitude.

He rushed forward and seized it in his arms, when, to his horror, the head slipped off and rolled on the floor, and he found himself clasping a white curtain, with a broom, kitchen knife, and hollow turnip lying at his feet! Unable to understand this curious transformation, he clutched the placard with feverish haste, and there, in the grey morning light, he read these fearful words:

YE OTIS GHOSTE,
Ye Onlie True and Originale Spook.
Beware of Ye Imitationes.
All others are Counterfeite.

The whole thing flashed across him. He had been tricked, foiled and outwitted! The old Canterville look came into his eyes; he ground his toothless gums together; and raising his withered hands high above his head, swore that deeds of blood would be wrought, and Murder walk abroad with silent feet.

He then retired to a comfortable lead coffin, and stayed there till evening.

4

The next day the ghost was very weak and tired. The terrible excitement of the last four weeks was beginning to have its effect. His nerves were completely shattered, and he started at the slightest noise. For five days he kept to his room, and at last made up his mind to give up the point of the bloodstain on the library floor. If the Otis family did not want it, they clearly did not deserve it. It was, however, his solemn duty to appear in the corridor once a week, and to gibber from the large stained-glass window on the first and third Wednesday in every month, and he did not see how he could honourably escape from his obligations.

For the next three Saturdays, accordingly, he traversed the corridor as usual between midnight and three o'clock, taking every possible precaution against being either heard or seen. He removed his boots, trod as lightly as possible on the old worm-eaten boards, wore a large black velvet cloak, and was careful to use the Rising Sun Lubricator for oiling his chains. Indeed, one night, while the family were at dinner, he slipped into Mr Otis's bedroom and carried off the bottle. He felt a little humiliated at first, but afterwards was sensible enough to see that there was a great deal to be said for the invention, and to a certain degree, it served his purpose.

Still, in spite of everything, he was not left unmolested. Strings were continually being stretched across the corridor, over which he tripped in the dark, and on one occasion, while dressed for the part of "Black Isaac, or the Huntsman of Hodley Woods", he met with a severe fall, through treading on a butter-slide, which the twins had constructed from the entrance of the Tapestry Chamber to the top of the oak staircase. This last insult so enraged him that he resolved to make one final effort to assert his dignity and social position, and determined to visit the insolent pair the next night in his celebrated character of "Reckless Rupert, or the Headless Earl". It was, however, an extremely difficult "make-up", and it took him fully three hours to make his preparations.

At last everything was ready, and he was very pleased with his appearance. The big leather riding-boots that went with the dress were just a little too large for him, and he could only find one of the two horse-pistols, but, on the whole, he was quite satisfied, and at quarter-past one he glided out of the wainscoting and crept down the corridor.

On reaching the room occupied by the twins, he found the door just ajar. Wishing to make an effective entrance, he flung it wide open, when a heavy jug of water fell right down on him, wetting him to the skin, and just missing his left shoulder by a couple of inches. At the same moment he heard stifled shrieks of laughter coming from the four-post bed. The shock to his nervous system was so great that he fled back to his room as fast as he could go, and the next day he was laid up with a severe cold. The only thing that at all consoled him in the whole affair was the fact that he had not brought his head with him, for, had he done so, the consequences might have been very serious.

He now gave up all hope of ever frightening this rude American family, and contented himself, as a rule, with creeping about the passages in slippers, with a thick red muffler round his throat for fear of draughts, and a small pistol, in case he should be attacked by the twins.

The final blow he received occurred on the 19th of September. He had gone downstairs to the great entrance hall, feeling sure that there, at any rate, he would be quite unmolested. He was simply but neatly clad in a long shroud, spotted with church-yard mould, had tied up his jaw with a strip of yellow linen, and carried a small lantern and a sexton's spade. In fact, he was dressed for the character of "Jonas the Graveless, or the Corpse-Snatcher of Chertsey Barn", one of his most remarkable impersonations.

It was about quarter-past two in the morning, and, as far as he could ascertain, no one was stirring. As he was strolling towards the library, however, to see if there were any traces left of the bloodstain, suddenly there leaped out on him from a dark corner two figures, who waved their arms wildly above their heads, and shrieked out "BOO!" in his ear.

Seized with panic, which under the circumstances was only natural, he rushed for the staircase, but found Washington Otis waiting for him there with the big garden-syringe; and being thus hemmed in by his enemies on every side, and driven almost to bay, he vanished into the great iron stove, which, fortunately for him, was not lit, and had to make his way home through the flues and chimneys, arriving at his own room in a terrible state of dirt, disorder, and despair.

After this he was not seen again on any nocturnal expedition. The twins lay in wait for him on several occasions, and strewed the passages with nutshells every night to the great annoyance of their parents and the servants. But it was of no avail. It was generally assumed that the ghost had gone away, and, in fact, Mr Otis wrote a letter to that effect to Lord Canterville, who, in reply, expressed his great pleasure at the news, and sent his best congratulations to the Ambassador's worthy wife.

5

But one day a few weeks later, Virginia was going past the Tapestry Chamber when she fancied she saw someone inside.

To her immense surprise, it was the Canterville ghost himself! He was sitting by the window, watching the ruined gold of the yellow trees fly through the air, and the red leaves dancing madly down the long avenue. His head was leaning on his hand, and his whole attitude was one of extreme depression. Indeed, so forlorn, and so much out of repair did he look, that Virginia, whose first idea had been to run away and lock herself in her room, was filled with pity, and determined to try and comfort him. So light was her footfall, and so deep his melancholy, that he was not aware of her presence till she spoke to him.

"I am so sorry for you," she said, "but my brothers are going back to school tomorrow, and then, if you behave yourself, no one will annoy you."

"It is absurd asking me to behave myself," he answered, looking round in astonishment at the pretty girl who had ventured to address him, "quite absurd. I must rattle my chains, and groan through keyholes, and walk about at night, if that is what you mean. It is my only reason for existing."

"It is no reason at all for existing, and you know you have been very wicked. Mrs Umney told us, the first day we arrived here, that you killed your wife."

"Well, I quite admit it," said the ghost petulantly, "but it was purely a family matter, and concerned no one else."

"It is very wrong to kill anyone," said Virginia.

"My wife was very plain, never had my ruffs properly starched, and knew nothing about cookery. Why, there was a buck I had shot in Hogley Woods, and you wouldn't believe how she had it sent up to the table. However, it is no matter now, for it is all over, and I don't think it was very nice of her brothers to starve me to death, though I did kill her."

"Starve you to death? Oh, Mr Ghost, I mean Sir Simon, are you hungry? I have a sandwich in my case. Would you like it?"

"No, thank you, I never eat anything now; but it is very kind of you, all the same, and you are much nicer than the rest of your horrid, rude, dishonest family."

"Stop!" cried Virginia, stamping her foot. "It is you who

are rude and horrid; and as for dishonesty, you know you stole the paints out of my box to try and furbish up that ridiculous bloodstain in the library. First you took all my reds, including the vermilion, and I couldn't do any more sunsets; then you took the emerald-green and the chrome-yellow, and finally I had nothing left but indigo and Chinese white, and could only do moonlight scenes. I never told on you, though I was very much annoyed, and it was most ridiculous, the whole thing; for who ever heard of emerald-green blood?"

"Well, really," said the ghost, "what was I to do? It is a very difficult thing to get real blood nowadays, and, as your brother began it all with his Paragon Detergent, I certainly saw no reason why I should not have your paints."

"Oh," said Virginia. "Good evening. I will go and ask papa to get the twins an extra week's holiday."

"Please don't go, Miss Virginia," the ghost cried. "I am so lonely and so unhappy, and I really don't know what to do. I want to go to sleep and I cannot."

"That's quite absurd! You have merely to go to bed and blow out the candle. Even babies know how to sleep, and they are not very clever."

"I have not slept for three hundred years," he said sadly, and Virginia's beautiful blue eyes opened in wonder; "for three hundred years I have not slept, and I am so tired."

Virginia grew quite grave. She came towards him, and kneeling down at his side, looked up into his old withered face.

"Poor, poor ghost," she murmured. "Have you no place where you can sleep?"

"Far away beyond the pinewoods," he answered in a low dreamy voice, "there is a little garden. There the grass grows long and deep, there are great white stars of the hemlock flower, there the nightingale sings all night long. All night long he sings, and the cold, crystal moon looks down, and the yew-tree spreads out its giant arms over the sleepers."

Virginia's eyes grew dim with tears, and she hid her face in her hands.

219

"You mean the Garden of Death," she whispered.

"Yes, Death. Death must be so beautiful. To lie in the soft brown earth, with the grasses waving above one's head, and listen to silence. To have no yesterday, and no tomorrow. To forget time, to forgive life, to be at peace. You can help me. You can open for me the portals of Death's house, for Love is always with you, and Love is stronger than Death is."

Virginia trembled, a cold shudder ran through her, and for a few moments there was silence. She felt as if she was in a terrible dream.

Then the ghost spoke again, and his voice sounded like the sighing of the wind.

"Have you ever read the old prophecy on the library window?"

"Oh, often," said Virginia; "I know it quite well:

> When a golden girl can win
> Prayer from out the lips of sin,
> When the barren almond bears,
> And a little child gives away its tears,
> Then shall all the house be still
> And peace come to Canterville.

But I don't know what it means."

"It means," he said sadly, "that you must weep for me for my sins, because I have no tears, and pray with me for my soul, because I have no faith, and then, if you have always been sweet, and good, and gentle, the Angel of Death will have mercy on me. You will see fearful shapes in darkness, and wicked voices will whisper in your ear. But they will not harm you, for against your purity the powers of Hell cannot prevail."

Virginia made no answer, and the ghost wrung his hands in wild despair as he looked down at her bowed golden head. Suddenly she stood up, very pale, and with a strange light in her eyes. "I am not afraid," she said firmly, "and I will ask the Angel to have mercy on you."

6

About ten minutes later, the bell rang for tea, and, as Virginia did not come down, Mrs Otis sent up one of the footmen to tell her. After a little time he returned and said that he could not find Miss Virginia anywhere. As she was in the habit of going out to the garden every evening to get flowers for the dinner-table, Mrs Otis was not at all alarmed at first, but when six o'clock struck, and Virginia did not appear, she became really agitated, and sent the boys out to look for her. At half-past six the boys came back and said that they could find no trace of their sister anywhere.

Mr Otis at once determined to begin a wider search. He dispatched telegrams to all the police inspectors in the county, telling them to look out for a girl who might have been kidnapped by tramps or gypsies. He went to the railway station to inquire of the station-master if anyone answering the description of Virginia had been seen on the platform, but could get no news of her. The station-master, however, wired up and down the line, and assured him that a strict watch would be kept for her. The carp pond was dragged, and the whole Chase thoroughly gone over, but without any result. It was evident that, for that night at any rate, Virginia was lost to them.

It was in a state of the deepest depression that Mr Otis returned to the House. In the hall they found a group of frightened servants, and lying on a sofa in the library was poor Mrs Otis, almost out of her mind with terror and anxiety, and having her forehead bathed with eau-de-Cologne by the old housekeeper. Mr Otis at once insisted on her having something to eat, and asked for supper for the whole party.

It was a melancholy meal, as hardly anyone spoke, and even the twins were awestruck and subdued, as they were very fond of their sister. When they had finished, Mr Otis ordered them all to bed, saying that nothing more could be done that night, and that he would telegraph in the morning to Scotland Yard.

Just as they were leaving the dining-room, midnight began to boom from the clock tower, and when the last stroke sounded, they heard a crash and a sudden shrill cry; a dreadful peal of thunder shook the house, a strain of unearthly music floated through the air, a panel at the top of the staircase flew back with a loud noise, and out on the landing, looking very pale and white, with a little box in her hand, stepped Virginia. In a moment they had all rushed up to her, and Mrs Otis clasped her in her arms.

"Good heavens, child! Where have you been?" said Mr Otis, rather angrily, thinking that she had been playing some foolish trick on them. "I have been riding all over the country looking for you, and your mother has been frightened to death. You must never play these practical jokes any more."

"Except on the ghost! Except on the ghost!" shrieked the twins.

"Thank God you are found," murmured Mrs Otis, as she kissed the trembling girl, and smoothed the tangled gold of her hair.

"Papa," said Virginia quietly, "I have been with the ghost. He is dead, and you must come and see him. He had been very wicked, but he was really sorry for all that he had done, and he gave me this box of beautiful jewels before he died."

The whole family gazed at her in mute astonishment, but she was quite grave and serious; and turning round, she led them through the opening in the wainscoting down a narrow secret corridor. Finally, they came to a great oak door, studded with rusty nails. When Virginia touched it, it swung back on its heavy hinges, and they found themselves in a little low room, with a vaulted ceiling, and one tiny grated window.

Embedded in the wall was a huge iron ring, and chained to it was a gaunt skeleton that was stretched out at full length on the stone floor, and seemed to be trying to grasp with its long fleshless fingers an old-fashioned trencher and ewer, which were placed just out of its reach. The jug had evidently been once filled with water, as it was covered inside with green mould. There was nothing on the trencher but a pile of dust. They all looked on in wonder at the terrible tragedy whose secret was now disclosed to them.

"Hallo!" suddenly exclaimed one of the twins, who had been

looking out of the windows to try and discover in what wing of the house the room was situated. "Hallo! The old withered almond-tree has blossomed. I can see the flowers quite plainly in the moonlight."

"God has forgiven him," said Virginia.

ACKNOWLEDGEMENTS

The publisher would like to thank the copyright holders for permission to reproduce the following copyright material:

Robert Arthur: "Footsteps Invisible" from *Ghosts and More Ghosts* by Robert Arthur (Random House, 1963). Copyright © 1991 by Elizabeth Ann Arthur and Robert Andrew Arthur. **Aidan Chambers**: "Room 18" from *Ghosts* edited by Aidan and Nancy Chambers (Topliner, 1969). Copyright © Aidan Chambers. **R. Chetwynd-Hayes**: "Brownie" from *The Third Armada Ghost Book* edited by Mary Danby (Mayfair/Collins Books 1970). Reprinted by permission of the Author's Estate and Dorian Literary Agency. **Agatha Christie**: "The Lamp" copyright © Agatha Christie Limited, 1933. **August Derleth**: "The Lonesome Place" by August Derleth. Copyright © April and Walden Derleth. Permission granted by Arkham House Publishers, Inc., Sauk City, WI, USA. **John Gordon**: "If She Bends, She Breaks" from *Ghost after Ghost* edited by Aidan Chambers (Kestrel, 1982). Copyright © John Gordon. **Jan Mark**: David Higham Associates for "The Gnomon" by Jan Mark, from *Shades of Dark* edited by Aidan Chambers (Patrick Hardy Books, 1984). Copyright © Jan Mark 1984. **Lance Salway**: "Such a Sweet Little Girl" from *Ghost after Ghost* edited by Aidan Chambers (Kestrel, 1982). Copyright © Lance Salway 1982. Reproduced by permission of the author c/o Rogers, Coleridge & White Ltd., 20 Powis Mews, London W11 1JN. **Catherine Storr**: PFD for "Christmas in the Rectory" from *Ghost after Ghost* edited by Aidan Chambers (Kestrel, 1982). **William Trevor**: PFD for "The Death of Peggy Morrissey" from *The Eleventh Ghost Book* edited by Aidan Chambers (Barrie & Jenkins, 1975). **Robert Westall**: "The Haunting of Chas McGill" from *The Best of Robert Westall, Vol. 2: Shades of Darkness* (Macmillan). Copyright © The Estate of Robert Westall 1998. Permission granted by the author's estate.

Every effort has been made to obtain permission to reproduce copyright material but there may be cases where we have been unable to contact a copyright holder. The publisher will be happy to correct any omissions in future printings.